Wed To The Devil

AN ENEMIES TO LOVERS BILLIONAIRE ROMANCE

VIVIAN WOOD

Acknowledgments

A big thank you goes out to all the wonderful ladies that helped make this book shine! Honey, Patricia, Sammy, and Amanda, this book would not be the same without your love and care.

Chapter One

DARE

I swing my gaze around the packed living room of the Morgan Estate, sipping my tumbler of whiskey. Clusters of men in suits stand around, talking about their new crypto investments. Women in elegant cocktail attire bend their heads close together, whispering about their handsome tennis instructors. I take in the crowd, absorbing how self-centered and shallow they must seem to an outsider.

Talia could probably take them down a peg or two, given the chance. Or maybe it's just me that she accuses of being an out-of-touch rich asshole. Lucky me, I guess.

Sweeping my eyes over the burbling crowd once more, I sigh and look at my watch. Talia excused herself to find the bathroom quite a while ago.

I can't help but wonder what is keeping her from returning to my side like a good little wife.

I'm distracted for a moment by a woman falling over with a yelp. She's giggling and holding up her wine glass, expecting someone to refill it. As I look on, her red-faced husband helps her up and forcefully steers her out of the room, muttering angry words into her ear the whole time. Everyone else is happy and drunk, seemingly having forgotten that only fifteen minutes ago, they were watching a showdown.

My twin brother, Burn, and I stood in the middle of a large circle of people, parrying and thrusting, trying to cut each other to pieces with our words. It was a surprise to me that this whole party was even taking place. Burn threw it together at the last minute, to dig in the fact that he is marrying the girl he stole from me.

But I got the last laugh. When I pulled Talia close and announced that we had been married this very day, Burn gave me a look that would turn any other human to stone.

I smile to myself and slide the melting ice cubes in my glass of blond whiskey with a faint clink. It was a very satisfying moment and I'm still floating on a cloud of satisfaction.

My Uncle Felix cuts through the crowd with his sharp elbows. A concentrated little frown is on his face and he shoots one lady a disdainful look as he shoves his way past her, brushing off his hands where he manhandled her shoulder.

"Damn bartender says that they are out of scotch," he grouses.

"Did you hear anything more from the lawyers about the site where we plan on drilling? From what the lawyers have told me, the state of Maine is being an extraordinary pain in the ass about giving us a fucking inch."

I arch a brow and shake my head. "No. I haven't heard anything from them all week. Then again, I've been pretty distracted with Talia."

My eyes rove around the gathering. The crowd ripples and a swell of laughter bursts free from a large group of men in the corner. Talia is nowhere to be seen and I can only hope that she hasn't been waylaid by a distant cousin or something. All of my extended family are a bunch of grasping, greedy vultures and Talia doesn't know that makes her vulnerable to their invasive insinuations.

My uncle is not even looking out at the crowd at the moment. He has a slumped posture, his arms crossed, his expression rather dour.

"You need to get your head out of your new wife's pussy and pay attention to what is going on. The lawyers have to be reminded that they work for us. You wouldn't think that they'd need a reminder that a big paycheck is waiting for them at the end of this journey, but you would be surprised at how lazy they can be."

I glance at him, my eyes narrowing. Try as I might, I can't find my usual vim and vigor for venting my feelings about the millions of dollars wasted on lawyers. I just nod and shrug, adjusting my tie as I look around the room again. "Have you seen Talia? She left almost twenty minutes ago. I'm afraid that Daisy has gotten ahold of her or something."

A brief moment of anger flashes over Felix's face. I'm not sure whether he is angry about Talia or something to do with Daisy, but in the next second it's gone from his expression. He shrugs and spreads his hands wide, gesturing around him. "I have been standing here with you. I'm sure that your new wife can hold her own."

I squint and run my tongue over my teeth. "I'm not sure about that. She isn't hardened like us. She's still a soft touch."

Felix rolls his eyes. "If you can't trust your wife to go to the bathroom by herself, you don't have a wife. You have a child."

A derisive snort leaves my nose. "Helpful. I should go look for Talia."

Felix looks like he is about to say something else but I

turn and shoulder my way through the crowd toward the door. I head out into the crowded hallway, looking left and right. All I see is a sea of blondes and brunettes. Not a single flash of coppery red hair to be seen. I turn left and head down the hallway to the library. Talia could have gone to any of the restrooms on this floor, but this was definitely the direction that I last saw her heading in. Turning the corner toward the library, I immediately see Frick and Frack. Their dark heads of hair stick out above the crowd, their shoulders ending at the top of everyone else's heads. They are facing away from me, moving silently through the crowd, their eyes scanning every face. But I see no sign of Talia anywhere near them.

Where the fuck is my wife? My pulse starts to speed up.

I head toward them, my eyes narrowing, my expression as serious as a fresh grave. Frack turns around, his face in profile looking like it was carved from granite. His dark eyes find me and he stops, muttering something out of the corner of his mouth to Frick. Her ponytailed head swings around and I see that they are moving toward me. It's funny because I have long thought that my size made people in a crowd nervous enough to move away from me automatically. But watching Frick and Frack approach me without so much as having to touch another suited or gowned partygoer is nothing short of amazing in a crowd this size. It takes less than a minute for them to be in earshot.

"Where's Talia?" I demand.

Frack scowls and Frick narrows her eyes. They are both impeccably dressed this evening in a pair of dark suits and starched white shirts. Frack moves towards me, his brow creasing.

"We were just searching for Mrs. Morgan. We thought perhaps she was with you."

My heart squeezes inside my chest. I give them a dirty look.

"She is not with me. And she's not with you. So where the fuck is she?"

Frick takes a deep breath and gives me a steadying look.

"We've been looking for her since she headed out of the living room without telling us. She's been gone for…"

Frick looks at her watch, flicking the cuff of her shirt back.

"Almost half an hour at this point. I think it's advisable that we consider her missing now. We need to examine all the security footage from the house's entrances and exits and try to determine if she left or was taken. Then we can figure out if we just have a search of the house to do or if we need to expand our options."

I grit my teeth. "How could you let this happen?"

Frick and Frack simultaneously bow their heads, the closest that they will come to admitting fault.

"We'll find your wife."

"You better fucking hope so," I snarl. "One of you, go get the security tapes from the security closet near the front door. The other one, go look for her outside. I will corner my father and uncle, herd them into the library, and try to ascertain whether either of them knows anything about Talia's whereabouts."

Frack nods and starts toward the front of the house. Frick immediately heads for the side door, exiting into the back gardens. My heart bangs against my ribs as I turn, looking for my father or uncle. I find my uncle standing very close to where I left him a few minutes ago. He is nursing a glass of whiskey and looking as grouchy as ever. I head straight toward him, pushing people out of my way. Felix sees me coming and takes a large swig out of his glass, hissing at the burn of the whiskey sliding down his throat.

"Felix, where is Talia?"

He arches a brow, managing to look completely expressionless.

"What do you mean?"

I stalk right up to him, grabbing his tie and yanking it up. His head snaps backward, his carefully combed silver and black hair flopping. I glare down at him, my aqua eyes probing him. His hands flap uselessly at his sides when I give his tie another yank, threatening to choke him.

Felix looks stunned. But that could easily be an act. It's impossible to tell whether Felix knows what is going on or not, though he seems perfectly innocent. His hands come up to my chest, pressing against it in a fumbling attempt to free himself. That only makes me double down and I pull his tie straight up, stepping his head back further, strangling him.

"Where is she?" I demand to know. "Did you have someone take her?"

All I can see in my mind's eye is a dark man wearing a balaclava and gloves with his suit, hauling a frightened looking Talia out of the back door of the estate. The thought worries me so much that I drive a fist into my uncle's stomach, knocking the wind out of him.

He gasps for air and writhes as I maintain my grip on his tie. Felix is roughly my size but gaunt, years of drinking and smoking making his muscles weaker than they should be.

I lean close to his ear and spit out the words. "If you touch her, if she so much as says you looked at her wrong, I will fucking gut you. I'll run you through and wipe your blood off on your own shirt."

Felix grits out, "I don't know where she is. I swear. I've just been standing here the entire time."

His distress is starting to make him break out in a fine sheen of sweat.

"Dare!"

I whip my head around and see Frack waving at me, motioning me over. "We found her. Come see."

The way that he says the phrase 'we found her' makes my blood cold as ice in my veins. Releasing my uncle, I turn and move through the crowd, which has now mostly turned to gawk at me. Everyone moves back, parting a wide aisle between me and Frack. I open my mouth to demand to know where she is, but Frack shakes his head.

'Not here," he says. "Come to the security room."

He turns and heads towards the front hallway. I am right on his heels, my thoughts running wild. Talia has been taken. That's the only thing that I can think of that Frack would need me to see for myself.

Or… Or an unknown assailant has wounded her or knocked her unconscious and then dragged her body away from the Morgan Estate and put her in a car.

No one but Talia and I know that she is pregnant, so some harm could come to the baby without the assailant even realizing it. I trudge forward, trying to steel myself for whatever I'm about to see. By the time that I step into the security room, nothing more than a closet really, I swear that every nerve ending I have is on high alert. My hands are clenched into fists, my lower back is sweating through my crisp linen shirt. I look at the wall of computer screens, seeing that each one covers a different angle of the security cameras inside and outside the house. One appears to be the upstairs hallway. Another shows a view of the inside of the multi-car garage, every one of my grandfather's precious collection of rare cars still in their bays. Most of the cameras capture footage of the exterior doors. I noticed just then that there is a nervous looking, young Hispanic man in a dark blue blazer, a white polo shirt, and a pair of dark brown khakis.

Frack moves toward him, gesturing. "This is Carlos. He is going to show you the footage."

My heart pounds. My mouth is dry. Carlos moves forward and gulps as he presses a button on a remote in his hand. Frick taps the top of a particular display to draw my attention to it and I see that it is the feed showing the outside of the back exit into the garden.

"This is from forty minutes ago," Frack says.

I watch as the door opens and Talia emerges from the building. At first, she just stands near the door, leaning against the bricks and looking out at the gardens just beyond. But then she fidgets a bit and pulls her cell phone out of her tiny purse.

She tosses her hair, looking at her cell phone. I don't know exactly what she is reading, but her eyes widen. Her hand flies up over her mouth and she looks horrified. She fidgets again and shoots an angry look at the house. Then she looks down and reads some more. When she's done, she drops her hand, her cell phone still loosely grasped in it. She leans back against the house and closes her eyes for a moment.

She just stays like that for the longest time. Then apparently,she makes up her mind and starts heading towards the front of the house.

The video jumps, suddenly showing the front door footage. I see Talia stalk out toward the front door and then she stops, looking around. She waves to one of the waiting chauffeurs, who is perched on the bonnet of his black Lincoln town car. He straightens and she says something to him. But though the security camera does record sound, it is too far away to make out what she says.

The young man that she called to bows, doffing his hat. He is a fit looking guy with sandy blonde hair and he is just a little taller than her.

He says something unintelligible and then she hurries over to the car, popping open the passenger side door and sliding in. He climbs in, too, and turns the car around, giving us a good view of his license plate. He pauses before he drives off, his brake lights soon the only thing visible in the darkness.

My whole body goes rigid as I watch the video. I don't know what Talia read on her phone that made her run away without a word. A million thoughts pour into my brain, tumbling over one another. It could be some sort of threat to her well-being. Or some kind of lie about me, I guess.

Whatever it is that made her run, I have to track my wife down and bring her back, whether she likes it or not.

My future hangs in the balance.

"Fuck," I mutter. I run a hand through my hair, gritting my teeth.

"She obviously left of her own accord," Frick says. "That's a pretty good thing, as far as I'm concerned."

I shoot him a sour look. "I need you to hunt down that chauffeur. She's not stupid enough to run off alone. She had help, that I am sure. Find out everything he knows about where Talia could have gone."

"Of course." Frick bows her head and leaves the security footage there with Carlos, who looks as though he is trying to blend in with the wall. I stroke my chin and stare at the darkened screen in the surveillance room.

What do I know about Talia and where she would run to?

I know that she has an aunt. I know her friend Olivia is heavily involved with her day-to-day life under normal circumstances. And I think she said she volunteers at some charity… For the life of me, I can't remember exactly which one or even what type of organization it was. Dogs and cats? Sick old people? Breast cancer awareness?

It honestly could have been any of those or a million other bleeding heart sad sack charities.

I pull out my phone and call Rob. My personal assistant picks up on the second ring, sounding more than a little perplexed. "Dare? Do you need something?"

"Remember the background check I had you run on Talia and all her known associates?"

I hear a sharp intake of breath. "Yes… I hired your usual private investigator to run down all the people in her life. There were many."

"I need to know everything you know. Including any locations that she would run to if she were in danger."

There is silence for a few moments. "And is she in danger?"

"Maybe," I growl. "Or maybe she is just trying not to be found. Who the fuck knows what goes on in her mind?"

"But she's gone missing," he says, his voice puzzled. "That's what you're saying?"

"I have security camera footage of her sneaking away from the estate. Talia stole off into the night without a word."

Something crackles on Rob's end of the phone line. "What the fuck?" he asks. "Why would she just leave like that?"

"I don't fucking know!" I explode, gnashing my teeth. "All I know is that we have to get her back. So I need you to look up places that she's been associated with in the past. I will send my security team to each and every location you dig up."

"Of course," he says. "I have the folder that the private investigator gave me right here. I'll compile the list and send it to you shortly. Do you need anything else from me?"

"No. Or… I don't know. Let me call you back. Right now, I can hardly think of anything but where Talia could possibly be. I am going crazy trying to remember if she ever mentioned any people or places to me. I can't believe that I don't even know where she would run to for safety."

"Well, you've only been married for a few hours…" Rob says. I can hear the uneasiness in his voice, though.

"I've got to go." I hang up the phone without another word because I realized that I am literally shaking with rage and no small amount of fear.

What the fuck is Talia thinking? There'd better be a damn good reason for this little rebellion.

Olivia and Aunt Minnie. Those are two names that I have heard Talia repeat over and over again. I have the vaguest sense of who Olivia might be. A quiet blonde with oversized glasses and an ill fitting dress swims up in my vision.

But I know next to nothing about her. I have no idea what her phone number is or where she lives and while I can have my security team look into it, it will take some time. Talia's Aunt Minnie though…

I certainly know where she works. I try to remember if Talia said that they lived together. I think that they did, before I proposed.

I text Rob and ask for the address of their little house. He responds fairly quickly with the address and I am out the door as soon as possible. I leave instructions with the security team to coordinate their efforts with Rob. I feel sweat pooling at my back, running down my spine.

The rev of the Porsche drowns out the persistent thumping beat of my heart. I clench the leather wrapped wheel and peel out, glad that I have a stick shift. It allows me some measure of control, a feeling that I desperately crave just at this moment. Working the clutch and speeding up or slowing down in response to the curves in the road takes my mind off of the sick cycle of racing thoughts. In minutes, I speed through downtown, running red lights recklessly and barely avoiding collisions with other vehicles. I am certainly not new to speeding or switching lanes heedlessly. But by the time I pull up in front of Aunt Minnie's bookshop with a squeal of tires, my engine practically roaring, I'm having heart palpitations. What if Talia is not here?

She might have run here because she didn't think it through. But a sneaking suspicion comes over me that she wouldn't be so thoughtless. I bound out of the Porsche the second I can throw it into park. I leave the keys in it in my rush to get inside.

I stalk up to the storefront, noting the weathered brick and the wide glass display window. To the right is a plate glass door laid into a wood foundation. Stepping close to the display window, I notice that it is covered in gold and silver sparkling glitter. The words 'enchanting', 'fairytale', and 'happily ever after' are written in white cut out letters and taped in the corners of the window. Bending down to see through the sparkles, I cup my hands around my eyes to seal out the intruding light. Right in front of my face is a white shelf covered in glitter with several fairytale books displayed nicely. I can make out several dark, shadowy blobs just beyond it that might be bookshelves. But though I strain to see more, nothing beyond that appears to me in the gloom.

Pushing off the thick window, I head over to the glass door. Though it's obvious that the store is closed from the quaint sign that has been turned to 'closed', I still try to see in. I can only make out vague and shadowy shapes, possibly another bookshelf on my right and a cash register beyond that. But again, nothing clearer. I shape my hands into fists and bang on the door, rattling it.

"Fuck!" I swear. "God dammit, Talia. Where the fuck are you?"

The bookshop looks back at me as I stagger backward, holding my arms out wide. I grimace and turn my face up, beseeching silently.

I don't believe in anything more powerful than money. There is no God that can save me now or deliver Talia to me. But still, I bring my hands together, folding them and bowing for just a moment. Genuflecting, if you will.

Then I turn on my heel and stalk toward my car. A few seconds later, a cold voice stops me in my tracks.

"Dare?"

It's a woman's voice, much older than Talia's. I whirl to face it and there is her Aunt Minnie, glaring at me from the doorway of the bookshop. She is dressed in a flowing violet robe and her hair falls around her shoulders like a cloak, gray and wild, bordering on scraggly if it weren't quite so thick. Her eyes glint blue and I see the resemblance in her proud nose as she tosses back her hair.

"Are you Dare?" She asks.

I cross my arms. "I am. Are you Minnie?"

Aunt Minnie looks me up and down, her mouth puckering slightly. "I am. What are you doing here? And where is Talia?"

I spread my hands wide and shrug. "I came here to ask you the very same thing. I thought she might have come here." I watch Aunt Minnie closely, expecting her perhaps to fidget or act as though she is hiding something. But she merely seems perplexed.

She raises a hand and beckons me closer. "Come here."

I stride closer, glaring at her. She doesn't even flinch, just sizes me up.

"Talia left without saying where she was going?"

I feel a flash of heat spread across the back of my neck.

"That's why I'm here."

"Ah." She leans against the door frame and considers me for several long moments. Her silence seems to crackle in the still air as I wait, heart thumping in my chest.

I need her to say something, to tell me where Talia is. I crack my knuckles.

"Where is Talia?" I ask.

"Hm." She straightens, pushing off the doorway. "I don't know. She's not here."

"Did she call you?"

Aunt Minnie looks down her nose at me. "If she had called me, I don't think she would want you to know it. You seem to have a short fuse. Maybe her disappearing is a sign. Maybe you should give her a little bit of space."

"Fuck that," I snarl. Leaning closer, I expect her to shrink back. She's much smaller than me, her weight much more slight.

But Aunt Minnie doesn't budge. She narrows her eyes and manages to look completely unimpressed by me.

"Don't." She puts up her hand, stopping me in my tracks. "What are you going to do? Huh? Are you going to beat me up?"

I feel a flash of heat on the back of my neck once more.

"I'll do whatever I have to do to find Talia," I rasp out. "I will search everywhere for her. She can't hide from me."

Aunt Minnie gives me a wry chuckle. "I have no doubt that you believe that. You are very much your father's son. You know that?"

"That isn't exactly a compliment," I grit out.

"I didn't mean it to be one!" She fires back, as sharp as a honed blade. "You Morgans are all the damned same. When Talia told me she was marrying you…" She clamps her mouth shut, her chin wobbling as she whips her head from side to side. "I tried to tell her."

"I don't know what the fuck you're talking about!" I snap. "I'm just trying to find Talia. I'm worried about her!"

And furious with her, but there is no need to get into that just now.

"Well, I don't know what to tell you," Minnie bites off. She scowls at me and crosses her arms, withdrawing at last. "She hasn't called. And if she had, I wouldn't tell you. You won't find Talia by darkening my doorstep, you big bully."

"A lot of help you are," I hiss at her.

Turning, I start pacing toward my Porsche again. I hear Aunt Minnie's voice call out as I am rounding the trunk, my eyes locked on the driver's side door handle.

"Give her space! I raised her for twenty three years. If Talia is mad, the worst thing you can do is invade her privacy."

I fling the car door open and shout at Aunt Minnie as I climb in.

"Talia gave up her privacy when she agreed to wear my fucking ring. She's *mine* now. My little wife, carrying my fucking baby."

Aunt Minnie gapes at me as I slam the door to the car. I realize belatedly that Talia probably hasn't told her aunt about the baby yet and I probably just ruined any chance at a special moment between them.

But it's not my fucking fault.

It's Talia's fault for running away.

I'm going to find her. And by god, I'm going to punish

her for this little stunt. I'm going to put her across my lap and spank her plump ass until it glows red as a cherry.

And then I'm going to fuck her until she knows that I own her, body and soul, for as long as we both shall fucking live. Every inch of Talia is long since bought and paid for.

The engine roars to life as I gun it, heading off into the darkness to find my wife.

"I really can't thank you enough for the ride." I swallow, looking at the young man that helped me escape from the party. He takes off his chauffeur's cap and scrubs a hand through his hair, looking aggravated.

"You didn't say why you needed to leave. And I am not asking you to tell me. I just want to know that you're safe." He peers out the windshield at the random block of houses I've had him stop the car at. "Are you sure that this is where you want to be dropped off?"

I nod and pull my wallet from my purse. It's a tiny thing, just large enough to accommodate my ID and debit card and a little bit of cash. I take the forty dollars that I have and offer it to the driver.

"I'm sure. Please take this."

He shakes his head and glances out the windshield again. It's fully dark and the houses on the street are a little run down.

"I don't feel right leaving you here. And I won't take your money."

Giving him a smile, I put the money on the seat between

us and open my door. "It's for the best. Trust me, when my husband comes looking for me, you don't want to know where I am."

"Your husband?" He asks. "But is he really going to track me down?"

I shrug and get out of the car. "Maybe. I can't say. Thank you for the ride, though."

Before he can protest anymore, I slam the car door and turn away, walking quickly down the cracked sidewalk. The college where Olivia works is only a few blocks away in the other direction, but I need to be cautious. Even though the chauffeur acted as my white knight just now, who knows how he will behave under the pressure of Dare Morgan. My heart speeds up as I think of just how angry Dare is right now.

Rushing along the unkempt sidewalk, I swallow and try to hold my head high. My husband will no doubt be furious when I disappear. But he has lied to me and deceived me for most of the time that I've known him.

Dare Morgan deserves what he gets.

I take the long way around, doubling back and retracing my steps several times before I walk up to the college campus. It's late on Wednesday night and the campus is hushed, only a few students rushing to and from late-night studies and their respective dorms. In the daytime, I know that this small college has several sets of multistory red brick ivy-covered buildings. I rush past the brick and stained glass chapel and the looming administration building with its great dome looking down on the rest of the campus. I have to get to the massive science complex, the place where I know Olivia will be working late. She always works late on Wednesdays and Thursdays. I approach it from the back, heading straight across the immaculately trimmed grass and up the steps to a white marble building.

There are a few lights on in the building. I make a note as I climb the stairs that the lab that Olivia runs is definitely one of them.

I try the door and find it open. Inside, my footsteps echo on the white marble floor as I head up the stairs, straight to Olivia's lab. I make it all the way to the door of the lab before I find a locked door. I peer inside through a long rectangular window, knocking on the door. Olivia is bent over a lab table, carefully pipetting a liquid from a beaker to a small tray of samples.

At the sound of my knock, she snaps upright, her blonde head turning toward the sound, her eyes wide. I give her an urgent wave and she pulls out a pair of earbuds from her ears as she sets the science equipment down. She rushes over to the door and opens it, her puzzlement clear on her face.

"Talia! What are you doing here?" She looks at her watch, squinting. "It's after ten p.m. I was just about to wrap up my experiment and head home."

I glance behind me, licking my lips. "Can I come in?"

"Of course." She steps back and waves me through the door. I glance around at the table in her lab and the desk with everything neat, tidy, and extremely organized. Olivia is a little bit of a neat freak. Perhaps it was a necessity in her job as a researcher in this lab.

I close the door firmly behind me and then turn to her. She reaches out to me, rubbing my bare arm.

"God, are you cold? It's freezing outside!"

"I didn't have time to grab my coat. I sort of ran away from the Morgan estate and Dare. I…"

My eyes well up with tears and I inhale a shaky breath. Olivia looks a little horrified and guides me over to her desk, where she plucks a navy cardigan off the back of her chair and hands it to me. I take it thankfully and swallow against the lump in my throat.

"Talia, what's going on? Why did you run away from Dare?"

"Because... Because he's a liar!" I spit out. "He paid someone to break into Aunt Minnie's store. And he paid them to make it look like Aunt Minnie was being threatened by the sketchy guys that she took her loan out from. But that's not all... Then Dare paid actors to come into the restaurant where I was working and mistreat me. He's... he's horrible."

With that, I dissolved in tears. Olivia quickly wraps her arms around me, rubbing my shoulder.

"Oh, Talia." She inhales sharply. "I had no idea. Really. If I had known that he would do something so horrible, I would never have advocated for you to accept his marriage proposal. Honest."

I let myself cry for a full minute, great gasping sobs as I lay my head on my best friend's shoulder. But after that, I control myself, wiping at my face and struggling to voice my thoughts.

"I don't know what to do," I admit. Olivia grabs a handful of tissues from a box on her desk and hands them to me. I blot at my face, which is hot and wet from crying.

"But it's okay. You're going to be okay. You are with someone that loves you and cares about you," she says soothingly.

I give her a one-armed hug and then separate from her. "I need to think. I need to be alone and figure out my next step. Where can I go so that Dare won't find me?"

Olivia looks pensive. "What about my grandfather's old cabin up in the woods near Ketchum mountain? I know we haven't been there in ages. But my mom still rents it out on occasion. It's not really the warm summer season, so I'm pretty sure that the cabin will be deserted. And there's no way to find you if you're out there. I mean, it's hard enough to find the cabin on a map, much less know that you're there."

I inhale, blowing the breath out as I nod. "I hadn't thought of that. It's been so long since we even went there… I was probably fourteen the last time I laid eyes on that place."

"Well, since Grandpa passed away, my mom has put a little money into fixing his old cabin up. She's made sure that it is fortified against the cold as long as whoever is staying there runs the wood stove the entire time."

For a moment, I picture the two of us as teens, laying in the grass by the cabin and giggling about our crushes. It almost makes me smile, despite the dire circumstances I'm currently facing.

"You really think that I could use the cabin?" I ask anxiously.

Olivia grabs her cell phone off her desk and starts to text her mother. "I am like ninety nine point nine percent sure. You can also take my car. I have to be back here in a few hours, but in the morning, but that doesn't stop you from going. And depending on how long you decide to stay out there, I can join you on Friday evening."

I feel a little bit sick, a wave of nausea washing over me. I pull out the office chair from Olivia's desk and sit down, trying to breathe deeply.

It's nice that my best friend has some place for me to run to. But the very fact that I am already running away from the man I married only earlier today is almost enough to make me want to throw up. The deception… The lies… How Dare fucked me and then looked me in the eye and promised that there were no secrets between us…

I grip the desk and try to breathe in deeply through my nose and exhale slowly through my mouth.

Olivia perks a brow, peering at me over her cell phone. "You okay?"

I shake my head. "I am very much not okay. I can't believe that I fell for Dare's lies. He just completely blindsided me. And I was willing to be his pretty little wife. Honestly, I blame myself as much as Dare. I knew he was a snake when I met him. But I never thought he would turn his fangs on me."

She frowns deeply and then puts her cell phone away in her pocket. "My mom says that no one is staying at the cabin. So we are all good there. I think you'll need to stop at a convenience store on the way there for firewood. But other than that, the house is clean and ready for guests."

Nodding my head, I swallow. I try to push the idea of Dare out of my head. Right now, I have to focus on what's right in front of me. I can't be worried about how angry he will be when he finds me gone.

If he hasn't already, that is.

Olivia grabs a coat and slides it around my shoulders, then urges me to follow her. She passes me her keys, pointing out the key to the cabin as we walk down the echoing halls of the science building.

"What am I going to do for clothes?" I ask aloud. Not really addressing Olivia, more just wondering.

"Well you can have whatever I have in my go bag." Olivia pushes the door open and I step out into the icy night air. She hustles me down to the back of the building, where I see a mostly empty parking lot. Her car is at the back of the lot and I walk across the newly paved parking lot. "What do you mean go bag?" I ask.

She eyes me skeptically as we approach her car. "You don't have a go bag? What about if there is an emergency?" She reaches over to my hand and grabs a key, popping the trunk of her car. We walk up to the trunk and she opens it further, lifting a duffel bag from the car. She unzips it and shows me the contents. It looks like a few clothes, a bag of toiletries, and a big heavy blanket. She lifts the blanket and shows me that there is a box of protein bars underneath and a few bottles of water.

My brows rise and I look at her with some surprise. "Prepared for anything, huh?"

Olivia shrugs and gestures around us. "For emergencies, just like this one." She presses the keys into my hand again and jerks her chin toward the driver side door. "Let me give you the address of the cabin. You need to get it now while you still have cell service, because there isn't much when you get up into the mountains. The same thing goes for food and groceries and anything else you get in the convenience store. You need to get it like twenty miles from the cabin, because when you get closer, there is just nothing out there. And don't forget the firewood."

I give her a hard hug, surprising her a little. She hugs me back and then lets go. Olivia moves to open the driver side door and looks at me expectantly. "Get moving. If I know anything about the Morgans, I know that they have unlimited resources. And when Dare figures out that you're gone, he will undoubtedly use those resources to find you. The sooner you go, the sooner you'll be out of the range of his reach."

"Thank you, Olivia." I give her a small, sad smile. "I will drive back into the range of cell phone service Friday morning just to check and see if you left me any messages. Okay?"

She gives my hand a squeeze and then steps back. "Okay. Everything that I hear, I will send along via texts. Just be safe, okay?"

"Thank you, Olive."

She gives me the same reserved smile. "Of course, Leah. I would do anything for you. That's what sisters are for." Nodding, I gather myself up and start the car. I close the door and back out of the parking space. Olivia waves to me once, standing in the parking lot. I wave back at her and then drive away.

IT'S ALMOST two AM by the time I turn down the bumping, gravel road in the pitch black darkness. There are tall pine trees on either side of me, covered in a thick blanket of snow. About twenty minutes ago, the snow started to fall, obscuring the view from the windows. It started off a light snowfall but has increased until now, when I'm driving five miles an hour, the brights on the car flashing, bouncing wildly off the newly fallen banks of snow that have fallen on the ground as far as the eye can see. I'm determined to make it to the cabin itself. But at this point, I have both hands clenching the wheel, leaning forward to peer out the window as I go.

I squint and try to get closer to the windshield. It's only a little about six inches from my face at this point so I'm not sure how to see the road any better. My GPS on my phone tells me that I have arrived but I just keep crawling forward until the cabin seems to appear right before my very eyes, solidifying in the burgeoning snowstorm. I slam on the brakes and my heart jumps into my throat. Putting the car in park, I unclench my hands from the steering wheel. As I shake out the tension that has been building in my fingers, I look at the cabin.

I can make out the front porch just fine, a window beside the rustic front door. But I can't see the lines of the roof. There's too much snow in the air to gauge the true size. I remember this cabin being pretty small when I stayed here last but I just suck in a deep breath and blow it out.

Taking the keys out of the ignition and turning off the car's lights, I open the door into a blast of freezing cold air and immediate dampness as snowflakes hit my bare skin. I grab the keys and my cell phone and drop them in my pocket, then try to head around the back of the car, opening the trunk and wrestling the gray gym bag free. I run towards the porch, my teeth starting to chatter already. I pile the gym bag by the door and go back to the trunk for several stacks of firewood and two small paper bags of groceries.

It takes me three more trips to wrestle the firewood and groceries onto the porch and close the car trunk. It is blindingly cold, my fingers feel numb and I scrape my whole right hand up on the rough raw logs. It's everything I can do to manage to fish the keys out of my pocket and find the front door key.

To my relief, the door opens without much fuss. It creaks open and I drag my bag inside first, then the groceries, then the wood. I barely get a glance at the little two room cottage cabin before I close the door and lock it. Beginning to shake all over, I wrap my arms around myself and look around the room. Here directly in front of me is a small sitting area with a couch and the wood burning stove. There is a small kitchen, a tiny bathroom, and a closed-door that I remember leading into a bedroom. The place has been jazzed up, all the windows cheerfully decorated in red gingham, the couch a basic gray corduroy but relatively new and clean. There is a huge pile of blankets and sheets and pillows on the couch.

Blowing on my hands, I decide that the first order of business is to start a fire in the wood burning stove. It takes me a couple of minutes and a lot of discarded newspapers from a box labeled fire starters. But I manage to get the fire going and I leave the door open wide, enjoying the heat that it immediately brings to the room. I hold my fingers out and the fire warms them quickly. Sliding my gaze around the room, I try to decide what to do next.

Outside, the heavy snowstorm becomes a downright blizzard. I can't see anything at all and the entire world just looks like a blank white screen. That's definitely not a good sign. Or maybe it is… If I find it difficult to get my car out of the road and back to Harwicke, Dare will certainly have trouble finding me.

Wishing that I were wearing a pair of comfy sweats instead of this fancy dress, I spend the next few minutes putting the firewood in a pile by the stove and putting away my meager groceries. I realize that most of the power in the tiny cabin isn't on. But that is easily enough remedied because there is a large sticky note over an electrical box with a set of switches. When I slip them on, the whole cabin lights up at one time. That's good to know. Especially because I was just wondering about using the tiny bathroom and thinking how cold it was going to be in there. I turn the tiny heat lamp on in the bathroom for a minute and then go check out the bedroom. It's barely more than a tiny room, a double sized bed built into the far wall and a bookshelf full of aging paperbacks stuffed in it.

The bedroom has a tiny space heater, too, and I crank that on, more worried about how freaking cold it is right now that I am about conserving any kind of power. Grabbing my bag, I rifle through the contents and change into a pair of yoga pants and a basic black sweatshirt with the name of the college that Olivia works at on the front. Olivia, God bless her, remembered to stick thick socks in the bag. I hustle into my new outfit and then hurry to the bathroom, thinking all the while about how badly I have to pee. I do my business and then wash my hands in the freezing cold tap water, leaving the tap running just a bit.

Thinking about the fact that I should leave the kitchen sink running as well, I move to the door. There is a rectangular mirror on the door, one of those cheap ones that you can find at any dollar store. I catch a glimpse of myself and stop, staring at my reflection. I turned to the side, slowly shaping my stomach with my hands. I swear, I didn't notice it before. But there is decidedly a noticeable little poof right below my belly button. And I don't mean it looks like I had too much to eat…

I have a baby bump. Lifting the sweatshirt, I move my body side to side, trying to figure out if I am going crazy or whether I could be showing so soon. By my calculations, I am only three and a half months pregnant… That's way too soon to be showing, isn't it?

I dropped the sweater back over my stomach and smooth it down, swallowing hard.

As if I needed another reminder that I carry the child that the Morgan clan would kill each other for. I definitely don't want to think about the lengths that Dare and Burn will go to if it means ascertaining their victory with their awful grandfather.

I make it out of the bathroom just in time to hear the sound of falling snow hitting metal. Padding over to the front window, I look out. I realize that I can't see anything at all. But I hope that sound was simply the snow falling off the roof and hitting the hood of the car. My mouth pulls down at one corner. I am definitely stuck here, whether I like it or not.

I head over to the groceries and make myself a peanut butter sandwich, scarfing it down once I realize how starving I am. At one point, I pause my sandwich making to check out a noise I heard that sounded like the house breaking and splintering in the corner. But when I go to check, it's just a noise.

It's funny, I have lived in the Northeast for my entire life and yet I don't think I've ever been so freaked out over every little noise as I am today. Maybe because I'm so keyed up, maybe there are just more odd and unexplained sounds now.

Moving the sheets and blankets to the bedroom, I sit on the couch and eat my sandwich. All the while, I am just coming to terms with the fact that I am leaving Dare. Leaving a Morgan man will not be easy. He will definitely demand repayment of his two hundred and fifty thousand dollars sooner rather than later. And then I will be on my own again, all alone, pregnant and not a little bit frightened. Aunt Minnie and Olivia made it clear enough to me that I wasn't choosing between marrying Dare or homelessness. But having a roof over my head won't really pay Aunt Minnie's loans. And I am not sure how well her loan shark will take it when I tell him that I need him to give the money back.

Do they even do that? Frankly, I don't know.

My eyelids grow heavy. The wood stove is putting off quite a bit of heat now and I'm quite certain that this is the first moment that I have not felt cold all night. Closing my eyes and resting my head on my arms, I drift off to sleep. As I fall, I can only think of how I am stuck between a rock and a hard place in my life.

Chapter Three

DARE

"And? Where is she? Where is my wife?"

The private investigator glances nervously around the coffee shop where he agreed to meet me. He looks nothing like what I imagine a private investigator looks like. He's young, extremely gaunt, with a shorn scalp, dark eyebrows, a lip ring, a tight black hoodie, and the honest to God tightest pair of black jeans I've ever seen. He looks at me and swallows.

I lean forward, almost leaving my seat, and snarl at him. "Where is Talia? Tell me right now or get the fuck out of my face."

This new investigator, the fifth that I have talked to in the last day and a half, leaps to his feet and backs up, putting his soft leather chair between us.

"Hey man, I'm sorry that your wife left you. But that's no reason to be a dick."

I get to my feet, my anger filling every inch of my being, crackling around me as I glare at him. He gulps and turns tail to run out of the coffee shop. I clench my fists and look at him as he runs around the glass walls of the coffee shop. He is a fucking idiot. But so were the four investigators that I talked to and fired before I came to talk to him.

"Sir?" A young barista asks me. "Are you okay?"

I glance over at her and she smiles coquettishly at me. She's blonde and thin, her big tits pushed-up in a tight little shirt that she wears under a blue and green apron. She's pretty, in an alternative, indie rock kind of way. Normally I would spend a few minutes here, talking to her, seeing how she feels about taking orders and spending a few hours in my bed.

But just now, I don't have time for her. There is only one pretty young girl on my mind, and her name is Talia fucking Chance.

No.

A shiver runs through me as I think of her new name.

Talia Morgan.

She will be back under my control very soon.

I flop a hand at the barista and stride towards the door, pulling my cell phone out. I check my text messages and see that Rob has finally gotten back to me about Talia's little friend Olivia. She is surprisingly difficult to track down and who I have yet to talk to about Talia's disappearance.

The text just reads 'found her home address...' Followed by an address on the other side of Harwicke, just down the street from Talia's old house. I walk straight out to my waiting chauffeur, climbing in the back seat and giving him the address. My heart beats fast and I can't keep the smile off my lips.

If Olivia knows where Talia is, I am about to break her.

I wait in Olivia's darkened kitchen until she gets home at ten thirty. The room is tiny, the worn flowered linoleum on the floor peeling at the corners, the paint on the cabin has gone gray with age, the ugly green countertop chipped and warped. It's not a nice place to wait, but at least it's quiet enough to do some thinking and hatch a plan for what I want to say to Olivia.

But by the time she gets home, the front door opening with a groan, I am waiting, sitting on the worn countertop. I hear the sound of her keys hitting the entryway table and the clunk of heavy boots as she takes off her coat and her shoes. I don't have to wait long for her to flick on the light, illuminating the shabby old refrigerator, the scant cupboards, and me. I lean forward, glaring at her. She gives me exactly the reaction I want because she splits the night air with a shrill scream.

She looks around, panicking. But I hop off the counter and fold my arms across my chest.

"There you are, Olivia. I've been looking for you. I think you know where Talia is."

She looks at me sharply and her eyes narrow on my face. "What are you doing in my fucking house? Get out. Now!"

"Now Olivia, I need you to shut the fuck up and listen to me."

"Get out! Get out right now or I'm calling the police. You can't just come into my house and wait for me here. It's creepy."

I shrug my shoulders. "You can call the police if you want to. We both know who the police really work for, and it isn't for the average Joe's in this city. I have the Chief of Police on speed dial. I can call them right now if that will speed things up."

Olivia licks her upper lip and glares at me. "You are intolerable. I don't know how Talia even stood you for as long as she did. I would have poisoned you, I'm pretty sure."

Something low in my body tightens. "Just tell me where she is."

She gives me a disbelieving laugh. "You've gotta be kidding me. Most men in your situation would be crawling on their hands and knees right now, kissing my feet and begging for that kind of information. But you have the nerve to come here and demand that I tell you where my best friend is after she ran away from you?" She makes an exasperated gesture. "You gotta be out of your mind. Like totally crazy."

It's not like I expected Talia's best friend to just roll over and give me Talia's address or anything. But she is making this harder than it needs to be.

It's time for the second phase of my plan. I will get the address from her the way that I get anything and everything that I've ever wanted in this life. Through deception and trickery and knowing the right people in higher places.

I shrug, uncrossing my arms and trying to look worried. "Talia's doctor called last night. She got the results of Talia's genetic testing back. That's the testing they usually do before a fetus is twenty four weeks old." The lie leaves my lips smoothly, although I haven't rehearsed a single word of it. I am relying on my confidence and Olivia's lack of knowledge to sell my deception. I lean forward, dropping my voice like someone that's actually worried would. "There may be something wrong with the baby. I'm not just trying to hunt Talia down for shits and giggles. There's really a lot riding on Talia getting to the doctor as soon as possible."

Olivia pokes her cheek out with her tongue, staring at my face and trying to decide if I am being truthful or not. I don't waiver and after a few moments, her shoulders sag the tiniest bit.

That could mean that Olivia has bought my lie hook, line and stinker.

"Dare, you should leave. Even if I knew where Talia is, and I'm not saying that I do know, I wouldn't tell you even if you threatened to kill me. I am loyal to Talia and I will be until my very last breath."

That surprises me a little. My eyebrows rise and I take a half a step back. "You're serious."

"Serious as a heart attack." She waves her hand towards the front door. "Now leave, before I call your bluff and get the police down here."

I snort. "Morgans don't bluff. But I do have a few other places that I can search for Talia. So I will see you around."

"I hope not. I really hope not." Olivia's voice is tight as she ushers me out of her house. Stepping outside into the frosty air, I turn up my coat collar and hustle toward my waiting SUV. When I get in, I tell the driver to start moving, anywhere but here is fine.

I need to be out of Olivia's line of sight long enough for her to make a phone call, which would complete my little act of deception. See, if Olivia is dumb enough to call Talia, my private investigator will tap her phone and give me the location of Talia's hideout.

Bing bang boom. Talia is caught in my web again. And I'm going to wrap her in a silk cocoon so tight that she'll never get free, no matter how hard she struggles.

I'm gone for less than five minutes before I get the phone call I have been waiting for so desperately.

"Yeah?" I answer. My private investigator Sam rumbles out an answer. "You are right. As soon as you left, Olivia started sending a flurry of texts. I'm going to patch you through right now. But don't worry, they can't hear us on the line. It's a one-way connection."

There is an audible clicking sound and then I hear Olivia talking. Her voice is hushed and frantic.

"Dare was here."

"Oh?" My wife answers.

The sound of Talia's voice pushes me to the edge of sanity. I was right, Olivia did know where Talia is hiding out. I'm going to have to click Talia's wings and cut her relationship with Olivia into ribbons in order to prevent this from happening again. Talia needs to know that she will never escape me, never live another day where she isn't Mrs. Morgan.

"He said that the doctor called and said that there may be something wrong with the fetus."

I hear Talia's quick inhale of breath. "Do you think that he was being honest?"

Olivia pauses before answering. "I don't think Dare has ever been honest a single time in his whole life. But I do think that you need to get this checked out. Assuming that you still want the pregnancy, it isn't worth risking the fetus' life on the assumption that Dare may be lying. He lies as easily as he breathes, but it's too risky not to have this checked out by a doctor up there."

"All right," I growl.

There is a clicking sound again and then the women's voices disappear. Sam asked the most obvious question.

"So what do you want me to do? I have the address. You want me to go up there and get her?"

I laugh, the sound cold and menacing.

"Oh no," I say. I smile at my private investigator's question, though he can't see my expression. "I'll go and get her. You've done your piece."

Chapter Four

TALIA

It takes longer than I thought to get up to the remote cabin in snowy rural Vermont. By the time I turn my Porsche onto the tree-covered, snowy private driveway, it's nearly light outside. The path is so filled with fresh snow that it becomes impassable just as the vague outline of the little cabin roof jutting out of the fresh snow appears.

But I am not about to let myself be slowed down by anything. Not weather, not distance, not anything short of death could keep me from Talia now that I know where she is.

It's a slog to get through the rest of the snow between my parked car and the cabin. But I push on and remind myself that inside this cabin is my little wife. The idea of her shock as she finds me knocking on her door is enough to power me through the thick snow without proper gear. When I finally step foot onto the cabin's front porch, my eyes narrow. I'm freezing and all my extremities are so cold as to almost be numb. But I knock the snow off my pants and boots, smiling to myself. I try the front door and find it locked but that's really no problem for me. I fish a credit card out of my wallet and make quick work of jimmying the lock.

Once inside the cabin, I am blasted with a wave of hot air. Talia is nowhere to be seen but I have a feeling that I am about to find her at long last. I close the door behind me, looking around the little sitting area and the kitchen. Then I see that there are two closed doors. I start to walk towards them when the door directly facing me creaks open. I see a flash of scared, pale face and a few strands of brilliant copper hair. Then I hear a muffled sound as the door is slammed shut.

Leaning down, I run at the door, ramming it with my shoulder. It gives way with very little resistance and I burst into a tiny bedroom. All I can see inside is my little wife, sitting rigidly on the bed, gripping the mattress with both hands. Her head is thrown back, her red hair streams out from her head in a wild mass, her expression is frightened and tight.

Her eyes are pleading with me.

"Dare," she says, her voice soft. "What are you doing here?"

In my chest, my heart thumps raggedly. I stalk towards her, not stopping when I reach her body. Instead, I push her down on the bed, my hand wrapping around her throat, moving my legs until they settle between her knees. I lean down and look into her eyes, close enough to her lips to kiss her. I can feel her begin to tremble all over and God help me, I can't get enough of her fear.

"You're my little wife now, darling girl." My voice escapes my lips in a seductive purr. I drop my body down against hers, my hips flexing into her body. My cock stirs when it meets her inner thigh. I grab her left hand and thread my fingers through hers, bringing it down to my lips and intentionally flashing the huge diamond engagement ring I bought her. "I thought I made myself clear. You can never leave me. We're man and wife now and it will be that way as long as we both shall live."

Her breathing comes in shallow pants. She licks her lips and looks up at me, as if trying to decide if it's worth fighting back against me. I encourage her by flicking my hips against hers, and lowering my mouth the last few inches to her lips. This is no sweet, tender kiss.

I kiss her with an intensity that I've never felt before. Brutal, harsh, completely lacking in any sort of kindness. My hand moves up to cup her chin and I suck in a breath as I plunder her lips. She opens her mouth to protest against the invasion. But I just angle her head and snake my tongue deeper into the crevice she creates.

I'm hungry for her, starving in fact. All but suffocating with the need for Talia to submit to me and give me what I'm asking for.

All of her.

Every last inch.

When I finally break the kiss, Talia sucks in a breath and looks at me with something bordering on hatred in her eyes. "I don't want you, Dare. This marriage was a mistake."

I run my free hand down her hip, squeezing her thigh painfully. I look in her eyes and utter, "You signed away the right to have anything to say. When I paid you, I bought the right to touch you how I want. To talk to you however I want. If I want to chain you to my goddamn bed? I will. So don't fucking test me, darling girl."

Talia gives me a glare and tries to push me off. I lean down and utter the next sentence against her lips.

"You don't have any choice anymore. I want to see the

pussy that I paid for. So spread those legs for me and smile while you take my cock."

She gasps. I push myself up and rip at her clothing, an ugly sweatshirt and a pair of black yoga pants. She tries to cover her breasts but I step back for only a second to shed my clothing too. Her breasts are heaving as I return to her body, prying her knees apart and pressing my thick erection against her inner thigh once more.

She's going to protest. I can see it in her eyes. I smirk at her and run my hand down her collarbone, tracing a line between her breasts.

She shivers and I can see myself as she sees me in that moment. A big, powerful man who hunted her down when she ran away.

A man who isn't interested in hearing the word *no*.

Talia gasps and kisses me hard, arching her body into mine and biting my lip hard. I growl and pin her hips with my own, thrusting against her soft warmth. She bites her lip and wraps her legs around my body, trying to draw me in.

I am uninterested in her attempts at wresting control from me. I pull away from her warmth, kissing her hard and then putting a hand to her chest to separate us completely.

Talia surges up and I put my hand around her throat, squeezing gently and looking her dead in the eyes. "Behave. I'll fuck you when I'm good and ready, not a second before that."

"You're the devil," she spits back.

"Don't I know it." I grin and flex my fingers against her delicate neck. "Now be a good girl and stay put while I explore."

She writhes beneath me, a fire in her eyes that is only matched by the fire inside me, threatening to burn me alive if I don't kiss the skin of her collarbone right fucking now. It's hot and sweet, with a trace of salt from the fact that it's getting hot in this tiny bedroom. When I suck hard for just a moment, a low hiss leaves her lips.

"Shh," I murmur. "If you make a sound, I'll stop."

I hear a muffled yelp as Talia struggles to sit up. I skim my fingers down her stomach, teasing the skin just below her belly button.

"Do you want me to continue?" I ask.

Her mouth pulls to the side. I can tell she wants to argue, to fling words at me. I still my hand, quirking a brow. She looks distinctly frustrated.

But instead of telling me off, she just shakes her head. I smirk at her and drop a kiss right between her glorious bare breasts.

"Good girl."

I palm one of Talia's tits, admiring its shape and the weight against my skin. The skin of her areola intrigues me; it's a whispered caress against my skin, just the color of a soft satin ballet slipper. Her breasts are on the small side but they're nearly symmetrical. I can't stop staring at them and touching them, rolling her nipple between my fingers until it grows hard and dusky.

She makes a stifled noise and I remember with stunning clarity that she is here too. Her nipple pebbles, creating an interesting texture beneath my fingers. I lower my mouth to her breast, dropping hot kisses around her nipple. Teasing, tormenting little bites to her velvety nipples that arouse me as much as Talia. She represses a moan and I stop, looking up at her.

"What was that?" I ask, cocking my head to the side.

She shakes her head quickly, her mouth bunching. I stare at her for a few seconds before I push her breasts together and lick, suck, and bite them both. She squirms, her breathing growing harsh.

I skate my fingers down between her thighs, carelessly shoving at her legs to open them, and tease one finger slowly up her slit. She's dripping, hot and wet, her body preparing itself for me. She convulses, sitting halfway up.

I'm quick to shush her. "Don't make me stop, darling girl. Not when I am enjoying your body so much."

I bring my finger up to my mouth, my eyes locked with Talia's while I lick her juices off as messily as possible. I swear that I actually see her pupils widen. Usually when I have sex, it's all about my pleasure. I'm in a hurry to give the nameless, faceless woman an orgasm so that I can come.

But right now, it's different.

With Talia… it feels different. I get as much pleasure from watching her squirm as I ever did from burying myself in any number of basic fucks.

I don't understand the emotions that swirl around us at this moment, but I drink them in, savoring them all the same.

She starts to lower her hands from their position over her head, frustrated at my lack of movement. At last, I move down her body, kissing and nipping her tender flesh, skimming down her ribs, her belly button, her hips. I slow down and pay special attention to the new swell of her abdomen.

Talia writhes and squirms, making a soft sound that is clearly not happy. I take the hint and move on, pressing her thighs wide as I drop kisses on the area that would normally be covered by the tiny triangle of her panties. Her hands touch my hair and I let her thread her fingers through my locks.

I mark her flesh on her inner thighs, inhaling deeply when I catch the sweet musk of her excitement perfuming the air.

"Fuck, Talia. You smell so damn sweet, darling girl. I

can't wait to taste you." My voice is raspy and low, my hands shaking slightly as I move back up to explore her body more extensively.

My kiss moves slowly down her body, tracing the curves and dips of her sculpted form until I reach the juncture between her legs. The sweet scent of her arousal fills my senses and I revel in it, inhaling deeply as I tease and tantalize the slick folds of her desire. Talia gasps and writhes beneath me, every inch of her body begging for more. She is fucking pleading with me to hurry up. But I take my time to savor each and every sigh and squirm.

I love having such power over Talia.

I answer her pleas by pressing forward, pushing my tongue against each ridge and curve until she is arching into my mouth with a convulsing sigh. Each taste and sensation sets off a wave of pleasure that shudders through both our bodies, leaving us panting as the intensity builds.

She clutches at my hair as I swirl my tongue around her clit. I lick and taste every part of her until she is quivering from head to toe. Then I stop, pulling away. Talia groans, her nails turning into weapons as they rake my shoulders.

"You're so impatient." I rear up and kneel between her legs, fisting my cock.

"And you're a bastard." Talia moans and writhes, her hand slipping down to her clit. I fling her hand away, pinning it back on the bed.

"Good things always come to those that wait for them," I whisper. "Have I ever left you unsatisfied, darling girl?"

Her eyes spark with defiance. "Hurry up and fuck me, Dare."

I shove my hands underneath her body and lift, pulling her closer and repositioning her. Fisting my cock again, I smirk.

"You asked for it," I grate out.

Talia's thighs shake as I put the flushed head of my cock at her entrance. I tease her pussy with shallow strokes, never fully entering her pussy. She wraps her legs around my back and tries to use the leverage to force me to stop teasing her.

That only makes me slow down my thrusts. She makes a guttural sound that is part enraged, part imploring.

"Dare, I swear to god," she mutters.

I grant her request, sinking my cock deep into her greedy pussy, fucking her hard for a dozen strokes. Then I pull out and press her knees wide as I smoothly switch back to sucking her clit.

"Oh god," she whispers, her hands burrowing deep in my hair. "Fuck!"

She tastes like nothing else in the world. She's sweet yet salty and full of passion. It makes my mouth water even more each time I swirl my tongue around her clit.

Talia gives her body over to me completely, finding new heights of ecstasy. Just before she reaches the peak though, I pull back slightly. I'm purposely edging her, giving her what she wants, but so gently that it's maddening. The contact is just enough so that we can still feel connected without sending her over the edge just yet.

"Dare," she whines.

I kiss and lick my way up her body, leaving a trail of love bites behind me until I reach the juncture between her legs. She shivers beneath me as I explore every inch with my tongue and lips and fingers. She cries out in pleasure, eyes fluttering shut as she absorbs every sensation that I give her.

When I reach the peak of pleasure, Talia is writhing beneath me, clutching me tightly and moaning my name in a desperate whisper over and over again. Her breathing is heavy and erratic as she clutches at my shoulders for leverage while pushing herself against me, begging for release from this exquisite torment that she has been subjected to.

I can feel her anger radiating off her like heat off a sidewalk after a summer storm.

Although I'm not sure what has sparked this sudden rage, I know better than to argue with her. Instead, I silently move back to allow her the space she needs to process whatever is going on inside of her head.

She stands in front of me, eyes blazing as she stares me down defiantly. I expect a scathing comment or an insult but instead, she surprises me yet again by lunging forward and pushing me onto the bed. She straddles my waist as I lie motionless, allowing her to take control of this situation.

Talia leans down and places gentle kisses on every inch of my body before finally moving lower and lower until she reaches my cock. She strokes it gently with one hand while licking and teasing it with the other. Waves of intense pleasure shoot through every nerve in my body.

It's almost too much for me to handle but despite the agony that is building up inside of me, I refuse to give in just yet. I refuse to let go until Talia is ready. As if sensing my struggle, she stops suddenly and flips over onto her back next to me on the bed before teasingly holding up one finger in invitation for more pleasure.

I don't hesitate for even a second before pushing myself atop her, our bodies pressed together as closely as possible until every inch is touching some part of the other's skin.

The raw power of our desire for each other is palpable in the air as I thrust deeply into Talia's body.

"You're never leaving me again, little girl," I utter. "You hear that? You'll die as my perfect little wife, Talia."

Talia huffs an icy laugh. "We'll see about that."

My strokes turn punishing. I have nothing left except enmity for Talia, and I prove it to her as I fuck her senseless.

"You're going to pay for trying to leave me," I grate out.

Talia tightens her grip around my shoulders as she feels the depth of my need for her. She nips at my ear with her teeth, running her tongue around the shell as if to emphasize her point. My eyes roll back in my head as I'm overwhelmed by the sensations that wash over me.

I move my hips faster and harder as I feel Talia's body respond to my movements. She encourages me, grabbing my ass and wrapping her legs around me tightly as I plunge deeper still into her. Her nails score my back as her moans get louder and louder. The sounds are a testament to the pleasure I'm eliciting from her body.

"That's right, darling girl. Moan for me. You know who you belong to, don't you?"

"Fuck you," she hisses, her eyes closed in conventration.

Each movement intensifies the waves racing through both of us until finally we crest together in the perfect moment of pure bliss. A second before I come, I pull out, jetting hot spurts of creamy liquid onto the flushed skin of her thighs. The orgasm seems like it lasts forever.

Fuuuuuck. God damn, she's so fucking good. I lean my head against her chest briefly.

"How does it keep getting better every single time we fuck?" I manage to gasp out.

Talia shakes her head, unable to speak.

I drop a kiss onto Talia's pebbled left nipple and use the too-sensitive tip of my cock to smear my cum over her skin. Marking her. Making her mine.

"My come looks so pretty on your skin, darling girl."

Talia gives a startled laugh and pulls me down to the bed for a deep, satisfying kiss.

As we lay there in the afterglow of our lovemaking, I find myself looking deeply into Talia's eyes. I cup Talia's jaw and brush her hair away from her salt-sticky skin. "You're mine. It's a good thing that you said yes to marriage, because I just marked you for life. You're mine. No other man will have you. You'll always be mine, darling girl."

She shudders as she looks me in the eye. "It's not that easy, Dare. You lied to me."

"I'll make it all better," I murmur. "Just kiss me and forget the rest."

I gently brush a few strands of hair away from her face before leaning down to kiss her again, needing to feel her lips against mine one more time. Her lips against mine are firm and unyielding. She's so fucking stubborn.

And so very sexy.

I cradle the back of her head in one big hand and kiss her crown tenderly. She looks up at me, eyes flashing dangerously. But it seems that the rough sex took the wind out of her sails.

She pushes against my chest and I wordlessly move to the side, letting her get up. She heads to the door and goes to what I assume is the bathroom, though I haven't laid eyes on it myself. But she does return, the same angry smirk in her expression.

She bends down and grabs the yoga pants off the floor. I sit up and reach out, narrowing her arm.

"Come here. Don't get dressed yet."

"Fuck you, Dare." She tries to tug her arm from my grip but I won't let her go that easily. Instead I move forward, stand on the side of the bed and put my hands on her hips to move her forward towards me. Her expression is one of hatred but I turn my face up, offering my mouth to her. She tosses her hair and licks her lips, her eyes darting at me.

"Kiss me," I tell her. Not an order, exactly. But I am not asking, either.

Her chin juts out and she leans over, giving me a peck on the cheek. But I am ready for that. I spear one hand in her hair, holding the other on the small of her back and kiss her lips.

This time it's less about dominance and more about the fact that I like the way she tastes. Lightly sweet, purely feminine, with an edge of salt and a note of honey. I kiss her passionately for a moment but when she doesn't make any move to kiss me back, I let her go.

"You're carrying my baby." I flatten a hand over her stomach and look up at her, wanting the words to sink into her brain. Though I hadn't noticed it much before, her belly is more curved now, less of a small flat plank than it was when we first met.

I have to say, I like it this way. I look up at her and she doesn't look nearly as defiant any longer.

"Yeah?" she asks, as though confused. "Maybe I made a mistake saying yes to your proposal."

I flash her a smirk.

"But you did. Now you'll never be able to escape me. But I don't want you to want that, either. I want this to be the most luxurious velvet-lined snare that ever existed. I want you to forget that you were ever caught and collared."

Talia looks away, her expression turning bitter. "I don't think that's going to happen anytime soon. Just because you found me and we had great sex doesn't mean anything really. You still deceived me. Now please, for the love of God, let me go."

She wrenches from my grasp and I don't try to fight her on it. She pulls on her yoga pants and hunts around for the sweatshirt, untying the knot in the arms. Then she pulls it on, all the while ignoring me as hard as possible.

When she turns and stomps out of the room, I finally stand up and redress myself in my slacks and my button up shirt. I don't know what her specific concern is just now, but I'm left feeling uneasy.

After putting my shoes on, I head back out into the tiny cabin. I find Talia curled up with a blanket near the wood stove, staring out the window blankly. She has no shoes on and no coat to speak of. Sweeping my gaze around the room, I check my watch. It's well past dawn, with the sunshine just streaming through the windows now.

"Come on. Get your stuff. We're going."

She looks at me like I've grown a second head. "Why would I go anywhere with you?"

Annoyance fills me and I cross my arms, shooting her a glare. "You're my wife. We have things to do. We can't be traipsing around the hills of rural Vermont. Let's go." Checking my watch again and pulling my cell phone from my pocket, I try to figure out where the nearest small airport would be. Somewhere big enough to land a chopper is all I require.

Talia doesn't move. She looks out the window again and grits her teeth. It's a new side of Talia that I haven't yet witnessed and I can't say that I am too crazy about it. "You are not being very helpful," I say to her.

That earns me a sharp glare. She stands up, wrapping herself in the soft white blanket. "Well, you are unbelievably selfish."

That stops me cold. "What does that mean?"

"You can't really think that I wouldn't find out about your deceptions and just be okay with it. That's insane."

I shrug. "I did what I did out of necessity. It's true. But in the end, you knew what you were signing up for. I haven't changed. I'm still the same person."

She gives a cold little laugh. "You are rude, boorish, temperamental, domineering, and selfish. Before anything else or anyone else, you are always on the lookout for yourself. It's disgusting."

My brows furrow. "What is that supposed to mean? Everybody looks out for themselves first. That's what being alive is all about."

She makes a soft noise of disgust and turns toward the window again, giving me her blanket covered back and the long copper mass of her hair. "You would say that."

"What is that supposed to mean? Are you saying that you don't look out for yourself first?"

She whirls, her tone exasperated, her face pained. "No! I don't. I think of other people first. And for someone that is going to be a father, you are going to have to learn to put someone else ahead of yourself for once in your damned life. You have to start looking out for other people, even if it's only me and the baby."

My mouth opens but I don't know what to say. For the first time since I met Talia, I find myself unsure.

Is she right? Do normal people walk around all the time with thoughts of how they affect others? That sounds awful.

"So?' She demands, stomping her foot.

"So what?" I ask.

"Are you not going to even try to apologize for coercing me into this marriage?"

"Would that make it better?"

She looks at me, pressing her cheek out with her tongue. "It wouldn't make it worse. I need to know that I can trust you and I can count on you. And you haven't shown me even the slightest bit of humanity. There has to be something else that's going on under your surface. But for the life of me, I can't figure out what it is. How am I supposed to trust anything with you? How am I supposed to trust you with a baby?"

I feel the back of my neck heat. I grimace and shrug at her. I have no idea how to answer any of the indictments she is spitting at me.

"Get yourself together. We're going. Maybe when we get back, we can have a conversation."

Talia whips around, walking past me and bumping my shoulder. The miserable look on her face doesn't make me feel exactly warm inside.

I pull out my phone and text Rob, telling him that we need to be picked up at my location. Then I glance behind me, where Talia is just packing her bag.

Her questions weigh on me, as I don't seem able to answer a single one of them. I hadn't frankly put much thought into being a father until just now…

Chapter Five

When I climb down from the helicopter, holding a hand up to shade my eyes, I stare out at a busy marina. Snow is falling on the ground all around me and I look around at the mass of the ships and the walkways that lead between them. Where are we?

I look at Dare and he comes around my side, putting an arm around me as he pulls me down toward the dock before us.

Prince Edward Island.

I suck in a breath and look at him, my eyes wide. "We're in Canada? How…? Don't we need to prove our identity or something when we are crossing the border?"

I glance down at the icy water as we walk over the planks that hold us a few inches above it. He gives a cold laugh and shakes his head.

"I have people that take care of things like that. Now come on, I want to get settled on the ship."

I start to ask another question but he glares at me, his hand tightening on my shoulder. "Not here," he grates out.

"We get on board, you can ask all the questions that your heart desires."

Swallowing thickly, I glance at the natural beauty all around us. There are large mounds that ascend on each side of the Marina, dropping right into the water. The sea itself is placid and calm at the moment, boats that enter and exit the individual bays of the dock do so slowly and create minimal wake.

Dare grabs my hand and hauls me down the dock, heading toward the largest and tallest row of boats. There are only three ships aboard on the dock he turns down and I look at each of them with no small amount of wonderment. Their gleaming white hulls rise out of the dark water. They don't have masts like a smaller boat would have. Instead they're just topped with a white navigation dash above a white plank and a huge tan wooden deck.

Dare doesn't even seem to think about the size of the boat; he's too busy dragging me along the dock and right up to the set of stairs leading up to the yacht. A man dressed in a crisp white uniform with white hair and skin like worn leather awaits us as Dare pulls me up the stairs.

Dare nods his head, looking at the man. "Captain Weathers."

The older man gives him a no nonsense look and avoids making any eye contact with me. Instead, he just looks at Dare and puts his hands behind his back.

"Sir. This ship is ready for you as you requested. But I will remain on board, if you don't mind. The weather is supposed to turn and I can smell a storm brewing."

Dare claps the man on the shoulder. "That's all right, Weathers. We got it."

Captain Weathers bows his head and shuts his mouth, but I can tell that he wants to press the issue.

Dare just jerks his head toward the dock. "When have I ever needed intervention out on the sea? Trust me. We're not going very far out. I just want complete privacy."

Captain Weathers slides a glance at me. But he doesn't say anything further. Instead, he just bows his head one more time and then heads down the stairs. Dare turns to me, cocking a brow.

"Can I trust you to find your way to the main state room downstairs? I've had an assistant furnish the state room with a new set of weather appropriate clothing for both of us. I suggest that you go change out of that get up." He gives my yoga pants and sweatshirt a disdainful look. "You're the wife of a billionaire, not a fucking fitness instructor."

I curl my tongue around my front teeth and shoot him a glare. But the idea of being alone for even a few minutes is appealing enough for me to agree.

"How do I get downstairs?" I ask. Glancing around, I try to see the staircase. Dare points to the back of the boat. "Head that way. You can't miss it. I will get us out on the ocean."

He turns away, pressing a hidden button near the stairs to draw them up and seal the hull. I roll my eyes and move toward the back of the boat, feeling awkward as I go. Though this ship is large, it is not so big as to keep me from feeling the water rolling beneath the boat. The tide shifts the boat every minute or so and I can feel it deep in my bones.

As I scuttle around the long white wall that makes up the middle deck of the ship, I look out over the water. From here, you can't see any land or even the mountains. But the ocean itself is an endless blank slate with a ripple running through it like an icy shudder here and there.

When I reach the back of the boat, I turn and see a white set of stairs heading up to the upper deck and beside it, a polished wood set of stairs leads below deck. Clutching at the matching wooden banister, I make my way down, leading heavily on the wall for support. I still feel the water moving somewhere under my feet and it unnerves me. It's odd to look around at the walnut finish on everything and yet feel that my feet might be carried out from underneath me at any moment.

Once I get down the stairs and walk down a cramped hallway made of solid floor to ceiling wood, I start to try the wooden doors on the right. I find a living room area, a maintenance room full of pipes, two small bedrooms, and another luxurious full bathroom. The final door I try is obviously the biggest state room. I swing the door open and my eyes widen as I take in the panoramic glass paneled view of the water line. Half of my view is above and the other half is nearly pitch black, gazing straight out into the fathomless deep of the ocean.

The room itself has a full king-sized bed and two bedside tables, a dressing table, and a little nook set up with a small circular table and two wicker chairs. All of the finishes in this room are mauve and dark gray and titanium, from the lights by the bed to the titanium drawer pulls on the bedside tables. The bed is covered in a mauve satin comforter and has so many pillows that I can't help but want to fall into it.

It only takes a minute to find the state room's hidden closet, tucked away in the back corner. It's stuffed full of sweaters and jeans. There is not a single strappy silk dress or a pair of Louboutin heels anywhere to be seen.

I pick out a dark gray cotton T-shirt, a heavy blue sweater, and a pair of expensive-looking jeans. I change out of my clothes and hurry into those picked out for me, adding a thick pair of gray wool socks and warm winter boots too. Everything fits perfectly and I have to wonder at the person picking out my wardrobe. They've never accidentally stuck the wrong size in with any of my clothes. I appreciate the work that it takes.

When I'm dressed, I head into the bathroom and do a little bit of washing up. I notice that the same face cleanser and moisturizer are here as I found in the lofts back home. Again, the person that stocked these is very good at paying attention to details.

Once I'm finally done, I head into the bedroom and sit down on the bed. I blink and look out the window. The marina is quite a ways behind us and we are steadily moving away from it, the wake of our ship bubbling and snapping behind us. It's hard to keep my eyes up and away from staring into the darkness below the waterline, but I try my best because it seems like staring into the abyss.

The whole bedroom is warm and cozy as a glove and I lay back on the bed for a minute, just letting myself rest for a second. Beneath me, the waves roll, constantly undulating softly. My eyes shut briefly, or at least they think they do.

But when I open them again, it's because I hear a sound that pulls me from my light slumber. I push up off the mattress, rubbing sleep from my eyes. The view outside is dark and indicates that it is probably mid afternoon.

I also notice that we are not moving at all anymore. I stand up and go over to the panoramic window, searching for land. From this point of view, I can see nothing but this water.

Now that we are no longer in the marina, wind ripples across the ocean, whipping waves in its wake. I stare at the waves and try not to feel seasick when the ripples I can feel beneath my feet do not match up with the waves I am looking at currently.

"Are you going to stay down here all day?"

I whirl, not expecting to find Dare leaning against the

doorway, looking me up and down. I can feel myself flushing although I don't know exactly why.

I toss my hair, giving Dare an annoyed look. I put my hand onto my hip and shrug my shoulder.

"What is it that you want from me, Dare?"

He pushes off the doorframe and heads into the room, watching my face closely. "Isn't that obvious?"

I give an exasperated sigh. "Apparently not."

He starts pulling at his dress shirt, unbuttoning the top few buttons. "I want you to follow through on your promises, darling girl."

I swallow hard and look at his hand as he unbuttons his shirt slowly, prowling around me. I'm not sure what to expect from him at this moment and I have to admit that he is making me nervous.

"And what is it that you have been promised?"

"Everything, Talia. Everything that a wife is supposed to do."

Dare turns away from me, pulling his shirt off and dropping it on the bed. Then he pulls off his shoes and strips off his dark pants, leaving him completely naked. He doesn't bother to hide a single thing, letting me stare at his well muscled ass and his mouthwatering abs as he stretches a little.

Then he pulls the closet open, finding a simple white T-shirt and a pair of dark jeans. He pulls the jeans on and the shirt over his head. I can't help but notice the fact that it fits against him perfectly, practically molded to emphasize his triceps and well toned chest. My tongue darts out and I lick my lips, feeling a little guilty.

After all, I am suddenly lusting after Dare, the very man I claim to hate. I try to remind myself that despite his good looks and my attraction to him, he is the enemy. He is the very definition of a bad person. Maybe it's the pregnancy hormones that are coursing through my body that are playing with my mind. I drop my hand to my abdomen, pursing my lips.

As I do, my stomach unexpectedly growls so loudly that Dare hears that. He finishes dressing himself and then turns around, looking me up and down.

"I take it that you're hungry." I shrug a shoulder but the truth is that I am famished, though the feeling seems to have come from out of nowhere.

Dare nods to the door. "Come on. We'll go into the ship's kitchen. There's bound to be plenty to eat up there."

He crosses the room and heads out, never doubting for a moment that I will follow. Unfortunately, he is truly the one in control just now. Out here, where no one can hear me scream or notice if he simply threw me overboard, I am in Dare's sway.

I follow him around the darkened hallway and up the stairs. He heads around to a small door that is discreetly located behind the staircase to the top floor. He sweeps it open and ushers me into a surprisingly large space with a long walnut dining table and matching set of walnut benches on one side of the room. On the other side is a little galley kitchen and a bar cart. Dare points at the table.

"Sit down," he says. I step out of the cold and close the door, noticing that there is a great quantity of natural light piercing through several cleverly hidden skylights. I sit down at the table, realizing just then that I am a little shaky. I don't know if it's from hunger or if it has something to do with the sea itself. But at this moment, I am definitely glad to be seated.

Twin waves of nausea and hunger hit me, one after another. I suck in a deep breath and don't even know what to do about the intense wave of nausea I feel.

Dare jostles some jars around and then appears before me, setting a tray of fresh made bread, butter, thick slabs of cold roast beef, mini-gherkins, and several other things all lined up in little bowls. He puts my slice of bread on a tiny plate and offers me a butter knife. Then he goes back to the bar cart, getting two cans of soda. He holds them up as I smell the bread, my mouth watering.

"You want ginger ale?"

To my surprise, I answer, "Yeah. That would actually be perfect."

He returns with two cans of ice cold ginger ale and sets them on the table before taking a seat across from me. He looks at my untouched food with some puzzlement.

"Well? Yes. What are you waiting for?"

I press my lips together and repress any kind of reaction. Instead, I smear a bit of butter on my bread and then add a few of the gherkins to my plate. Dare pops the top on my ginger ale and pushes it towards me as I take a bite of the bread.

I close my eyes, unable to stifle the chorus of groans. The bread is very good, still warm from the oven. When I open my eyes again, I find Dare looking at me with a smirk.

"Is it good?"

I roll my eyes. "I haven't eaten all day. I don't think I realized that I was even hungry until about four minutes ago."

He reaches across the table and pushes the soda can closer to me. "Drink some of this. My mom used to get really seasick and she always swore by this brand."

I pick up the can, noting that it is an old brand, the label in French instead of the English I was expecting. I bring it to my mouth and take a sip, letting the sweet fizz dissipate before taking a swallow. For a minute, I eat in silence, polishing off the bread and drinking half of the Canada ginger ale. I don't know what it is, whether it's just some combination of the food and drink or whether his mom had it right, but I feel my nausea disappear with a puff of smoke.

Dare eats his own piece of bread with a slice of roast beef, watching me all the while.

"So? Was my mom right?"

I shrug and make a face. "Maybe. We'll see."

He looks down, busying himself with another slice. While he's piling butter and what looks like strawberry jam on one end, he asks his question casually. "What the hell is your deal? Why would you run away like that?"

I put my hands on the table, eyeing another slice of bread. "What exactly are you asking? Are you trying to deny that you tricked me and trapped me into this marriage? Or do you just want to know how I found out about it?"

He gives me a sharp look. "I would love to know your source."

My mouth lifts a little at the corners. "Of course you would. You want to know who ratted you out so you can keep them from telling your secrets in the future. Have I got that correct?"

He sets his knife down a little too hard and glares at me. "I don't need the sanctimonious bullshit. I want to know who is talking out of school, though."

I smirk at him and then pull my cell phone out of my back pocket. I fire off a text to let Olivia know that I am okay, then start to turn my phone off. But I power it back on and find the messages. I hand my phone over to Dare, looking like the cat that ate the fucking canary.

I study his face while he reads the text. He's a much better poker player than I am because he doesn't flinch or look worried in any way. He just reads the text and then tosses my phone on the table.

"Well?"

"The number is anonymous. It could be anyone. But I have good money on my twin brother. Sounds like him."

I drag the phone back across the table and put it in my pocket. "I don't think you can guess that from a couple lines of text."

He shrugs. "This is actually good. Burn is already working to pry us apart. It means he is worried about the outcome of the inheritance race."

He shoves another piece of strawberry jam covered bread in his mouth and brushes his hands off.

"Burn isn't responsible for your actions. He didn't make you hire someone to scare my Aunt Minnie half to death or come into the restaurant and annoy me. That was you. You did that. I don't really care about the rest."

He rolls his eyes. "That's not really the point."

"No? What about that whole thing about how we were going to tell each other the truth about everything? Was that a lie too?"

His lips twitch and his eyes dance with something dark and wicked. "You're only allowed the truth when it's convenient for me. The sooner you learn that, the better it is for you."

I pull my arms across my chest, narrowing my eyes on his face. He looks me up and down and chuckles.

"I can't trust you. I don't know how I'm supposed to have a child with you when I have to worry that you will do something horrible to me."

He shrugs his shoulders. "I don't see what the big deal is. Trust me or don't. You're still married to me. You're still my wife. I'm still going to be a father, whether you like it or not."

My lips thin. I can't figure out how to explain to him that there should be trust between us. He makes me so angry when he orders me around and treats me like a little kid asking for special treatment.

Dare spears his hand and stabs the table with one finger. "You seem to be forgetting what our agreement is. This is a marriage of convenience. You are making things extremely messy with your emotions. I'm telling you right now, it's easier if you just try not to feel as much about anything. I've been stuffing my emotions down for many years and I must say that it has given me excellent results."

"How can you enjoy anything if nothing feels that good to you?" I demand.

My answer seems to catch Dare by surprise and he furrows his brow. "What do you mean? Don't I seem like I am having a good time?"

I make a noise of aggravation and bang the table with my fists. "This is another problem that we haven't even talked about. I want more than some petty, shallow relationship. Don't you want that? Don't you need someone that you can confide in and rely on? I know I do."

Dare stands up and takes a swig out of his can of soda. For a second, I think that he isn't going to answer me. He lifts the tray with all the food from the table and turns toward the galley kitchen. To my surprise, he waits until he is a few steps away and not facing me before he answers my question.

"It's not essential, no. I learned years ago that if you trust nobody, you won't ever be disappointed. Maybe you should start thinking about doing the same."

Then he throws down the tray with a clatter, turning and stalking out of the kitchen. I'm left with his words bouncing around in my head. Trust no one. Life will be less disappointing.

I don't know if I should feel sorry for him or if his words are more accurate than I could possibly know.

Chapter Six

DARE

After another fitful night of sleep, I steer my yacht another hundred miles north up the coast. By the time I anchor in a sheltered bay, I'm as broody as a teenage boy. Things between Talia and I have been frosty since last night, to say the least. But I left the little town of Harwicke with such haste that returning without getting on the same page will be extremely difficult.

After dropping the anchor and making sure that the boat won't go anywhere, I head down to find Talia. To my surprise, I spot her on the back of the boat, leaning against the railing and staring off into the distance. She has borrowed one of my oversized coats and she looks tiny in it, her copper mass of hair looking brilliant amongst the bleak colors of the black sea and the white rocky shore beyond.

She turns around and spots me looking at her. Her cheeks flame bright pink and she turns away again. Something inside of me tightens, excited that she noticed me. I don't fully understand that feeling but I head to the back of the boat, leaning against the railing beside her. Talia pushes her hair out of her face and looks at me, her eyes stunningly blue.

"Have you come to yell at me more?" She asks coolly.

I rub my jaw and then shove my hand through my short, dark hair. "That's not my intention."

She rolls her eyes and turns back to the ocean, leaning over the railing. "No? Then what is? What do you want from me?"

"You already asked me that question. And I've answered it. I want exactly what you promised me when you let me slide that ring onto your finger."

She lifts her left hand and looks at her ring dispassionately. It's huge and glittering, gorgeous by any standards. But I have the feeling that she is currently thinking about pulling the ring off and chucking it into the ocean.

I feel like I'm at a loss for words. I don't want to comfort her, exactly. But I do wish that I could find something to say that would appease her. Make her more malleable and less resistant to the changes in her lifestyle that I have forced on her.

It's frustrating because we only seem to communicate well through fucking each other's brains out. When I'm not balls deep inside her, the odds of her wanting to scratch my eyes out are pretty good.

"You wanted to talk about those text messages," I say. I'm a little surprised that the words escaped my mouth but the way that she looks at me, her head turning suddenly and her eyes filling with question marks… I like the way that she regards me.

Talia turns, her mouth twisting. She leans away from the railing, using her hand to hold herself up. "I'm listening," she says, finally.

I purse my lips and choose my words carefully. "I only did what I had to do to convince you that marrying me was your only alternative. I could tell that you had too many options. So I just peered down the field. Maybe the guys I hired went a little farther when they busted up your aunt's bookstore. But I wouldn't take it back. It got me the results I was looking for. It made you accept my proposal."

Her face tightens as I speak. Her lips thin.

"I feel like you deceived me. I feel like I was led down the garden path. I would have liked to have made that decision of whether or not to accept your proposal on its own merits. But you didn't have any faith in me or in the value of your plans. Even now, you can't say that you're sorry."

I glance away over my shoulder out toward the sea. I squint at the bright light and exhale a long breath.

"I could've made a different choice. I did what I felt I had to do. I can't apologize for something I am not sorry for."

With an exasperated noise she pushes away from the railing, starting toward the front of the boat. But I reach out a hand and grab her wrist, pulling her to a stop. She looks back at me and there is hurt echoing in her eyes.

Seeing that written all over her face makes me want to wipe it all away. For some reason, when Talia is vulnerable and I know that she is just letting me see it, something in my chest wrenches.

"Listen. I don't know who sent you this text. It could have been my brother, my uncle, my dad. My life is full of people that could betray me at any moment. But I think it is important that we don't let them get between us."

She tugs at her arm, her expression disdainful. "They aren't doing anything to us. It's your actions that threaten to come between us. You are the one who lies and schemes and throws up walls. That's not my doing. You have to see that for what it is."

Ever so slowly, I draw her closer, her strength nothing compared to mine. When she is pressed against me, I flip our positions, putting her back against the railing and leaning down to rub my thumb along her jawline, her throat, her collar bone. She looks up at me wordlessly. I look deep into her eyes and bend to kiss her, the slightest brush of my lips over hers.

It's a confession, as close to an apology as I ever get. When I am finished making my case, she looks at me with an unfathomable expression. "You're mine now, Talia. Mine forever." I bring my hand up to run it through her hair but she catches it, grabbing it down until it lays directly over her heart. She puts her hand over mine, searching my gaze intently.

When she whispers the next words, my heart beat speeds up. "I'm a person. A whole separate person. I know that you have become accustomed to a certain lifestyle where you look out for yourself first all the time. But I don't want to live that way. I won't. So I'm asking you to stop and consider what I might be thinking and feeling about you right now. Do you think it would be something that would make you proud?"

I open my mouth to answer and feel as though she has just slapped me. Talia's face doesn't change but she doesn't look away either.

What she thinks about me, how she feels? The idea is foreign to me.

When I look at Talia, I see a woman who is scared shitless and trying to act as though she isn't afraid. I tilt my head and scrunch up one side of my face. I guess if I were in her position, a total outsider that is only in my world because she got knocked up, I would probably be just as scared as she is. She's just one tiny person against the world. Talia starts to pull her hand out of mine, her mouth turning down into a slight frown. But I hold her there for just a moment longer, my eyes meeting hers.

At last, she touches my face with her free hand, cupping my jaw gently. She gives me a small smile and says, "Something to think about."

Talia pushes me back and I go willingly this time. She goes into the kitchen and closes the door, leaving me to stare out into a darkening sky and a chill comes across the water that forebodes the coming storm. Much later, when I've locked down the command center of the boat and bolted down everything on the upper deck, I head downstairs and find Talia curled up on one corner of the couch in the living room.

Her eyes are fixed on the windows, two oblong cutouts that show the surface of the ocean around us. The wind is picking up outside and waves are battering the hull of the ship. Although I can only see a little glimpse of the sky above, I imagine that it is full of storm clouds and at any moment they will begin to pour rain down on us.

I enter the living room, if it can be called that. It's only ten feet wide by twenty feet. One side is taken up by the long couch that Talia sits on and an extensive set of bookcases. On the other side, there are leather lounge chairs and a lightweight table. In the corner, there is a small bookshelf full of board games. I grab a heavy wooden box from the shelf of board games and bring it over to the table, where I open it to reveal a simple wooden chess board.

Talia notices me and watches me with some interest, but her eyes keep going back to the window. She monitors the weather outside and her brow furrows with concern.

"It's going to storm," I say. I take a seat in the leather chair beside the table, concentrating on setting up the chess pieces.

She gives me a funny look. "You think?"

I scowl down at the pawns that I line up but I don't

respond directly to her jibe. "You seem to be worried about it. But all the hatches are battened down. We are anchored in a sheltering bay. We have nothing to worry about."

She quirks an eyebrow at me but she just presses her lips into a thin line. After a moment, she turns her head back to the board game that I'm setting up.

I glance up at her, keeping my face smooth and expressionless. "You play?"

She scoffs at me. "Of course I play. I went to school for liberal arts. I work in a bookstore. In what world would I not be able to defend myself on a chessboard?"

I nod to the chair on the other side of the table. "All right. Show me."

She gets up, unsteady on her feet. As she wobbles, I notice her hand go to her belly. It's funny, but I think I notice a vague swelling there. Not enough to remark upon but it is there nonetheless.

I don't want to get my head bitten off for commenting on her shape at just this moment, so I bite my tongue.

Talia sits on the chair, pulling one of her legs up underneath her. She looks up at me, licking her lips. "Am I white, then?"

She gestures to the board, where I have set up the white pieces on her side and the dark pieces on mine. I shrug my shoulders. "I thought I should give you the advantage of the first move."

Her lips twitch. She raises a hand and moves a pawn forward, seamlessly segueing into the first game.

I move several pawns. She moves a couple and then her knight comes out. It's a bold move and the game progresses quickly. Talia is a very good chess player, quite aggressive and quick. It's been so long since I have played that she knocks half of my pieces off the board before she corners my queen. She's two moves away from a checkmate, looking quite smug as she moves her pieces around the board and slays my queen. At length, she puts my king into check several times and eventually I knock the piece over, conceding the game.

Talia sits back, putting her hands on the armrest and giving me a defiant smile. "That was easy," she announces.

I haven't ever seen this side of Talia before. Smug, superior, self assured. It's annoying but also vaguely attractive. It reminds me of Daisy, truth be told.

"I think we should play again. And this time, we should make it more interesting. A wager."

This seems to pique her interest. "What will we win or lose? And before you say it, I have no interest in playing strip chess so don't even bring that up."

I flash a smirk. "I was thinking that we would play for something more simple. I need us to come to an understanding before we head back to Harwicke. So perhaps we could play for one answer for each piece we capture."

Her eyebrows fly up in surprise.

"One answer? To any question we ask?"

I nod. "That's the idea."

She purses her lips. "I don't know. It's hard to believe that you will be honest with me now. How do I know that you won't just lie if I ask you anything that pushes your boundaries a little bit?"

I suck in a deep breath and release it slowly. "I promise to be honest. For this game, at least."

Talia studies my face, her mouth bawling up tightly. She keeps looking at me for half a minute, making me fidget.

"Look. I need to know that I can leave you unattended and turn my back for more than a minute without you running away again. I feel like one of the reasons that you can't trust me is because you don't know anything about me, not really. So I am offering you a free pass to ask any question that you want."

She toys with a pawn and nods slowly.

"Okay. Let's set up the game again. You can be black this time."

As we reset the board and swap sides, Talia appears pensive. I start to worry that she is going to pry into my past and try to figure out what makes me tick. Having someone else poke around inside my brain makes me fidgety and shifty. But Talia is looking at me expectantly.

"What?" I ask her.

"You're white," she says, gesturing to the board. "You go first."

The back of my neck heats and I grimace. I think about the moves available to me and then select a pawn to move forward. She is quick to make her first move, glancing at me with a tiny smirk. I won't give her the satisfaction of getting under my skin so I just move another pawn. The game progresses fairly quickly until she captures the first pawn.

Talia sits back, holding the pawn between her thumb and forefinger and giving me a considering look. She leans forward and places the pawn on the side of the board and then gives me a cool little smile.

"I think you know exactly what I think of your deception and what you did to force my hand when it comes to this marriage. So I will just let that lie. But I want to know... What happened to the agreement we made to be completely honest with each other? No, wait. I have a better question. What was going through your mind when you looked me in the eye and swore you'd tell me the truth?"

Ouch. She went right for my throat with that question. I wave my hand over my chin and give her a long look.

"I guess I was thinking that you would never find out that I guided your hand in accepting my proposal."

Talia bleats out a laugh. "Guided my hand? That's rich. If you can't even admit that you lied, I'm not sure that a game of chess will solve anything at all." She begins to stand up, pushing up from the armrests of the chair. I grit my teeth and glare at her.

"Wat!" I say. "Just sit back down."

Talia freezes where she is, arching a brow. My lips thin but I manage to force the words to leave my mouth. "I lied. Okay? Now will you sit back down?"

She collapses back into the chair and flips her hair out of her face. Before she can say anything, I reach out and move my rook several places.. Her eyes tighten on my face but she leans forward, putting her elbow on the table and concentrating on the game. After a moment, she moves her bishop a few spaces. I immediately capture it with my rook.

I steeple my fingers and consider my question for half a minute. "What will it take for you to move on from this?"

"From what?"

"My… deception. What will it take for you to let it be in the past in the rearview mirror?"

She toys with her queen, watching my face carefully. "I don't know. I feel like I've been foolish when it comes to you. I'm embarrassed, actually. And frankly, I don't trust you not to hurt me if the choice is between doing something that hurts me and doing something that benefits you."

She is staring at me, putting the feelings out there on the table between us, plain as can be. I'm completely taken aback by her sentiment.

"I thought that I had made my priorities perfectly clear when I married you and gave you my name. Something that hurts you hurts me, too, I suppose."

She bangs her fist on the table. "That's not enough, Dare! How can I ever trust you when I wonder if I'm just a pawn to be sacrificed in your chess game?"

I lean back, realizing only then that the rift between us has become something larger. It's gone from being a gully to a gulf.

"As far as I'm concerned, you are Mrs. Morgan. I made vows and I take the 'till death do we part' bit quite seriously. I never wanted a wife, but now that I have one, I intend to keep you."

Talia stands up, her gaze direct and intense. "You made promises in the past that you didn't keep. I can let that go, but the only way you can make up for it is by showing me that you want to change."

She starts to move past me, but I grab her arm and pull her onto my lap. She struggles but I lock my arm around her waist and grab her chin between my thumb and forefinger, forcing her to look at me.

"If it will keep you from running away, I'll do better. Okay?"

Her blue eyes are wide and they study my face. She frowns for a moment and I think she's about to push me away. But then her eyes drop to my mouth and she wets her lips.

I haul her closer and kiss her hard, stealing the breath out of both of her lungs. Then I turn her loose. She stays on my lap for a few fleeting seconds, the corner of her mouth tugging down in a frown.

"Okay, Dare. I don't forgive you for lying. But I won't run away again. That's as much as I can give you."

God, her weight on my lap and her soft curves against my body are almost too much for me to handle. I start moving my head, angling for another taste of her luscious mouth. But she waves me off and clamors off my lap, standing.

"I need to eat again," Talia says. "I feel a little faint."

Repressing a sigh, I stand up and shoo her from the room. "Let's get some food for you."

She vanishes out of the doorway in a flash, eager to leave our conversation behind. I follow her, my steps heavy, wondering how long this peace between us will last.

Chapter Seven

TALIA

Once the storm clears, Dare sails the boat back to the dock. While he navigates the ship, I sneak peeks into the small cabin where he stays, absent-mindedly looking at his phone while he makes sure that the ship steers itself safely on its course.

At last, he puts his phone away and stares out at the sea, standing by the manual wheel for the ship. I can't help but wonder what he is thinking about. Honestly, I am impressed that he stays still for so long when the meditation session hits twenty minutes.

Is he thinking about us? Or perhaps what awaits us in Harwicke. That's the more likely answer.

I spend most of the rest of the day on my own in the living room, working on a book of tough crosswords that I found shoved in between all the Parcheesi sets and the Monopoly boards.

I get lost in my own thoughts, tangled up with twelve-letter words and clues about rivers that run through Paris. When I notice the ship gently pull to a stop, I look up and the sky above me is growing quite dark.

I head back up to the main deck and find Dare descending the stairs from the navigation deck. He arches a brow and he sees the crossword book still clutched in my hand.

"Where did you find that?"

I look down at the book and shrug. "It was on the board games shelf in the living room."

He gives me a dubious look for reasons completely unknown to me. Then he jerks his head toward the dock. "Come on. We have to go back to real life eventually. Might as well jump right in."

I follow him, allowing him to lead me from the ship down the steps to the dock. It's only then that I realize that this is not the dock we departed from. It's much smaller, only three other boats moored to one side. The other boats look like little toys next to the ship that I am departing. "Where are we?" I ask.

Dare keeps walking, his pace never slowing for a moment. "This is one of many slips that we own. We're just at the southern tip of Maine right now, only half an hour by car from Harwicke."

"Oh." I blink, realizing that the snowy ground might be one of the reasons why I am so confused. Though the massive mountains are missing from where we originally departed from, everything else could be the same. There is thick snow on the ground, a few people bustling down the wood planks toward their boats, and it is just as cold here as it was when we were in Canada a few days ago.

I step off the last plank onto solid ground and immediately feel the ground tilt. It's the weirdest thing; I think my body had just gotten used to the gentle swaying of the ship. Now my legs feel strange and rubbery without the slight movement of the earth beneath my feet.

Dare eyes me as I stumble forward, grabbing my arm.

"Don't worry. Happens to everybody. The feeling will be gone before you know it."

He hustles me up a well worn footpath and we come into the parking lot where, idling in the handicapped spot, is a big black SUV. As soon as we make it onto the wide concrete surface of the parking lot, the doors open and I see two familiar faces. Frick and Frack climb out of the car, their expressions all business as usual.

Frick opens the passenger door, giving me a cool smile. If she is upset that I ran away on her watch, she doesn't say anything about it. She gives me a little bow.

"Welcome back," she says.

For some reason, I blushed deeply. I don't say anything but I climb in the back of the SUV. Dare slides in beside me, pulling his phone from his pocket. When Frick and Frack are both back in the car, Dare says, without looking up from his phone, "Go ahead. You can fill me in on the improvements to the loft later."

I shift my gaze over to him but Frick just backs the SUV up and heads toward Harwicke. A few minutes into the drive, I grow tired of staring out the window at the coastline as we speed past. I look at Dare and he is still reading from his phone, scrolling and looking concerned. I pull out the crossword magazine from the boat and open the spot I have marked with a pencil. I work diligently for a minute before finding a clue that I am stumped by. I page through some of the other crosswords that have been filled in by what I assume is a feminine hand.

When the magazine is ripped from my hands, I look up, stunned. Dare is holding the magazine, his expression furious. "Where did you get this?"

I reach for the magazine, scowling at him. "I already told you. It was on the ship."

Dare closes the magazine, smoothing his hand over the front cover as if it were somehow invaluable. "This is my mother's magazine. My mother's handwriting is in it."

My pulse speeds up. I want very badly to ask what he means, but I don't think that Dare will be particularly forthcoming with his story in front of Frick and Frack.

He is still looking at the magazine, his hand touching the cover reverently. So I reach over and squeeze his forearm. He looks at me, his eyes somewhat unfocused.

I don't know much about Dare's mom or what happened to her, but I get the sense that finding an item that belongs to her means a lot to Dare. I slip my arm through his, leaning my head against his shoulder. For a long second, he is tense and wooden. But when he realizes that I only intend to comfort him and let him be, he seems to relax.

I make a note to ask him about his mother the next time we are alone.

The spell is fragile. It's shattered easily when Dare's cell phone begins to vibrate. He puts one hand on top of the crossword magazine, as if he needs to hold it down lest it blow away. The other hand answers the phone, putting it up to his ear.

"Yeah?"

He listens intently, cursing after a moment. "Fuck. All right. We'll be at the house in ten minutes. We'll talk about it then."

He sighs and puts his phone away, then awkwardly pats my hand where it rests on his arm.

"We have to go to the estate. My uncle has some plans that he needs me to look over. Remy is out of town so we should be able to get in and out of the estate relatively quickly."

I wrinkle my nose and shrug. Dare barely looks at me and

seems very distracted by his phone. I pull my hand out from his where it grips his arm and sit up, sad that our moment of understanding is gone. I look out the window, pouting a little as Frick drives us into Harwicke and all the way up the mountain, finally dropping us at the Morgan estate. When Frick pulls the car to a stop, I open my door before anybody can help me out of the vehicle. Dare offers me his arm as we step into the shadow created by the sun against the large stone building. But I choose to ignore it, blithely making my way into the house. Inside, the manor is exactly as magnificent as always. High ceilings, polished floors, the same royal colors and echoing great hallways as before. Dare starts forward, forgetting that I trail behind him until he is halfway down the hallway. He stops suddenly and looks back at me, his eyebrows rising slightly.

"Are you going to come with me?"

I shrug and give him an uninterested look. "I think I will go into the living room and check out the taxidermied animals. I can keep myself occupied."

His mouth pulls down but he glances at his watch.

"It should only be a few minutes. We just have to go through some documents. Felix needs my signature on some things and then I'll be done. You will probably only be alone for ten or fifteen minutes."

Giving him a frigid smile, I turn, bounding off to the living room area. Out of the corner of my eye, I watch Dare as he stands still, looking at me with uncertainty. But then he checks his watch again, shakes his head, and starts off toward the back of the house.

I'm about to head into the living room when I stop, looking at the doorway. Something is off about the shape of the wall here. I reach out to the wall immediately to the left of the door frame, feeling that there is a slight edge sticking up.

Using my nails, I pry up a few inches and to my surprise, it opens a large small doorway of no more than five feet by three feet.

It is patterned to look just like the rest of the wallpaper. If someone hadn't left the door ever so slightly ajar, it wouldn't even be visible. Sucking in a breath, I push the door open a few inches and peer inside. My heart hammers as though I am doing something illicit.

But no one has ever told me not to look in any secret doors I might find, so I guess technically I'm not doing anything I'm not supposed to be. The open door throws a light on the small, dark space. I squint and realize that it is actually a passageway. What it goes to, I have no idea.

Checking behind me to make sure that no one sees, I step into the chilly, dark space. I pull the door closed, leaving it open only an inch. Cold air rushes up to my skin and nips at my wrists and my neck where bare skin meets the heavy wool coat I am wearing. I shiver and move a little further down the passageway.

There are several holes cut out in the wall, tiny viewing portals. I peek into one and have a perfect view of the entire living room. It's silent and dark just now, the lights not even on. I look directly down and realize that the viewing portal is stealthily hidden just above the wainscoting.

This must be for servants to pass, I realize. I think I remember Dare mentioning that his family has lived here for centuries. I could easily imagine a young man in nineteenth century garb bending low to look through this peephole.

Wandering farther down the tiny hallway, I wonder where the passages go. Are they all over the house? Or do they just run to this room?

Creeping down the corridor on my tiptoes, I tried to be quiet as a mouse. I can hear the sound of someone clearing their throat in a far-off place. The air vent kicks on at the end of the hallway and I can hear the quiet hum. As I poke my head out of the end of the hallway, I look left and right.

I realize that going left would only lead me to the front of the house. So I turn left, cautiously making my way down the secret hallway. It's ice cold back here, with a constant draft moving around my ankles. I can feel it waxing and waning but I don't know what the forces may be behind it. I stop once and check the living room one last time before I cross another passageway which forks off to the right.

This hallway is exactly like the one I just came from, but it has one special exception. A door stands ajar, barely more than an inch. But because it's so dark in the hallway, it looks like a magical glowing portal. I move towards that as stealthily as possible, putting my ear to the wall next to the door and listening intently.

I hear that same man clearing his throat and coughing, the sound farther away this time. But it's almost definitely not in this room. I move the door open very quietly, noting that there are three paintings on the wall that I move back. The one facing me most directly is a powdered wig wearing descendent or ancestor of Dare's. He looks like an older, smudged photocopy of Dare. I step closer and examine the tiny gold plaque beside it. The old man is named Jeb Morgan. He wears a simple white shirt and an old-fashioned naval officer's coat with a number of medals pinned to the lapel on one side.

I look above and below and find that there, too, are portraits of Dare's ancestors. Mostly men, mostly wearing wigs and their finest suits. All looking off into the distance, gauging the future.

Finally I open the door enough to stick my head in there. The walls are almost filled with portraits, as many as five high and four wide. There are roughly the same shape and size, rectangular portraits of men alone or men on horses.

I know that there are no women on the walls in this room. Probably why this closed off space exists, frankly.

The middle of the floor is cluttered with busts on stands, marble and wood and obsidian portraits of proud male figures. I squint at the one closest to me, a marble statue of someone wearing a toga and looking off into the distance. I'm not sure how this is related to the ancestry of the Morgan family, but somehow I have no doubt that it is one of Dare's relatives.

Looking around the small space one last time, I pull my head out and start to close the door.

That's when Dare's voice reaches out and ensnares me.

"What are you doing here?" he asks.

His voice is low and threatening, almost certainly about to tell me that I shouldn't be here.

I spin around and shut the door with my back to it, my eyes going wide. Dare looks at me, his expression haughty and imperious. For a moment, I am confused. Is he just angry that I went snooping where I shouldn't have been?

"Well? What do you have to say for yourself?"

I gulp and look down at his outfit. Then I squint. I don't remember exactly what he was wearing when we left the boat, but either he has changed into a three-piece suit or…

Or he isn't Dare at all. Sucking in a breath, I put my trembling hands behind my back and straighten my posture. My head goes up, my shoulders go back, my chest sticks out. Just like Dare told me to stand whenever I was around someone that I wanted to impress or intimidate.

"Burn," I greet him carefully. "I suppose I should ask you the same thing. Why are you creeping around the secret passageways in your grandfather's house and trying to scare people to death?"

He looks nonplussed at the fact that I figured out his little deception so quickly. He stalks toward me, making his size evident when he looms over me. I draw a shaky breath and look up at him, determined not to look like I actually feel. That is, that I'm about to pee my pants.

Burn raises his hand to me, his fingers getting much too close to my throat for my liking. Then he diverts his hand at the last moment, catching a little of my coppery hair between his fingers and tugging it gently.

"I see that my brother brought you back unscathed from wherever you scampered off to. I was just telling Daisy that I didn't know if Dare would kill you or not."

My blood goes cold. Suddenly, I can only hear the sound of my heart beating in my ears.

Did I hear Burn right? Did he say that Dare would kill me?

I have to say something. I lick my lips and say, "I'm fine, as you can see. Thank you for your concern."

Burn smirks and moves closer to me, his body nearly touching mine. I move back but I hit the wall and Burn chuckles. "Talia, Talia, Talia. What are we going to do with you?"

He traces a line from my collarbone down to my breasts, looking me dead in the eye as he does it. I move to smack his hand away but he grabs my hand and pins me against the wall, resuming his slow unbuttoning of my coat.

The look in his eyes is fiery, with an edge of threat.

"Stop, Burn. I don't want you to touch me."

He smirks and stops, then he spews his hand into my hair and pulls my head back. "Why are you with my brother? Is he paying you? Or did he just promise you a cut of the proceeds when he manages to steal the inheritance from me?"

I lick my lips, struggling against his tight hold.

"Let go of me, Burn. You're hurting me."

He laughs. "You don't know the first thing about what it is to be hurt, little girl. But maybe you don't have to. What's he paying you? Whatever it is, I'll double it. Or if you wait until I win the inheritance race, I will triple your money. All I need from you is a promise that you will start birth control right away. The patch, the pill, the shot, whatever."

I look up at him, my brow furrowing. "What? No. Get off me. You are sick."

He grits his teeth, leaning close enough to my face that I can feel his breath against my cheek. "Either you let me pay you. Or I fucking kill you. I don't particularly care which one."

Something in me snaps. I rear back and bash my forehead into his mouth, screaming. "Get off me! Help! Get off me!"

Burn stumbles back, holding his hand over his mouth, his eyes going wide. A door opens at the end of our hallway and Clive steps through, looking perplexed. His gaze scans the small hallway and he sees Burn on the ground and me screaming bloody murder.

"Help! Clive, help! Burn is trying to kill me!"

Burn looks bewildered and absolutely scandalized by the idea that I would just immediately rat him out. Clive storms down the hallway, casting Burn a vicious glare. The butler grabs me, pulling me from where I am standing and practically carrying me back toward the open hallway.

I catch a last glance of Burn getting to his feet, his hands still over his mouth. And then Clive shoves me out the door, following me and slamming the door shut behind him.

Dare comes running around the corner, ready to do battle,

his fists balled up. Clive grabs me by the shoulders and pushes me toward Dare, looking ashamed though he didn't do anything wrong.

"Sir, I'm very sorry. If I'd known that you were here, I would have known to keep Miss Chance's location in my head. You see, I knew that Burn was here–"

"No offense, Clive. But if my brother wanted to fuck with Talia, he would have found a way to do it regardless of being watched or not. None of his actions are your fault."

I reach out, gently laying a hand onto Clive's arm. I'm hysterical, almost sobbing when I speak.

"You saved me, Clive. Thank you. I'll never forget it."

Dare looks at me, grabbing my coat and pulling me close, his eyes search my face.

"You're all right now. It's okay. I've got you." He cups my jaw, looking down at me, his eyes blazing with fury and concern. "Did he hurt you?"

"He… He grabbed me. He wanted to pay me to run away from our marriage. And he– he threatened to kill me. I think if it weren't for Clive, he would've…" I shake my head, tears welling in my eyes. "Done something more."

Dare turns away, his body as tight as a bowstring, his eyes riveted on the door that we just exited. But I grab at his arm, scared that he will either trounce Burn or Burn will beat the shit out of him. Either way, I don't want to be the cause of it.

"Dare, please. Stay with me!"

He moves toward his twin brother, murder in his eyes. I pull Dare away from Burn, my tone turning pleading.

"Please don't leave me. I need you, Dare."

Dare freezes and then turns his head back to me. I lift his arm, using my shoulders underneath it. Then I hug his body, realizing only then that I am shaking so hard that my teeth began to chatter.

"Don't leave me. Please."

Some of the tension goes out of his body and he closes his arms around my shoulders, pulling me against his chest. I know that I am supposed to be faking my reaction to keep the twins from killing each other. But it feels so good to have his familiar scent around me, his warmth revitalizing me, his big strong body sheltering me. I close my eyes for a second and let out a shaky breath.

"Okay," he whispers into my hair. "Okay. I'll deal with my brother later. Clive, tell the driver to pull the car around. We're leaving."

Dare sweeps me up into his arms and carries me out of the mansion.

Chapter Eight

DARE

It takes everything in me to drive Talia back to our loft and carry her upstairs without turning around and going back to the estate. The fact that my brother thinks that he has the right to touch my fucking wife makes me sick with a frenzied kind of anger.

I am poisoned with fury, unable to think straight. I can't stop myself from picturing just how amazing it will feel when I grab Burn by the collar and put my hands around his throat, staring into his eyes as I choke the life out of him.

But I can't do that just now. No, now I have to carry Talia through the loft, not stopping until I manage to deposit her in our bed. She is still shaky and watching me with wide eyes. As if she doesn't quite trust me, but I am better than the alternatives.

"You didn't have to carry me all this way," she says, her voice barely a whisper. She shrugs her long red mane out of her face and purses her lips, her eyes still scanning my face. "I could've walked."

I look up at her, my blood still pumping hot through my

veins. Talia struggles out of her jacket and I lean in, cupping her jaw.

Something has changed. Something has shifted inside me.

Something that was triggered by her words. *I need you, Dare.*

I've never been needed before, never been relied upon. The responsibility of being Talia's husband is all striking at once, enormous and sudden and sucking the breath right out of my lungs.

I need you, Dare. It's like she found the secret words to activate my soul.

I bend and brush my lips against Talia's, my fingers tightening on her face.

"I will kill him," I utter. "For laying a hand on you, Burn assured his own death."

Talia winces and reaches up a hand, delicately threading it through my hair. She hesitates for a moment before answering.

"You can't kill Burn. What he did was unthinkable and unforgivable. But he doesn't deserve to die for it. He is a bastard, no question about it. But I don't think you killing him and then ending up in jail is going to help anyone. Not me, not the entire Morgan family."

"It doesn't matter. Burn has a history of touching things that don't belong to him. First Daisy. Now he tried to take you from me. I won't just stand by like a helpless fool and let him steal my wife."

Talia frowns a little. "Dare, you've already won that battle. We are married. I'm your wife. One of the reasons that I married you was because I think that Burn is a cheater that cannot be trusted. You said so yourself."

"Burn knows that you are mine," I growl. "*Mine.* He knows that you are my wife. I think he delights in the idea that he can take any woman that I have and steal her away with enough charm, money, or force."

I see her quick inhale of breath. "I know you don't want to lose me to Burn. I know that you two have a complicated history and he has burned you in the past. But that's not taking me into account at all." She takes my hand, lacing her fingers through it and bringing it to her chest. She looks at me intently. "I have agency. I have the ability to make choices for myself. I am telling you right now… I have no interest in running to Burn's arms. The only way that you can lose me is by being dishonest with me and not respecting me. You don't have to worry about competition from your brother. Especially not now, after he assaulted me. If I leave, it won't be because Burn charmed me. Do you understand?"

My heart hammers against my chest. I hear what she is saying, but her words don't fully sink in.

Still, I agree without really thinking. "I understand. That doesn't make me want to kill Burn any less, though."

Talia smiles and puts her hand against my cheek briefly. "Just remember the inheritance battle. I doubt that Remy will award you the company for killing your own brother. Even your family seems a little too uncouth for that."

She pushes me away with gentle hands and moves to the edge of the bed, finally standing up.

"What are you doing?" I ask.

She moves over to the closet, passing me a sideways glance as she goes. "Changing. There is a pair of silk drawstring pants in here and an oversized cashmere cardigan that are really calling my name. Unless you have other plans, I was going to try to close my eyes for a minute. I think I'm having an adrenaline crash. You don't mind, do you?"

I squint at her but shrug. "No." I stand and watch her as

she undresses, looking back at me a couple times with a harried expression.

"Are you just going to stand there and watch me?"

She pulls her sweater over her head and I look at her smooth, flawless skin on her back. She's not wearing a bra at all and while she hurries to put a shirt on, something primal stirs in me.

Lusts perhaps, but something deeper than that. I don't have a name for the emotion that looking at Talia makes me feel. Possessive, yes. But something more than that, too.

Some emotion that is new, one that flits beneath the surface and sinks too quickly for me to fully examine it.

She seems to have cooled off completely by now. Her shaky hands are gone, her voice is calm and even. I check my watch. "If you're going to take a nap, I should get caught up with work and touch base with a few people. I don't want to leave the loft again today. So maybe I will have a private chef come in and cook for us."

Talia tugs on her shirt and then rubs herself in a white cashmere cardigan. She looks at me, her expression hard to read.

"That would be nice," she says.

I prowl over to her, slowly putting my hand out and wrapping it around her waist. Drawing her in slowly, I look down at her. Her head falls back, her face bewitchingly beautiful.

For the first time that I can remember, I want to kiss her lips. There is no expectation behind the movement when I brush her lips with my own. Just that odd possessive feeling again. I enjoy the press of her body against mine, the way she inhales sharply just before I kiss her. The feeling of having completed a goal when I look into her eyes.

She is mine. I really do believe her when she says that she isn't interested in Burn.

I want to deepen the kiss and push her backward to the bed. I want to hear her call my name.

But I don't. Instead I reluctantly turn her loose. "I'll be here when you wake up."

Her brow furrows in confusion but she just nods. "Okay. I'll see you for dinner."

Walking out of the room is hard. Closing the door behind me is nearly impossible. But she needs rest. And I have plenty to do in the meantime.

When Talia finally stumbles out of the bedroom, wiping sleep from her eyes, she finds me in the room that I've claimed for my office. I glance up from the paperwork that I have been paging through, jogging the boring balance sheets and looking her up and down. She changed into a loose white cotton dress and kept the oversized white cashmere cardigan on. She crosses her arms and saunters into the room with a curious expression on her face.

"What smells so good?" She asks.

My lips twitch and I stand up, moving around my desk. "I thought that you might like having some Italian food for dinner."

Her brows knit. "You're cooking for me?"

I smirk at her and roll my eyes. "I don't cook. But I do have a number of personal chefs on my payroll that are available at a moment's notice. So you get the best of both worlds: great food and the pleasure of my company."

She pulls the edges of her cardigan close over her chest, giving me a considering look.

"I'm actually pretty hungry. When will the staff be ready to serve dinner?"

I put an arm out, touching Talia's hip ever so briefly. She looks at me, her eyes narrowing a minute momentarily. But I only guide her out of the office and toward the kitchen.

"I instructed her to have everything ready to go when you woke up. So now is as good a time as any."

Talia eyes me as I usher her toward the kitchen, but she doesn't say anything. We soon emerge from the hallway into the living room and walk around to the kitchen. The staff I've brought in have a number of pots and pans full of half finished food on the stovetop and kitchen counter. She turns when she hears us coming, her chef's coat starched and crisp. She wipes her hands on a kitchen towel as I wrap an arm around Talia.

"Patrice, this is Talia. Talia, this is Chef Patrice."

Patrice bows her head, a tiny smile blooming on her face. "It's a pleasure to serve you." She waves a hand, gesturing to the small dining room just off the kitchen area. "If you're ready, I can serve you right away."

"Thank you, Patrice," Talia says. She grabs my hand and squeezes it, looking at me strangely. I gather that she means that I should also thank the chef.

"Er, yes. Thank you. We'll be in the dining room."

Patrice bows and turns toward the kitchen counter. "I'll be right in with the first course."

I hurry Talia over to the dining room, my own stomach rumbling. The air is heavy with garlic and I'm interested to see what our private chef has come up with.

After pulling out a chair for Talia, I take the seat immediately to her right. The dining room isn't large, only really having room for the most basic rectangular table and three chairs. This chef has already set two places, complete with silverware and plates and two full wine glasses of water. Talia looks at the set up, her eyes wide.

"This is pretty nice," she says.

I slide her a smirk and shrug. "Usually I would have this

chef serve wine pairings. But I figured since you can't drink, it would be a waste."

Talia starts to respond to that but Chef Patrice sweeps into the dining room, two plates in her hands and a kitchen towel hanging over one arm. She comes around and sets down the plates before us, giving us a light smile.

The first course is several slices of cantaloupe with a salty sweet ricotta. She bows. "Please enjoy."

She leaves us to taste her food. I look over at Talia to gauge her reaction. But she has already picked up a fork and spears her melon, dipping it in the ricotta.

Just before she puts it in her mouth, she makes eye contact with me and blushes. "I'm really starving," she explains.

Looking her over, I give her a wry smile. "I'm just surprised to see you with a healthy appetite. After what you endured this morning with my brother…" I shrug. "I wasn't sure you would recover. And yet here you are, looking well and eating quite graciously."

She arches her brow. "I don't think that my hunger has much to do with whether or not your brother assaulted me or not. I think I just forgot to eat last night and now I am starving."

Talia pops another piece of cantaloupe into her mouth and chews. I purse my lips and taste the melon, finding its pairing with the ricotta pretty mouthwatering.

She fidgets, cleaning her fingers off with her cloth napkin. "I wonder what Burn would have done if you hadn't heard me scream."

I look up at her, trying to control my emotions. The last thing in the world I want is to let her know how unthinkable the idea is of Talia being brutalized while she was in my care. I push out a silent breath.

"The thing that matters most is that you are okay." I push my plate away, picking up my water glass and emptying it in a few swallows.

"So… What, then? You're just going to let Burn get away with this, just like everything else in his life?"

Her words are bitter. I want to yell at her, to express the frustration that is simmering inside. But she's already gone through so much today that heaping more on her plate would be incredibly cruel.

"Talia." I lock gazes with her, reaching across the table and snaring her hand. I speak slowly and quietly, every word as grave as death. "I will deal with Burn. He will absolutely get what is coming to him for daring to touch you. He knew what he was doing and who you belong to. But he did it anyway. So you can rest assured that I will see justice done."

She drops her gaze and pulls her hand from my grasp. "Okay."

She says it like she doesn't quite believe me. But I am not really interested in challenging her preconceptions at the moment. The chef appears and clears our plate, reappearing with two handmade pastas, covered with aromatic bolognese sauce and a dusting of parmesan. Before the chef can speak, I raise a hand and thank her. She catches on, backing out of the room without another word. Talia doesn't wait for permission. She grabs her fork and digs in eagerly, twisting up the pappardelle noodles carefully before shoveling a bite into her mouth.

The bite is bigger than she thought it would be and she glances at me apologetically, chewing quickly and holding her hand up to hide the way that her mouth is stuffed full of food. A second later though, she moans. "Oh, my God. This is so good."

I pick up my fork and twirl a bit of pasta in the tines. "I'm glad that you approve."

She swallows and then wipes her mouth. "I've never had anything like this before. Is this a popular Italian dish?"

I nod. "Bolognese is an Italian specialty. It is usually made by little old grandmothers with over twenty four hours to cook down the meat and vegetables into the stock."

Talia nods and then seems to have a displeasing thought. "I see."

"You see what?"

She shrugs a shoulder and piles another bite onto her fork. "It just occurred to me that our baby won't have a grandmother. That's kind of sad."

Her statement knocks the wind out of me. I look up at her from my plate, my brows descending in a worried frown. "No, it will not. It will have a million other advantages though. I think it will be just fine."

She nods slowly, picking at her food now. "Your mom died when you were little?"

To avoid answering the question, I take a big bite of my pasta. I leave her question hanging in the air, taking time to consider how to answer her question.

I swallow and say, "That's right. She passed away when I was ten."

Talia stares down at her pasta. "What was your mother's name?"

I repress a sigh. "Caroline."

"If you don't mind me asking, how did she die?"

"Pancreatic cancer. It was really quick. I think I knew about three months before she died that she even had cancer. And the next thing I knew, my father and Remy were holding my hands at the graveside when they buried her." I put my fork down, my appetite leaving me. "It was a long time ago though."

"Where is your mother buried?" Talia asked.

My mouth curves downward. "I think that's enough talk of my mother's death for one day, don't you think?"

Talia glances at me sharply. The look on her face says that she has a dozen more questions. But before she can ask a single one of them, I stand up, my face a carefully blank slate. I throw my napkin on the table and storm out of the room, needing some space.

Chapter Nine

TALIA

Nibbling on my lower lip, I peek inside the doorway of Dare's office. He's sitting behind his desk, jotting down notes in a legal pad, his crisp white shirt open at the collar. He's looking particularly appealing to me today, though that might be just my hormones playing tricks on me.

Clearing my throat, I step more fully into the doorway and knock on the open door. He turns his steely blue eyes on me, pinning me in place without even moving.

"What is it, darling girl?" he asks. He uses his pet name for me, which turns my legs to jelly and makes my heart beat in double time.

Swallowing, I lift my chin. "What exactly am I supposed to do all day?"

Dare puts down his pen, pushing the pad of paper a few inches away from him.

"What do you mean?"

"Can I still mind the cash register at Aunt Minnie's bookstore? And what about my work with Hope House? There are still children going through tough times. I may have access to an unbelievable amount of money now, but Hope House is still one step away from bankruptcy."

He leans back in his chair, his fingers drumming on the edge of his solid wood desk. "I thought you would relish the idea of taking it easy."

Walking over to his desk, I cross my arms. I'm gearing up for a battle. But I need to play it cool, not yell or lose my temper.

"I'm a hard worker. Always have been, always will be. It's dyed in the wool, never coming out. So I can let my job at the restaurant slide. Gladly. But the other two activities, Aunt Minnie's and Hope House? Those never paid me. They both give me things other than money."

He blinks. A ripple of doubt runs across his face. "Like what? Money and power are the only currencies that anyone who's anyone trades in these days."

My lips thin. I draw in a breath to bolster myself.

"Working at the bookstore provides me with the security of knowing that I am making sure that my Aunt Minnie doesn't lose her shirt. And Hope House… The kids need someone to be in their corner. They make me feel like I'm… being useful."

"Useful?" He huffs out half a laugh.

"Yes." I can feel my cheeks beginning to burn. "It's important to be of service to people that need you."

Dare snorts. "That sounds like crazy talk. I thought you would just take up a quiet hobby. Collecting art, maybe. Or be a patroness of the arts. My friend Calum owns a ballet company. Maybe he can get you started supporting some ballerinas."

I can feel my heart sink and all the air leave my lungs. All the joy I have found in the last few days disappears in an instant as Dare's words hit me like a punch in the chest.

He looks at me, expecting me to acquiesce to his demands. But there is no way I'm giving up what has become so important to me. Each week, I go to Hope House and work with those kids, helping them through their crisis; it brings me incredible satisfaction and peace of mind. Besides, Aunt Minnie desperately needs me working at the bookstore.

She won't hire anyone else to help around the store.

"You're wrong," I reply firmly, meeting Dare's gaze head on with a confidence that surprises even myself. "I am not going to give up my job at the bookstore or volunteer work at Hope House. You may think I should be some fine lady of Harwicke, but that is not who I am and what I want."

Dare's eyes flash with anger and disbelief.

I stand there, unable to believe what I'm hearing. Dare wants me to give up my job at the bookstore and join charity boards? What kind of life is this? After all that I've done to make it here - working hard, getting into college, supporting myself - he expects me to just throw it away?

I can feel anger rising within me but before I can say anything Dare continues. "It will be good for you," he says. "You'll have more free time and won't be so tired from work."

He doesn't understand my passion for books or volunteering with children in Hope House. It brings me joy and a purpose that I can't get anywhere else. How can I possibly give that up?

I want to tell Dare all this, but I can't bring myself to. I just stand there feeling helpless and a little lost, not sure what my next move should be.

"I like volunteering with children in crisis at Hope House. What is your issue with it?" I ask. He says, "I don't have a problem with it, but you need to think bigger. As the wife of a billionaire, Talia, you have the ability to sit on the boards of charities. You can effect changes at a much higher level."

Maybe if I'm lucky I'll find something else here in Harwicke - something to fill the void left by giving up my job. But right now, I can only stare at Dare in silence, wishing he could understand how much it would mean to me if he just let me keep doing what I love.

But I guess that won't be the case for now. All I can do is take a deep breath and try to move forward, even when it feels like my heart is breaking in two.

"Dare..."

He looks up at me, his eyes scanning my face and his mouth tightening slightly.

"I can see you working up the nerve to say something. Spit it out."

Tossing my hair, I frown. "You don't even realize it, but you are taking something from me. Telling me to set my sights higher than merely volunteering at Hope House takes away the joy I get from being there with the kids. I wouldn't expect you to understand."

Dare arches an eyebrow. "I don't. But maybe..." He stops for a second, his lips pressing together. "Show me."

I sit on the corner of his desk, crossing my legs. He puts his hand on my leg, sliding it up my thigh. I blush and bite my lip, trying not to squirm at my husband's touch.

"Really?" I ask.

Dare's lips twitch. "I can almost guarantee that I won't like it nearly as much as you do."

My heart flutters as I realize this could be my chance to do something meaningful. Dare's giving me a single tiny crack in his otherwise impenetrable shell made of wealth and privilege. I would be crazy to push him away now.

"Okay," I say softly. "Let's do it."

Dare smiles knowingly and squeezes my leg gently before releasing me.

"Just like that?" I ask, narrowing my eyes on his face.

He shrugs. "If it will make you stop nattering on about your life's purpose, I can give you one afternoon."

WE ARRIVE at the children's shelter, the loud sound of laughter and cries of joy ringing around me. Most of the older kids were in school today, but a few younger ones remain, accompanied by volunteers.

As I step into the shelter, I'm met with warm smiles and hugs from the familiar faces - people I have grown to know over time. We exchange pleasantries, catching up on recent events before saying hello to the children who run up to greet me and shower me with hugs.

Gathering us all together in the giant playroom, I guide Ansel— a seven-year-old boy whom I've befriended— towards a table filled with colorful blocks. He looked excited yet apprehensive as he eyed the construction toys.

Dare kneels down beside Ansel and watches the boy with an apprehensive gaze. I smile at Dare, giving him what I think is a soothing look. I'm honestly just impressed that he allowed me to talk him into coming to Hope House.

"Have you ever played with blocks?" Ansel asks me. He stacks three blocks and then looks at me skeptically. "My friend Jake says that you probably haven't done lots of normal stuff because you are a fancy rich lady."

My cheeks color. It's everything I can do not to stare at Dare. I have this feeling that if I glance his way, I'll crack up. Instead, I focus on speaking softly to Ansel, giving him my full attention.

"What do you think you could build with this?" I ask Ansel. I pick up a block and place my hand lightly on his shoulder, giving him a smile of reassurance.

He hesitates before answering, "I don't know. Maybe a castle?"

I smile wider. "That's a wonderful idea!"

Ansel begins to assemble the blocks slowly. Soon other children join us at the table, eager to be part of the activity. They crowd around Ansel and I, offering their help and advice for Ansel's project as it starts to take shape.

Ansel's eyes widen in surprise as he sees the group of children approach. "Thank you so much for your help!" He exclaims.

The children listen attentively as Ansel describes his plans and offers constructive suggestions.

"Look how high it is!" Ansel crows.

"It's incredible," one of the other children says.

"Very good," Dare manages

Ansel smiles, looking around himself.

A volunteer sweeps into the playroom and announces, "We have a new arrival. Everyone, meet Solana."

She nudges a small girl forward. Solana has long black hair and dusky brown skin, coupled with beautiful doe-brown eyes. She's wearing an oversized and wrinkled blue smock over a long-sleeved white tee-shirt. She clings to the volunteer's pant leg, looking around with wide eyes.

"Solana, it's okay," I coax the girl. "You can come play with us."

"I have blocks!" Ansel crows, waving a red block at Solana.

The volunteer pushes Solana forward a step. She looks like a newborn deer walking for the first time and stares at us as if we are a foreign species.

I lean forward and extend a block to the girl. "Have you ever played with these? Do you want to show us what you can build?"

Solana's gaze darts to Dare, taking in his size and stature. As I watch, she runs to straight to Dare, throwing her arms around his waist and resting her head against his belly. His eyes go wide. His posture stiffens. He glances at me, confusion evident in his gaze.

My mouth curls up at the corners. "She likes you, I guess. Right, Solana?"

Solana nods her head, hiding her face.

"I can't believe that anyone is so trusting," Dare replies, rubbing her lightly on the back.

"I've never seen a kid act like this," I comment.

The volunteer gently says, "Solana has had a tough week at home. She needs extra care and attention."

"Of course," I'm quick to respond. "We're happy to take over. Right, Solana?"

The girl only seems to burrow further into the black silk of Dare's shirt.

Dare blinks in surprised confusion, his cheeks turning a deep red. He hesitates only for a moment before wrapping an arm around Solana's shoulder while offering her a gentle smile of reassurance. I watch as he tries to appear composed and confident despite clearly being out of his comfort zone.

"It's okay," Dare whispers, "Everything will be alright."

Solana seems to relax a bit, although she still looks away shyly. I can't help but stifle my laughter at the sight; here is this towering figure trying to comfort this young girl, both of them clearly so uncomfortable yet still managing to find some solace in each other.

Solana gazes at Dare, her eyes brimming with admiration. Dare is taken aback by the intensity of her stare, but he welcomes the feeling all the same; not quite understanding it, but embracing it all the same.

"What do you want me to help you build first?" He asks as he sits down next to her.

She throws him a coy smile and points towards a pile of wooden blocks. "This tower!" She exclaims confidently, despite her obvious insecurity.

Dare chuckles at her enthusiasm and begins assembling the pieces. An undeniable warmth fills the room as they interact; his kindness radiating off him in waves. I can't help but smile, watching them come together.

Solana inches closer to Dare, her gaze locked intensely on him. She watches in awe as he deftly places the blocks of the tower. She hastily begins to mimic his actions, grasping a block and carefully setting it atop the structure.

Dare abruptly notices, throwing an astonished look of surprise before swiftly grinning back at Solana. "I'm glad you're enjoying it," he whispers softly.

"Hey, I'm just playing with blocks." I bite my cheek to keep myself from grinning and stack a few blocks.

He takes it in stride and begins talking to Solana.

"What kind of things do you like?" he asks.

Solana blushes and replies, "I like reading and playing piano."

"Do you have any brothers or sisters?" Dare inquires.

The shy girl shakes her head slowly and answers in a whisper. "Just my mom and dad."

Dare smiles warmly. "That's cool. I have a twin brother, but when he was annoying me as a kid, I would kind of wish I was an only child. You get all the attention and you don't have to share your stuff."

She gives him a grave look. "Maybe."

He shifts the topic.

"What are some of your favorite places?"

Still whispering, Solana says, "I like the park near my house and the library where I go for story time."

Dare listens intently as she talks about things that matter most to her, never interrupting or judging.

I can't help but feel emotional myself; such moments make me remember why I do this work— why we choose to volunteer at shelters in our spare time despite our busy schedules— because these brief opportunities matter more than anything else when it comes to giving back to those who need it most.

"What else do you like to do?" Dare asks, trying to make small talk.

Solana's face lights up. "I love gymnastics!" She spins around and begins doing cartwheels across the playroom floor. Dare watches in amazement as she performs one complex move after another. When she finally finishes, he applauds thunderously and grins giddily at her accomplishment.

I step back and laugh, marveling at the scene before me. This is why we chose to volunteer at shelters— to be able to share these kinds of moments with others.

At one point, Solana looks up at me with a huge smile on her face and says "Dare's cool!" I can't help but chuckle at this; it warms my heart to see how much she is enjoying their conversation.

Dare's gentle demeanor brings out the best in Solana, and watching them together fills me with hope for the future. If he's this great with kids he doesn't know, I can't wait to see how good he is with the baby I'm carrying.

We spend some time conversing with Solana, and I'm eager to join in.

"So, what do you want to be when you grow up?" I inquire.

Solana's face brightens and she answers energetically. "A doctor, an astronaut, a detective..." She motions around the room at her toys and grins. "I can do whatever I want, because I'm brave!"

Dare takes all of this in stride, eager to learn more about Solana just as I am. He doesn't talk much—which makes his presence even more powerful—but he listens intently as Solana talks about her interests and future aspirations.

One of the volunteers comes in and tells us that it's time for the kids to come upstairs for a snack and a nap. It's fine, because it's around the time of the end of our visit anyway.

Solana pulls Dare into a warm embrace, and he slowly brings his arms around her. "Take care," she says softly.

He steps back, giving her a small nod as he struggles to swallow the lump in his throat. "You too."

The genuine emotion between them makes tears prick my eyes. Despite only knowing each other for a few moments, they've formed a connection that even I can sense. We reluctantly say our goodbyes.

The drive home from the shelter is quiet; neither of us feel like talking much after such an emotional day. Dare seems to be lost in thought, and I'm not sure what he's thinking about.

Dare squints through the window, desperately seeking the truth. "What will happen to Solana if she isn't adopted?" he asks meekly.

"Solana comes from a very sad situation. Her parents died recently, and there don't seem to be any relatives that have offered to take her. Her future is nothing but a question mark at this point. Hopefully, god willing, an aunt or uncle will turn up."

He quirks his head. "Surely there are plenty of decent parents waiting to take in a bright kid like her."

I feel my chest grow heavy with sadness. Rubbing the

sore spot the feeling creates, I give him a wistful smile. "Finding homes for kids over the age of three is often nearly impossible," I reply. "It's heartbreaking to contemplate that she might never find a family. It kills me to think about it. She'll be stuck bouncing around from one foster home to the next until she ages out of the system. Those experiences will haunt her for the rest of her life."

I feel my throat closing up. Solana's sorrowful gaze flashes in my head. She must know what is happening, but at her young age, she can't quite put all the pieces together.

He goes quiet, looking away out his own window. After half a minute of waiting, I shrug and lapse into daydreaming about my own future. The silence stretches on for ten minutes at least.

When Dare finally speaks, it isn't to talk about Solana at all. Dare says, "I'm moving the company headquarters out of Harwicke."

My eyes widen and my head whips around.

"What?! Why would you do that?!" I exclaim.

Dare gives me a hard look and replies firmly. "It's way past due time to make a change. There will be no innovation or radical changes in the same place the company has been for over a hundred years. Morgan Drilling is dying a slow, painful death here. I'm thinking practically."

"What about the rest of the town?" I ask incredulously. "The shelter is only open because your company keeps the town of Harwicke alive. Without your company, the town will wither and die. Hope House will be forced to close its doors."

"That is... unfortunate," Dare says. "I don't think I should be blamed for that, though."

I gape at him. "Do you not understand that your decisions affect people?"

He looks at me like I'm a puzzle he can't figure out. "It's only business," he says simply before lapsing back into silence.

I shake my head in disbelief, not knowing how else to make him understand.

Chapter Ten

DARE

I'm not sure what to expect as I show up at our loft with a closet full of new clothes for Talia. But I am certain she won't be pleased with my gift. And I'm right - her anger swells as soon as she sees the boxes and bags filled with everything from dresses to lingerie.

"What have you done?!" She shouts, her eyes blazing. "You burned my stuff? All of it?"

I shrug nonchalantly, but inside guilt swirls in my stomach. It's true - I had taken all her old clothes and had them incinerated without consulting her first. But it didn't seem chic enough, and I wanted to make sure she was wearing the best quality.

"It's no big deal," I say, trying to sound casual. "I'm just trying to help you look your best."

She glares at me before finally giving a sigh of resignation. "Fine," she mutters. "But this doesn't mean I'm going to like it."

Despite her initial protests, I can tell deep down that Talia is excited about all the new clothing options - it's evident in the eagerness of her eyes as she paws through everything.

When she finishes admiring each piece of clothing, I clear my throat and speak up:

"Now that you've seen everything, why don't you get dressed? We're going out for dinner tonight."

Talia's eyes widen and she looks up at me in surprise. But to my relief, there isn't any anger this time - just a small smile playing on her lips.

"Alright," she says softly before turning to head off to the bedroom. "I'll be ready in no time."

And with that, Talia begins getting ready for our evening out - an evening where I know we'll have a bit more fun than usual, thanks in part to the new wardrobe I've so thoughtfully provided. Sure, it might not make us best friends anytime soon - but at least it will be a start.

I look over at Talia, who is staring out the window as we drive to dinner. She looks so peaceful and beautiful at this moment, she really takes my breath away. Lucky for me, I have something special planned for just this moment.

Reaching into my pocket, I pull out a silky bag. Within the bag is a stunning necklace encrusted with diamonds. The second I laid eyes on it, I thought that its beauty can only be matched by hers.

Plucking the necklace from the bag, I wait until she faces out the window before I slip it around her neck.

Talia's eyes widen in surprise when she feels me fastening the clasp behind her neck. She turns to face me, touching the necklace with awe-filled fascination. "It's heavier than I thought it would be."

My eyebrows fly up. "That's all you are going to say? No, 'thank you, Dare, I love it'?"

A deep crimson floods her cheeks. "It is a gorgeous necklace. And I am thankful for it. But what is it *for*?"

I smooth my touch around the back of her neck, causing a shiver to slide down her spine.

"It has no value beyond the fact that I knew it would look beautiful against your collarbones."

I run a single fingertip in a tiny arc across her bare skin. Talia looks me in the eye and her whole body shudders. Sweeping the copper hair off of her shoulder, I bend down and place a burning hot kiss against the base of her neck.

The sudden, shocked inhale I hear satisfies me on a primal level. I chuckle as I sit back.

I gave her a smirk as I watch her eyes flick over the necklace. She's intrigued, but she's trying to hide it. "You know plenty of women would be falling all over themselves for this?" I ask, raising my eyebrows.

Her response comes quickly and with fire in her voice that tells me she isn't going to be one of those nameless, faceless women that came before her. "I am not like them. I don't need your gifts to make me happy," she says

I cock my head. "You make a good little wife, Talia. I didn't expect it, but I'm beginning to enjoy having you by my side."

She rolls her eyes and looks away, shaking her head. But I see a pink flush creeping across her cheeks.

We arrive at the restaurant and she steps out wearing her dark gown and a heavy fur coat. It's coupled with a dark frown, refusing to look at me at all. I grab her hand and tug her forward across the sidewalk and into the bistro.

At the restaurant, a suit-wearing maitre d' shows us through the loud, dimly lit restaurant. Every table is full. White-shirted waiters artfully twirl trays full of drinks, dodging around the tables full of restaurant patrons.

We are shown to our table, which is a large circular booth at the center of the restaurant. The company clients I agreed to meet with are already tucked into the booth and sipping their cocktails.

As I greet them, I tug on Talia's hand, needing her to sit down and move inward toward the clients first. It's all about power. I chose this booth at this restaurant for a reason.

She gives me a puzzled look as she does it, her lips pinching and her eyes flashing.

"Go ahead, darling," I purr. I flash a smile that's as sharp as a knife.

Her eyes tighten but she slides into the booth. I smooth my tie down as I seat myself. I slide a hand into her lap and grip her knee, pasting on a smile. Talia does the same after I give her knee a hard squeeze.

I address the clients, who look like cookie-cutter versions of the same Wall Street businessman. Three expensive white or blue shirts, rolled up at the sleeve. Three dark wool jackets tossed into a pile separating Jamal from Talia. Three tumblers of liquid courage clutched in their hands.

"Gentlemen. May I introduce you all to my new wife, Talia? And Talia, meet Gus, Ken, and Jamal. They are clients that require quite a bit of finesse…" I gesture to the restaurant around me. "To be content."

"Congratulations, Dare," Ken says, looking at Talia like some prize-winning horse. "Never thought you were much of the settling down type."

Talia's mouth pinches. I pat her knee under the table.

"She convinced me," I lie blithely. "Didn't you, darling girl?"

If looks could kill, I would be dead from Talia's toxic glance. She doesn't make much of an expression, but her eyes are angry.

Pulling my hand off of her knee, I direct my attention

back to the three clients. "Should I order a round of gin martinis for the table?"

"Damn right," Jamal says. "Let's toast how well our two companies are doing right now."

"The market is literally ravenous for our products," agrees Gus. "It's a beautiful time to be young and ambitious. It seems like the sky's the limit. Hell, maybe I should get my own woman." He wiggles his eyebrows at Talia. "Do they have more of your model at the store where Dare bought you?"

Talia's smile vanishes. Her mouth bunches up and for a second, I think she's about to expose Gus to her razor-sharp tongue. But she just looks at me, scooting toward me.

"If you'll excuse me, I'm going to try to find the lavatory."

I stand up, offering her my hand. Talia ignores the gesture and struts off toward the bar. As she walks away, her ass looks amazing in her little black dress.

"Jesus, man. All that red hair. She must be a real firecracker in the bedroom," Jamal says.

My lips tip upward. "You have no idea."

Talia is gone for quite a while. I sip my martini and try to pay attention as the men take turns telling crazy stories of going clubbing and hooking up with wannabe-models. After a while, I see Talia heading out of the restaurant, putting her head down in a failed attempt not to attract any attention.

I fold up my napkin and excuse myself from the table. Weaving my way between patrons and waiters, I catch up with Talia just as she slips out the door. Snaring her hand, I pull her to a stop just outside the restaurant.

"Talia."

She looks back at me and pulls her hand free of my grip, exasperated. "What?"

I can feel my neck growing hot. "Where are you going?"

"I'm leaving." She tosses her head, her jaw locking. "Away from this macho 'I own the world' bullshit. It's gross."

I snort. "Just because the guys are a little douchey—"

"They are *awful*." Talia crosses her arms, shivering against the cold night air. "And the fact that you expect me to sit there like a complacent sex doll while you all talk about how much money you have… It's totally immature."

My mouth falls open. This was not the reaction I expected her to have. I don't know exactly why I brought her; her feelings were an afterthought.

Talia looks at me, shaking her head. "Honestly, Dare. I expected more of you."

"You expected more of me? That's a ridiculous thing to say. You didn't marry me because I'm perfectly respectable. You married me because I could pay your bills. And I married you because you are pretty enough, meek enough, and you happen to be carrying a child with my DNA."

She clenches her jaw, eyes flashing. "I'm not some pretty trinket that you bought. You can't just bring me out on special occasions to amuse your friends. I'm a person, Dare. I can hear *and* I have feelings."

I open my mouth to defend myself, but she holds up a finger.

"I really hate that you think of me as meek. You have some old-fashioned notions of a biddable, quiet little wifey. And I'm here to tell you that I'm not going to fit into that mold."

I grab Talia by the shoulders, snaking one hand up behind her head, and shut her up by sealing my mouth over hers. At first, she makes a muffled noise, protesting as I kiss her. Then she opens her mouth to me, her tongue sliding against mine. She tastes so fucking sweet that I growl into her mouth.

But she wrenches herself away from me, her chest heaving. Her eyes are sparking like bottled lightning.

"No." She wipes at her lips as she drags in a breath, her color high. "You don't even know me, Dare. How can you kiss me? How can you act like you want to fuck me?"

"You're my wife," I grit out. My hands clench the fabric of her dress at her waist. "How can I pretend that I don't want to rip your dress off and—"

She pushes at my chest with such force that it almost hurts. "Let me go, Dare."

She looks disgusted with me. I clench the fabric of her dress in my hands tightly for a second. Then I ease my grip and allow her to wriggle free.

"You're handsome. I'm sure you know that. But you know what else you are?" She pulls up the hem of her top. "You're not a good human being, Dare."

"What does that have to do with anything?" I ask.

She points a finger at me. "You are selfish. And you're self-obsessed. And if you're not careful, you're going to tear our marriage into pieces."

Talia gathers her skirts and spins toward the street. As she heads toward the curb, I scrub a hand across my mouth.

What does she want? What could a girl like Talia even expect from a guy like me?

I watch her receding figure, a note of insecurity lodging itself in my chest.

Should I be different?

Looking at the bright lights of the city, I admit to myself that I don't know.

Chapter Eleven

TALIA

I sigh to myself as I stack a peanut butter and jelly sandwich on top of a faded beige melamine cafeteria tray. The tray sits on a metal sheet pan that holds twelve such trays, all identical down to the shiny red apples and the servings of baby carrots. Lunch time at Hope House is almost always the same.

Longing for some work that will keep my hands busy, I volunteered for making sandwiches and doling out baby carrots. The tiny kitchen is downright depressing. It clearly used to be a closet of some kind, a room without windows. Somebody stuck a large photo of an aerial view of a Hawaiian island and the surrounding ocean up with thumb-tacks. Trying, I guess, to imitate the feeling of having a view to gaze upon.

It's a lucky thing that I'm so distracted by my own thoughts. I hum along with the ancient radio, which has been stuck on the disco oldies station since my very first volunteer shift.

"Mmm. Baby, baby," I sing absently. "Where did our da dah…"

I trail off, unable to focus on the song. In truth, all I can think of is Dare.

My mind keeps turning the events of yesterday evening over and over as if tumbling them in a rock polisher.

Dare brushing his too-hot fingers over the hollow of my throat after he fastened the clasp of the icy diamond necklace around my neck. His fingers digging into the sides of my kneecap as he sat, thigh pressed against mine.

The way his eyes sparked electric blue at me when he gripped my wrist. A tendril of desire snaked around my body and wound itself tight, its thorns embedding in my delicate flesh.

I shiver as I remember the hot, flushed feeling coursing through my veins. That is the problem with Dare: his body is so desirable. But in the very next second, he opens his mouth and poison leaks out.

Sighing heavily, I push my hair out of my face. I have to pull myself together. At least if I am going to be useless, I might as well be able to help with the mind-numbing activity of finishing these lunches.

Fishing another slice of bread out of the half-full loaf bag, I grab my knife and slather a blob of peanut butter onto it. The kitchen door opens and I turn, my hand reaching for the strawberry jelly jar.

Aunt Minnie sticks her head in, beaming at me. Her hair is the same untamed mass of grays sticking out from her head almost like a halo. And she's wearing some sort of forest green velvet robe with several strands of thin silver chains around her neck.

"Ah! There you are, Talia."

I drop the knife in the jam jar and plow into her, not knowing until this moment how much I've missed her. Her arms wrap around me as I bury my face in the soft fabric gathered at her shoulder and squeeze her.

"I've missed you," I whisper.

She chuckles. "I can see that. I've missed you, too, for what it's worth."

When I pull back, Minnie sees the ring on my right hand. She gasps and grabs my fingers, twisting my hand around so the giant gemstone glitters.

"What is this? It's so huge!" she asks. "Surely that's not your engagement ring."

My face grows hot. "Ah. It's not a big deal."

"The hell it isn't. Most peoples' houses don't cost as much as what you are just casually wearing."

I suck in a breath. Her words were not meant as a slight, but they landed like an arrow right in my heart.

"I didn't buy it. Dare just sort of handed it to me."

As if that somehow makes it better.

Minnie finally lets my hand go. I fiddle with my ring, unsure how to tell her that I am married. Only *technically…* but still. Minnie moves back a couple of steps, looking me up and down.

And her gaze stops on my ever so slightly distended abdomen.

"Are you…?" She looks up at me, baffled.

I turn red as a beet. "I'm pregnant, yes. "

Her eyes bug out. "Christ, Talia. You're more than a couple of months along, too."

She shoves her hand through her unkempt mane and looks distressed.

Not the reaction I wanted. But perhaps the one I expected. I duck my head, the words for defending myself eluding me just now.

"What the hell is going on with you? I can't believe that

you didn't tell me about your pregnancy sooner. What other major events in your life do I not know about?"

I can't even look at her. Tears prick the corners of my eyes. I turn around, picking up the peanut butter sandwich I was making. Anything to keep my hands busy and occupy me while I try to repress my emotions.

"I'm sorry," I say softly. "There was a lot of drama surrounding my pregnancy. I wasn't really able to talk to anyone about it."

The lie slips out of my mouth easily and takes me by surprise. I talked to Olivia and Dare about my pregnancy. I just didn't include my aunt.

Aunt Minnie looks at me for a beat before her posture softens.

"When are you due?" she asks.

Giving her a tentative smile, I smooth a hand over my belly. "July fourteenth."

She nods, still looking skeptical. "I hope you'll include me in your baby's life."

Her words steal the breath from my lungs.

"Oh, Aunt Minnie." I leave the sandwiches behind and step forward to hug her tightly. "I would love nothing more."

She rubs a hand over my back, kissing my hair. I feel so safe in her embrace and realize that I haven't felt cared for in this exact way since I left Aunt Minnie's bungalow.

"Good. It's settled, then," she murmurs.

We stay like that for what seems like forever but is only probably a minute. Then Aunt Minnie steps back, her expression regretful.

"I have to go to the bookstore. I hired a girl to replace you, but her hours are very strictly limited. I promised her that I wouldn't be late today."

A preteen girl pushes open the kitchen door, interrupting Aunt Minnie.

"Talia? There is a visitor downstairs who wants to talk to you. I can finish up here if you want to go see what he wants."

"Hm. Okay." I don't know who it could be. I'm not expecting anyone. "Thanks, Molly."

Molly shrugs a shoulder and starts making the sandwich I never finished. We head outside and to the dark staircase. Aunt Minnie smiles at me and squeezes my hand, slipping away up the stairs toward the street. I head down, the stairs creaking and protesting with every step.

Who would be here to talk to me? The question makes my heart beat a little faster.

When I walk into the playroom, I immediately see Dare. He's sitting on a couch, looking extremely uncomfortable. Solana is on his lap, her dark hair shining, her face hidden as she presses it into Dare's expensive light blue Oxford. He sees me and gestures down at the little girl, a puzzled look on his face.

I smother a laugh as I approach. "I see your biggest fan found you."

His sharp glance could pierce right through me.

"Do you want to take her?" Dare asks.

Shrugging a shoulder, I try to appear as though I'm not about to burst into howls of laughter. "It looks like you've got it covered."

A young boy runs up to me, his dark eyes assessing me. I take in his thrift store clothes and the inflatable beach ball clutched under his arm. I see his gaze trip over my giant wedding ring and then see his eyes narrow as he passes judgment on me.

For the first time, I feel like maybe I am overdressed in

my black suit jacket and strappy black maxi dress. I should have taken my ring off at the very least.

"Who are you?" the little boy asks.

"Talia." I kneel down, putting myself at eye level with the boy. "I work here sometimes. What about you? What's your name?"

His jaw juts out and his mouth puckers up. "Will."

"That's a great name. And you have a beach ball under your arm… I love playing with beach balls. I like how they float in the air for a second when you toss them."

Will frowns. "Yeah."

"Do you want to play? You could stand over there and toss the beach ball up. Maybe we could keep it from hitting the ground. See how long we can do it for." I slide Dare a look. "How many times do you think we can pass it?"

Dare clears his throat, prying Solana from his chest. "I don't know. Maybe… four? What do you think, Solana?"

"A billion!" Will shouts, running to the spot I pointed out. "We can do a billion-trillion times, I bet."

He hits the beach ball with a soft pfft, arching it into the air. I rush to hit it before it touches the floor, tapping it on the bottom a few times to boost the ball into the air. I pass it back to Will, who laughs and hits it to the side.

Dare sets Solana on the floor and stands up, reaching over to catch the ball. He taps it up a few times, then passes it very gently to Solana.

She looks nonplussed but hits the ball very hard in my direction. Luckily, the ball shoots up and then falls slowly. I hit it back to Will.

We manage to keep it going until Molly comes tromping down the stairs, cupping her hands to her mouth. "Lunch is ready! Come upstairs!"

Will catches the ball and then hits it to me. He runs to the staircase, looking back breathlessly. "Hold the ball while I eat. Okay?"

I catch it, holding the ball up. "Definitely. It will be right here when you get back."

He pauses, looking at Solana. "Aren't you coming?"

The little girl shrugs, her gaze darting to Dare. "I don't know."

"You should go eat, Solana. Dare isn't going anywhere. Right, Dare?"

Dare glares at me and smiles thinly. "That's right. I'll be here."

Will runs over to Solana, grabs her little hand, and hauls her upstairs. As soon as they are gone, Dare folds his arms across his chest.

"You are going to break that little girl's heart."

I smile at him, walking over and collapsing on the couch.

"Are you going somewhere in the next half an hour?" I ask.

He glares at me. "No."

"Then what's the harm?"

"I don't want to…" He pauses, then releases a melodramatic sigh. "I don't want to make the little girl promises that I can't keep. And I don't want Solana thinking that I will be here for the entire day. I don't want her to expect a lot from me."

"Because that would set her up for disappointment."

"Yes!" Dare hisses.

"I see." I pat the spot next to me on the couch. "Come sit here with me."

He looks at me, narrowing his eyes. But when I don't add anything else to my statement, he does head over to me, his big frame taking up most of the remaining space. He spreads out, his expression a little tart.

"Happy?"

I touch his knee, looking into his eyes. "Yes."

Dare's brow knits. There is momentary confusion in his blue eyes. He seems to be expecting me to add more, to say something else.

When I don't, he sits back, his shoulders dropping a fraction.

I squeeze his knee. "You know, for someone that talks a big game about marriage lasting forever, you don't seem particularly comfortable with me. How can we ever be an old married couple if we aren't comfortable with each other?"

Dare pushes his cheek out with his tongue. "Do you think that is our biggest concern right now?"

I shrug. It's not small enough to be unnoticeable, either. "It's something worth thinking about."

He represses a sigh and wraps his arm around my shoulder, pulling me closer. I'm ready for an invasion, for him to kiss my lips and distract me. But to my surprise, Dare merely places a kiss on my head and attempts to sit silently with me. My breath hitches but I force my body to relax, folding my head against his chest. My position feels awkward but I'm not about to protest. After all, Dare is merely trying to comply with my demands.

I close my eyes for a few moments and inhale deeply, appreciating his masculine scents in my nose. Dare is a radiator, heat pouring off his body. I move infinitesimally closer to his body, letting my body warm up, soaking the warmth into my bones. He sighs again, his hand cupping my shoulder, his fingers tracing figure eights into the skin of my upper arm.

I remind myself that this is the stillness that I have been demanding for so long. I should just be able to enjoy it.

A muffled shout outside the window makes me seize up.

Dare moves me off his lap, standing up with a tense look on his face.

"What is that?" he mutters.

He moves over to the window and pushes aside the tattered lace curtain, looking out. Unable to help myself, I scramble to my feet and join him.

My eyes immediately land on a woman's curvy frame and thinning black hair. My immediate instinct is that this woman needs help.

Peering out the window, I see her standing about ten feet away, sandwiched between two larger figures. Two men, one in a faded red track suit and one in a dark green hoodie and jeans. They each have one of the woman's arms and are shouting at each other as they yank on her. She wears a thin wool duster over a skintight black dress and shivers against the icy air as she looks back and forth from one man to the other. Her eyes are wide and her fear is palpable.

"She's coming with me," one of the men bellows. "I'm telling you, she's my girl."

"I'll kill you both first," the other man growls back. He rips her away, the force of his yank making the woman stumble.

My heart beats fast. I head to the basement door, thinking only that the woman must be saved.

"What the fuck are you doing?" Dare hisses. "Don't you dare open that door."

His words give me pause. I stop, looking back at him with alarm.

"I have to save her, Dare."

Our argument draws the attention of the trio of people.

"The fuck, man," one of them says. "I don't need this."

He lopes off, leaving the other man to drag the woman

away, muttering as he goes. I run back to the window and watch as they go, flattening my palm against the glass.

"I can't believe you didn't let me help her. She clearly needed it."

Dare grits his teeth. "You are four months pregnant, Talia. There is no way in hell that I was letting you walk into a situation like that. Someone could have pulled a knife or a gun. You could've been really hurt… or worse."

My face feels hot. I pull away from the window, crossing my arms and feeling quite petulant.

"It would have been fine. I have been coming here to volunteer at this very house for half my life. I've managed perfectly well until now."

Dare's hands drop to his sides and he clenches his fists. "You are carrying my baby, Talia. That child is worth a billion dollars. Don't forget that."

"I haven't forgotten!" I snap. "Even if I wanted to, you haven't given me the chance. I can barely breathe, let alone forget."

His expression turns murderous. "That's it. Get your coat."

"Why?"

He leans toward me, his words precise and cutting to the quick. "Because we are leaving."

"We can't leave!" I protest. "I'm in the middle of working a shift!"

Dare pulls out his phone, texting for half a minute. Then he looks up at me, his tone brooking no arguments.

"There are three nannies on their way here right now to work for the entire weekend. Now go get your fucking coat. We are going away for a while."

I blink. "What? Where?"

Dare's face gets so red that I shrink back from his touch when he grabs my wrist. "No more questions."

My pulse hits the roof. I swallow and nod, hurrying to get my coat. Before I can do anything else or even let the other adults know I'm leaving, Dare hauls me out of the house and pushes me toward the waiting SUV.

Chapter Twelve

DARE

It isn't until I am steering the yacht out of the harbor that I begin to feel in control again. It's a drizzly day, the sun hiding behind heavy clouds all day long. I grip the polished wood steering wheel as I look out over the sea. All I see beyond the deck of the boat are shades of gray sky and deep blue-black water.

Everything is so much simpler at the helm of my yacht. There are no backstabbing brothers, no imperious grandparents, no sketchy characters looming far too close to Talia for any kind of comfort. And because I have turned off my phone and directed all business to my personal assistant, there are not even any urgent business matters that demand my attention.

Here, it's just me and the ship. When I want to change direction, I do so with an easy twist of the wheel. There are five screens in front of me that give me a sense of what is coming. Other than that, the yacht gives me no orders and suggests no directions.

I'm the one in charge.

It certainly makes me feel better than being told that I'm

selfish. There is no one here to make a fuss about my personal priorities or to call me an asshole for putting myself first.

It's nice, though it feels a *tiny* bit hollow.

The softest scuffing noise makes me turn around. The steering wheel is on the highest deck of the boat. I left Talia sitting in the warmth and comfort of the main deck's viewing area. Lined with sleek black leather couches and enclosed by glass walls, it allows one to look out at the sea in any weather and while wrapped in luxury.

The scuffing sound comes again, followed by the faintest moan. I slow the yacht and head down the steps, spotting Talia as soon as I open the door to the viewing area. She's on her knees, bent over a small wastebasket, emptying the contents of her stomach.

I walk over and touch her back and she stiffens, straightening and wiping her mouth on the back of her sleeve. "I would like some privacy," she says softly.

I kneel beside her, reaching in my jacket pocket and withdrawing a handkerchief. I offer it to her, looking at how pasty she is. I imagine she would blush a deep red right now if her face were not drained of nearly every ounce of blood.

Talia takes the handkerchief, her eyes fluttering closed for just a second. Then she bends over the wastebasket again and heaves. I can do nothing but pull her long hair from her face, closing my fingers around her hair like a hair elastic and drawing it to the back of her neck.

When the bout of seasickness passes, Talia wipes her mouth once again.

"Let's get you to bed," I say. "Come on."

Without waiting for her response, I hook her under each arm and haul her to her feet. It only takes the work of a couple of minutes to guide her downstairs into the largest bedroom, to peel off her coat, and to take off her shoes. Talia grabs the wastebasket from the bedroom and drags it into bed with her.

I head into the bathroom, rooting through the medicine cabinet until I find a bottle of anti-nausea medication. Returning with a couple of pills and a bottle of water, I offer them to Talia.

She looks white as a sheet when she turns to me. "What are you offering me?"

"Something for motion sickness."

She lifts her hand as if to scoop up the pills, but hesitates. "Is it safe for the baby?"

My lips twitch. "Yes. I checked the last time we were on the yacht. It is perfectly safe."

She swallows, eyeing the pills for a moment longer. Then she takes a sip of the water and swallows the pills.

I take a seat beside her on the bed, watching her expression carefully. She catches my examination and arches a brow.

"What are you expecting me to do?"

Shrugging a shoulder, I lean closer and brush a fiery lock of her hair away from her face. A tiny frown creases her brow as she watches me as closely. Like I'm a predator, and if she turns her back, I might pounce at any second.

"Stop looking at me like that."

Her face shows her confusion. "Like what?"

"Like I'm a lion and you're the human who has made the mistake of thinking you can tame me. I'm not going to bite, Talia."

She starts to say something, a quick retort. But then her body goes rigid. She lies down and closes her eyes. I notice that she still looks withdrawn and pale as a ghost.

Her lips are clamped together, her expression tense. I brush another lock of her hair away from her face and wait.

After several minutes, the bout of nausea passes. Talia opens her eyes, exhaling.

"At least I didn't throw up that time," she grouses.

"No."

Her lips thin. "Why are you still here? I thought you would have returned to captaining the ship by now."

All she gets from me in exchange for her remark is a vague shoulder shrug. "And yet, here I am."

She blinks, stifling a yawn. "Where are we going?"

"The destination is not the point. We are just sailing for the sake of the journey. And I know that we'll be left alone here. There are definitely no vagrants here, sharpening their knives and waiting for people that look like us to cross their paths."

"Vagrants." She releases a soft snort. "No one is targeting *me*. People that look like you, maybe."

I narrow my eyes and cross my arms, leaning back. "I don't think so, darling girl. You're my wife now. You wear my ring. You dress like you have money. You blend in with the upper class so well that the boundaries disappear completely."

Talia's eyebrows rise. She runs her hand over the hair on the pillow beside her head. "You think so?"

I nod.

She yawns. "That's good, coming from you. You're a snob."

"I'm discerning," I fire back. "And you agreed to marry me over my twin. So who between us is the pickiest one?"

She blinks several times, her eyelids growing heavy. "Not sure."

I lean over, pulling the comforter up around her body.

Talia's eyes flutter open and her lips curve into a smile. She turns over on her side, her hand seeking out mine on top of the covers.

"I'm tired," she admits.

"Just relax." I begin to rub slow circles into her back using my free hand. "I'll take a sleeping wife over a sick wife any damn day."

She closes her eyes, gripping my hand. I start to move away, but she clutches my hand harder and whines.

"Stay for a few minutes," she whispers. She nuzzles my hand, imploring me. "Please."

My jaw tenses. Her plea is an arrow straight into my heart. Talia is begging me to stay and protect her while she sleeps.

What kind of monster could say no to that?

"Of course," I grate out. Resettling myself on the bed, I skate my gaze down her body. I tug the comforter up around her shoulder and gently comb my fingers through the hair at her temple. She makes a soft sound in response, a quiet *mm* of what I assume is pleasure.

No, not pleasure.

Safety.

She feels safe knowing I am watching over her.

Sucking in a breath, I stare down at Talia's sleeping form. I like her when she's like this, all sleepy and curled up next to me. When we first met, I would have never thought that I would be right here, with Talia gripping my hand while she sleeps.

The sheer pleasure of realizing that Talia needs me, that she wants me to be close... If my frozen heart is on a glacier, this feeling is a block of ice shearing off and falling away into the nearby water.

I press my free hand to my chest, feeling as though something is loosening and unlocking. Breaking free.

Whatever this sensation is, I want more of it. I've only had the tiniest bit but the feeling is addictive.

When I stand up to shed my jacket, Talia makes a sleepy noise of protest and opens her eyes.

"What–"

"Shh." I lie down beside her, spooning her, and pull her close. "Go to sleep, darling girl."

A shudder runs through her, but her eyes sink closed once more. She grabs my hand and pulls my arm around her waist, tucking it against her chest.

Is this her way of marking me? Of telling me that I'm hers?

Fuck.

Burying my nose in Talia's coppery hair, I inhale her scent and try to be calm. As the even sound of her breathing lulls me into the lightest of dozes, a solitary thought swims to the surface of my mind.

Is this what Talia wanted when she called me selfish? It must be.

Chapter Thirteen

I'm in the library on my hands and knees the next day, trying to retrieve the chess piece that I carelessly knocked on the ground. The problem is that it seems to have gone skidding into a dark corner and is lurking behind one of the leather couches. I kneel, leaning over the furniture, my hand searching the crack between the wall and the leather back of the couch.

My long white sundress is pulled up around my knees to allow me freedom of movement. But I lean just a little further and hear ripping fabric.

I startle, looking down to see that the deep slit in the dress's silk skirt has begun to tear. When I straighten and move to grab the spot where it's torn, I hear a louder, longer ripping sound.

"Seriously?" I complain, as if my dress can answer for itself. "Fucking fuck."

Dare clears his throat. I look up, my eyes going wide, as though I had done something wrong. He smirks.

"What's going on here?"

My cheeks color. "I knocked a chess piece behind the

couch, I think. And then when I was trying to retrieve it, I ripped my dress. Stupid, expensive, flimsy piece of *crap* fabric."

Dare looks me up and down with a smug smile.

"You're pregnant, Talia. You shouldn't be trying to get anything from behind the couch."

"I can get it," I huff. "I'm not that awkward and ungainly yet."

Pinning me in place with his gaze, he prowls toward me. He walks right up to me, biting his lip and making direct eye contact. I look up at him and reach out to touch his hip. His entire stomach is taut and rippled with muscle.

Dare rubs his thumb against my lower lip. Electricity sizzles in the air between us. I open my mouth and suck his thumb between my lips, feeling a tingle of excitement low in my body. When I release his thumb from my mouth with an audible pop, he growls and pushes my shoulder back against the couch.

Dare falls to his knees before me, leaning in and kissing me so passionately that it's on the edge of being painful. My breath freezes in my lungs. Suddenly, every nerve ending is firing, every brush of his fingers against my skin sets me on fire.

He cups my cheek for a second and then threads his fingers in my hair, fisting my hair and tugging my head back. I gasp as he kisses and sucks at the tender skin over my pulse. The feeling of being taken is overwhelming and total. I surrender as Dare's big hands yank at the skimpy straps of my dress and rip the fabric in his rush to expose my breasts. Automatically, I bring my hand up and try to block my nipples from his gaze.

But Dare growls at me and uses a hand to knock my hand away. He brings both of his hands to shape my oversensitive breasts and kisses each one with a hunger that takes my breath away.

His five o'clock shadow against my pebbled nipples is like lighting my whole body on fire. It sends a jolt straight down to my aching clit and I start panting.

I try to move my hands to cover myself, but Dare holds me down, pressing me into the couch with his strength. His body takes up the space all around me and his shoulders block out the light as he covers me. He licks and kisses and bites my breasts until I squirm.

Then Dare pushes my shoulder back an inch, locking eyes with me. I shiver as his ice blue gaze skewers right through me.

"Turn around. I want you on your knees, leaning your face against the couch."

I swallow, my eyes going wide. I start to protest, opening my mouth. But his snarl stops my words.

"I thought I said turn around."

Nodding at his tone, I push myself off the back of the couch. Dare moves back to let me turn myself around but then stops me when the front of my thighs touch the bottom of the couch. He reaches around me and presses one hand to my belly and the other to my throat. He nuzzles his face against my neck and whispers in my ear, making a shudder slide down my spine.

"You're mine," he grates. "My greedy little wife. You're such a good girl. Let me show you how you get treated when you make me happy, darling."

He kisses my neck and then pushes my forward, urging me to rest my arms against the couch cushions. As soon as I bend over, Dare lifts my skirt up around my hips and pulls my panties down. I 'm hungry to feel his cock inside me, filling me so perfectly. Images run through my head of how his cock is going to stretch me out, how in a matter of moments I'll be clenching and calling out his name.

Dare shocks me by putting his hands on my ass and spreading my ass cheeks, then putting his face down and kissing my inner thigh, mere inches away from my pussy and ass. I stifle a yelp.

"Dare!" I gasp.

He chuckles as he guides my knees apart with his hands and runs a single fingertip along my pussy seam. I clench forcefully and he kisses my inner thigh again.

"Easy," he murmurs into my flesh. "Let me feast on you, darling girl."

"Oh god," I whimper. I don't know whether to be embarrassed or excited that he has me bent over, exposed, and moaning. I am both at once somehow and I feel almost intoxicated with it. "Dare..."

His gentle touch as he trails his fingers over my pussy makes my pussy spasm.

"You're so needy, Talia. Do you feel how wet you are for me? How ready? God, I can't fucking get enough of you."

Dare's words make me clench. When he swirls two fingertips around my clit in a lazy motion, I swear my eyes roll up in my head. My entire body shivers.

He's got me right where he wants me and he's not letting go anytime soon.

Dare kisses my left ass cheek and works his fingers around my clit. My hands clutch the couch pillows. I let out a low moan of pure need.

"Does that feel good?" he whispers. "I want to hear you tell me how it feels to have my fingers in your pussy."

"Yes," I pant. I make another half a groan, pressing my ass toward Dare's hand. It feels so wrong to be enjoying this, but I can't stop. "Fuck, baby. You are killing me."

"Baby?" he asks with a chuckle. "I didn't realize that I'd get a pet name if I got you all wound up like this. I might have done it sooner if I knew."

His taunt passes in one ear and out the other. He continues to circle my clit with his thumb and I completely forget to answer. My pussy is so wet right now and he just keeps teasing me, building anticipation, stoking the flames.

"I'm going to fuck you with my fingers," he murmurs, his voice low and deep. "Then I'm going to fuck you with my tongue. And finally, I'll eat that pretty ass of yours. You're going to scream my name while I fuck you with my tongue."

A gasp tears through my mouth. Dare's idea of dirty talk is absolutely filthy and it's fucking *working* on me. I drop my forehead to the top of the couch and squeeze my eyes closed.

He's trying to kill me and I am about to *let* him.

"Do you promise?" I grit out.

"Oh, sweetheart." He laughs. "I promise."

"Then do it, baby," I beg. "I need you to do it. I need you to fuck me with your fingers and your tongue."

"You asked for it, my little wife," he growls.

I know that he's never going to acknowledge my words. I also know that I don't care. I just want him to fuck me and make me come.

And he will.

His fingers continue to work around my clit. I feel my pussy squeezing and releasing around his fingers and I know that it's time.

Dare circles his fingertips around my clit one more time and then traces a line back to my entrance. He swirls one digit slowly around my passage.

He releases a groan. "Fuck, Talia. Do you know how fucking wet you are for me right now?"

I don't answer because I can't answer. I can't focus on

anything but the way he's touching me. He kisses my ass again and thrusts two fingers deep into my pussy. I cry out, taking pleasure in the rough, quick way he moves his hand now.

"That's it, darling," he says. "Take what you need. Take it all."

When Dare adds a third finger, I clench and start moving my hips, desperate. He fucks me with his fingers, using his other hand to angle my hips and control my movements. I dig my fingers into the couch cushions and listen to the sound of my wet pussy as it accepts his fingers. I am so wet now that Dare's fingers make a sucking sound as they work in and out, in and out. The sound alone is enough to make me come.

I move my hands down to feel my tits, gently tweaking my ultra sensitive nipples. I cry out, fucking Dare's hand, feeling like I'm right on the edge of ecstasy.

That's when Dare slows down. He pulls his fingers out of my pussy and wipes all of my juices up to the little balloon knot of my ass.

I make a strangled sound. "Dare!"

"Shhh." He drops a kiss to my shaking inner thigh. "I need you to stay still. I have to go get something but I don't want you to move an inch. I want to see you in this position when I come back."

"What?" I gasp. I turn and look at Dare, who points at the wall.

"Keep your face pressed against the couch, darling girl. I promise that you'll like what I bring back."

I turn around, my mouth gaping. What in the world is he going to do? Does it have to be *right now*?

Squirming, I listen to my thundering heartbeat. My pussy aches for Dare, but I'm a little miffed at him now. Why in the fuck is he leaving me wanting?

Two or three minutes pass, but it seems like forever. When Dare finally returns, I sneak a quick glance at him. He's holding a small translucent bottle and a small, smooth cucumber. He smirks at me when I gasp.

"Turn around, little wife. Let me see that beautiful view again. I'm going to sear the sound of you moaning while I touch your pussy and eat your ass into my fucking brain."

Whipping my head around, I widen my eyes. My heartbeat sounds so fucking loud in my ears. Dare kneels behind me once again, caressing the two firm globes of my ass.

"Damn," he whispers. I hear the sound of him opening the plastic bottle and I shiver. What could that be?

"Have you cooled off enough for me to start touching you again?" he asks.

The laugh that burst from my lips startles me. "Fuck you, Dare."

"That's exactly what I intend to do, sweetheart."

He slaps my ass hard and I let out a tiny yelp. I feel him touch my clit. Cool liquid drips onto my clit and I stiffen. Ah, that's what the bottle was. Lube.

"Relax, Talia," Dare coaxes. "

I let out a shaky breath. "I'm trying."

He leans down and presses his lips to the smooth flesh of my ass, just above my tight little balloon knot. The warm, wet sensation of his kiss makes me groan. I tense, but I stay in place. I don't move a muscle.

"That's my girl. I want to hear you come apart for me on my fucking tongue."

A gasp bursts from my lips. The promise in his words makes my pussy clench. I can't help the tiny bucking motion of my hips.

I feel Dare chuckle. He knows exactly what kind of effect

he has on me. "I can't hear you, Talia. I want to hear you say you're going to come for me."

"Yes," I gasp. "I'm going to come for you."

I can't believe I just said that.

Dare's hands come up to my hips and he pulls me back. I gasp when his tongue, hot and wet, slides up the crevice of my ass. He doesn't stop at my balloon knot. He slides his tongue up to the tiny puckered star. I gasp, pressing my forehead against the cold glass.

"I want to touch you so fucking bad, sweetheart. You must know that by now." His warm breath against my ass sends shivers down my spine. His tongue laps at my balloon knot. I gasp, pressing my forehead against the cold glass.

"I want to touch you so fucking bad, sweetheart. You must know that by now." His warm breath against my ass sends shivers down my spine. His tongue laps at my

He brings his hands up to my hips and he spreads my ass cheeks wide. I feel the sharp burn of his hot breath against the sensitive flesh of my ass.

Dare breathes in deep. "I can smell how wet you are, little wife. I can taste it. You taste just like the ripest berries bursting on my tongue."

Dare's tongue darts out and he flicks my balloon knot sharply. The rough motion makes me groan. I can feel my pussy tightening in tiny pulses.

"I can feel your pulse, Talia." The rough motion makes me groan. I can feel my pussy tightening in tiny contractions. "God *damn*, wife. Do you have any idea how much I love eating your ass?"

He flicks my balloon knot with his tongue again and my breath stops. Then he shocks me by teasing my pussy lips with something big and cold. I yelp, but Dare's hand on my lower back keeps me in place.

"Easy. It'll warm up soon enough."

Dare runs the cucumber tip up and down my crevice. It's slick with lube and though I don't want to admit it, it feels... intriguing. He circles it around my clit for a moment before he slides it down my wetness, sweeping it around my entrance, and pushes it into my pussy.

I gasp at the invasion. The cucumber feels big but the lube makes it slick enough to slide into my pussy with little force. I clench my pussy against the feeling.

He pushes it in slowly and pulls it out again. I groan and shudder as I feel it fill me. Dare leans in close and flicks his tongue against my balloon knot. At the same time, I feel the cucumber slide farther in.

"It's so big," I pant. "I can't take it, Dare."

"You can. You'll take it *all*. You'll fucking come all over my face." Dare reaches under me and rubs my clit. My pussy clamps down on the cucumber and my hips buck. Dare's finger slides over my engorged clit and his tongue flicks my balloon knot. He's relentless. "That's it, baby. Relax and let it wash over you."

I try to take him at his word. Squeezing my eyes closed, I shove out a breath. Every nerve ending is on fire and I can't help pressing back, needing Dare's kiss and touch all over my too-hot body.

He works his tongue into the star of my ass. I gasp as he alternates between swirling his fingers around my clit and moving the cucumber in and out of my pussy. Gripping the couch cushions, I can hear the messy squelch of Dare fucking me faster and faster.

"I need your fingers on my clit," I whisper breathlessly. "God, I'm so fucking full. Your tongue in my ass..."

I trail off, feeling feverish. As soon as I say the word, Dare pushes the cucumber deep inside my pussy, leans his face closer, and moves his tongue in and out of my ass. He pinches my clit, eliciting a startled moan from me.

I'm dying. He's fucking killing me.

"You're so tight. Are you going to come for me? I can feel your pussy clenching and releasing."

"Yes," I say. I'm shaking. I'm tingling all over. "I'm going to come, baby. I'm going to come. Oh... oh god..."

He groans and the vibration against my balloon knot makes me clench the cucumber inside of me. My pussy cinches down and my eyes roll up in my head.

"Come for me, Tally. Come now."

I can't. I can't. I can't. With a wordless cry, I come apart. Lights burst behind my eyes and my pussy tries to milk the cucumber.

Dare pulls the cucumber from my body. I'm still coming when he positions his rock hard cock at my entrance.

He slides his dick deep inside. My body is still on fire. I'm not sure if I'm just feeling the wave of orgasm still or if I'm coming again. Dare pulls out, plunges in, and fucks me hard and fast. All the while he's whispering dirty things in my ear.

I'm so hot. I'm so dizzy. I'm so full of Dare's hard cock. I don't know how much more I can take.

My pussy is clenching, milking the cock that's deep inside of me.

"I'm going to come, sweetheart. Your pussy is too perfect. I can't hold back."

"Come inside me, Dare," I breathe. "I want every drop. I want to feel your hot cock filling my needy little pussy."

"Oh, fuck, Talia. *Fuck*. I'm coming."

His voice is strained. He's gritting his teeth. He's riding me hard. He thrusts one last time, hard enough to plaster me against the couch. His cock is pulsing as it spills his seed inside of me. It's so intense, so fucking visceral. He keeps milking his hot cum into me, filling me up. I feel it dripping out of me before he even pulls out.

"Mmm," I gasp. "That was... that was..."

"Perfect," Dare growls. "I've never felt anything like it. Your pussy is perfect and it's all mine, isn't it? You're all fucking mine."

"Yours, Dare," I whisper. "All yours."

He pulls free from my body and spins me around, kissing me.

"For better or for worse," he says. "For richer or for poorer. For hotter and kinkier."

I giggle. "I don't know what that last part means, but it sounds promising."

Dare pulls me close and kisses me again. I kiss him back, closing my eyes and savoring the moment. He tastes like me. I love it.

I love him.

My eyes fly open. I stare at Dare, my expression panicky.

What kind of weird post-sex slip up was that?

He looks at me, brushing away a stray strand of hair.

"What?"

I bite my lip and shake my head. Before he can ask any more questions, I silence him with a kiss.

Chapter Fourteen

Talia is lying beside me, still completely nude, tracing indecipherable figures in the soft skin just below her navel. The sounds of lapping waves and the persistent rain permeate our bedroom. I've drawn the curtains and flipped on the soft light on the bedside table. Night has fallen now and the sky is still overcast, so there are no stars or moonlight.

Coupled with the silky comforter and fluffy pillows, it has created a very cozy atmosphere in our bedroom. Just now, it seems like we are the only two people alive. And because we just finished an amazing, athletic fuck, we are both slightly withdrawn and yet content to be together.

The feeling is new… and one that I must admit that I don't hate.

I peek at Talia. There is a frown on her face.

"Are you trying to figure out a complex math equation or something?" I joke.

Dusty pink tinges her cheeks. She looks up, her brow furrowing.

"Like you haven't noticed."

"Noticed what?" I stretch out, folding my arms behind my head and crossing my legs.

Talia snorts and rolls her eyes. "It's not like you to be nice."

Her words catch me like a blow to the solar plexus. I wince.

"I hate to say it, but I'm not being nice."

She spreads her fingers out across her abdomen. It has grown, the convex shape of it ever so slowly becoming more pronounced.

"Ah," I say. "Your pregnancy is beginning to show. So what?"

She looks up at me, her brow creasing with concern.

"Don't you worry about what the baby will be like? It seems more real to me every single day."

My eyebrows arch. "Worry? No, not really."

"It's different for you. You're not growing a whole person inside your body." Talia rubs her abdomen in slow, rhythmic strokes. "I feel like a crazy person right now. But I can't stop thinking that I'll look away and then suddenly, I'll be nine months pregnant. Or worse, that suddenly my son or daughter will be standing before me, a fully-fledged human being."

My brow furrows. I reach a hand over to her belly, spreading my fingers over her bare skin. "Are you worried you'll blink and miss it?"

She shakes her head. "No. I'm just completely freaked out by the fact that our baby is growing so quickly. As we speak, it's like… getting nutrients and developing fingers. It's wild."

I give a laugh of surprise. "When you put it that way, sure."

Talia scrunches up her face.

"It's still not real to you. I can tell by how laid back you are. If it was real, you would be freaking out."

I shrug. "Maybe."

Cupping her belly, I try to picture Talia heavily pregnant. But I can't. I can only see her as she is right now, lying next to me. I don't know whether that means I am shortsighted or if I'm just more interested in the present.

Her mouth bunches up and she looks at me.

"What?" I ask.

"Can I ask you a question?"

I take my hand off her stomach and shrug. "That is a question."

Talia schools her expression. "Will you tell me about your childhood?"

Her question kills my enjoyment of the moment. I screw up my face as I look at her.

"Why?"

She blushes but doesn't demur. "Because. I want to know about you, Dare. Right now, it's kind of like I'm married to a ghost without a past." Her lips thin. "And I would like to know what made your brother so terrible."

A chuckle rumbles from my chest. "I can't say why Burn is like he is. He certainly wasn't born like that. He was normal all through grade school and college. It wasn't until…"

Stopping abruptly, I shake my head.

Talia tilts her head and uses two fingers to lightly stroke my forearm. Her delicate touch sends a jolt down my spine and my cock stirs.

"Until what?" she prompts, her voice soft and sweet.

I grunt. "Until he stole Daisy from me. When Burn broke off the engagement by announcing to the family that he was marrying Daisy, he changed. In the blink of an eye, I lost him. He became someone I didn't know."

She traces figure eights into my skin but her eyes are locked on mine.

"You lost your brother and your fiancée in one fell swoop. How cruel. That must have been hard for you."

My only response is a shrug. I swallow, uneasy with anyone seeing just how furious and heartbroken I was. Maybe I still am.

Clearing my throat, I break eye contact with Talia and look off into the distant darkness.

Her voice is more hesitant when she speaks again. "The last thing I want is to pile on. But I would like to know when your mother passed."

I put a hand over my heart, unconsciously feeling a distant ache.

"Do you have to open and examine all of my scars tonight, Talia?"

She winces. "Sorry. I thought it was best to rip the bandages off all at once. Plus, you're usually quite… argumentative."

I heave a sigh. "You're getting me right after sex, when my defenses are down."

"That's the idea." She smiles.

I stretch, sitting up. Talia sits up too, hugging a pillow to her chest.

"All right. My mother died when I was ten. I don't really have that many memories of her when she was alive. Either she was very busy or she just didn't have much interest in us."

Her eyebrows rise. "Your father surely remembers. What does he say?"

Snorting, I stare off into the distance. "Tripp won't say her name, even if he is asked a direct question about her. Remy will, but his answers are usually limited to curse words. He has absolutely lost it when asked about her. Everyone is too scared to say her name in his presence."

Talia lifts her hand, ever so gently rubbing my back. I close my eyes, admitting to myself that my wife's touch does feel comforting in a way I hadn't expected before now. I almost feel a kind of relief to be saying these words out loud to someone other than Burn.

It's like scrubbing a boat's hull to remove hard water stains. It takes an immense amount of work, but afterward, the blindingly white fiberglass is its own reward.

"It must have been frustrating as a kid to have tons of questions about your mom and yet no one to answer them."

I purse my lips, dropping my head forward. "The day we found out about it, Burn and I were already in boarding school in Scotland. Remy's assistant Samantha called and told us. She said that Remy had decided it would be best if we stayed at school rather than come back for the funeral. So… that's what we did. The first time I saw my mother's grave was six months later, when I came home for summer break."

Talia's jaw drops. "Seriously?"

My neck heats and I stare out at the darkness.

"Yep."

"That's really fucked up, Dare."

She moves closer and twines her arms around my torso, hugging me. I don't know how to feel right now. On one hand, a part of my heart is clearly thawing in the warm radiance of Talia's affection.

On the other hand, I feel stiff and disjointed. It's like I have the ancient battle wounds, desiccated and dusty, still covered in stitches. And someone just went around with a giant pair of shears, hacking at whatever fabric they could find and reopening some of the cuts I had thought healed over.

She squeezes me tightly and my eyes flutter closed. I am reminded of the fable of the lion with the thorn in his paw, letting the tiny mouse help him and letting her live in exchange. I am choosing not to lash out in part because this tiny woman is trying to help me. Well, maybe help is the wrong word. It's more like Talia is trying to understand me, to get closer to me, even though she knows I'm dangerous.

Sliding an arm around her, I hug her. She buries her head against my collarbone, the pillow she was hugging falling to the floor, forgotten.

"As long as I'm alive, our kid will never have to face anything like that."

Her words are a promise that she whispers as she presses herself close to my chest. They hit me like a quick, hard punch in the ribs. I grimace.

Our kid.

It might not be visible just now, but Talia is growing my child inside her body right this minute. And one day? One day, that infant is going to be a kid, every bit as real as I remember being at seven years old, half a world away from here and suddenly cut adrift.

Mourning my mother.

I hold Talia close for a few more seconds before relaxing my grip. She pulls away, her head dropping back, her lips more appealing than they have ever been. Cupping her jaw, I kiss her, pushing her back onto the mattress.

Her body is lush and warm and willing. The breathy sounds she makes as I use my hands and my mouth to tease her and pull her toward the edge are so fucking hot, I swear that my very soul is on fire. I fuck her like a man who's going to the gallows, like I'll die if I don't feel her come around my cock as I drive it home again and again and again.

I clench my eyes shut as I come, the sensation like freefalling from the top of the highest cliff imaginable. Afterward, I stay inside Talia's body for a couple of minutes. She wraps her arms and legs around me and welcomes me like a sheltering cove during a storm.

And I'm just a tiny sailboat, blown into the cove by nothing but pure chance.

I keep my eyes closed and press my face against her neck, surrendering.

Chapter Fifteen

TALIA

When I wake in our loft a few days later, I am alone. Dare's preferred side of the bed is made up, but there is a square black box lying on his pillow. Beside it is a neatly-folded note.

Sitting up, I rub the sleep out of my eyes and pluck the note from the bed.

These belonged to my mother. Wear them tonight at dinner with my family.

The note is not signed, but it could only be from one person. Dare knows that I don't have any interest in going to dinner. But apparently what I want doesn't matter.

Frowning, I pick up the box and pull off the lid. Inside are two of the most jaw-dropping chandelier earrings I've ever seen. They are dripping with diamonds and sapphires, easily a million dollars each. I swallow hard and pick them up, weighing them in my palm. They're pretty heavy, just like you would expect real diamonds and sapphires and gold to be.

I run my tongue over my teeth. This seems to be something of a habit for Dare. We have a romantic weekend. He acts as though he hates his family. I comfort him.

And then I wake up to expensive jewelry and a note telling me to be ready for a family event.

It's a little old by now. I lift my hand, holding the earrings up to catch the sunlight streaming in the windows of the loft. I wonder if this is Dare's way of paying for my comforts and attention. Like you would pay a prostitute, maybe.

It certainly cheapens the whole experience if I think of it that way.

Nesting the earrings back in their box, I get out of bed. The rest of my day is taken up by beauty treatments and a nail appointment. My hair color is touched up, the ends of my hair are trimmed, my body is made smooth and hairless, my eyebrows plucked, my nails and toes painted a soft blue. I ask the aesthetician to send someone along with a rack of brand new dresses for me to choose from. Hours later, I stand in front of the mirror, looking at the stranger staring back at me with a puzzled frown. I'm wearing a strapless white chiffon Valentino dress with a matching white chiffon shawl. On my feet are a pair of white leather pumps. My long hair is artfully twisted into an up-do that looks extremely chic. Underneath the dress, I wear a piece of shapewear that hides the slight bump of my pregnant belly.

The new earrings shine at my earlobes and I wear a chunky gold chain to finish off my look.

All in all, it's an outfit that I wouldn't have dared to put on my body a few months ago. But being Dare's wife has boosted my confidence somehow. It's forced me to become more elegant, to say the least.

Dare knocks on the bedroom door, his eyebrows rising slightly as he looks me up and down. "You're gorgeous," he says. "I can't wait to rub you in Daisy and Burn's faces. They will absolutely die of jealousy and envy."

"I don't really think that I want to put myself in harm's way again by going to an event with Burn."

Dare walks over to me, grabbing my hand and drawing me in. He wraps his arms around my neck, looking at me quite seriously. "He will never touch you again," he swears. "You're going to be right by my side the entire night. I'm going to follow you everywhere, even if it means leaving a conversation. Not only that, but I've doubled up your personal security. So Frick and Frack will be paired with two other agents of their choosing. They know that Burn is a dangerous man. Trust me, I don't want Burn to even look in your direction. In a few months, when we win this inheritance race, we will never have to see them ever again. Okay?"

I swallow. "What if I say no?"

"I'm hoping you won't. Besides, I've made arrangements for the entire family to meet at Tusk."

My eyebrows rise. "Is there a reason why you picked that restaurant in particular?"

A mischievous light dances in Dare's eyes. "Because if I am going to spend the evening rubbing you in Burn's face, you might as well have a little payback of your own to focus on. I get the feeling that the people that you worked with at Tusk did not treat you particularly well. So now you can let them know that you've gone from someone they can kick around to being someone of real means and status."

I roll my eyes a little. "I didn't need you to help me stick it to my old manager. I was doing just fine by moving on with my life and forgetting all about him."

He shrugs his shoulders. "What is life for if not for petty little paybacks?

"You're impossible," I tell him.

He arches a brow and smirks. "But you like that, don't you?"

I wrap my arms around his torso and close my eyes, giving him a quick hug. Where before I hugged him to reassure him, this time I hugged him to give myself strength.

"Okay," I whisper. "If you say that I will be safe, I believe you."

He drops a kiss to the crown of my head, rubbing my back. Then he pulls away, taking me by the hand. "Let's go. We don't want to keep Remy waiting."

When we arrive at the restaurant, I am surprised to find it rather hushed when I step in the door. Usually the restaurant is loud and bustling. Waiters yell out last minute modifications to orders to the kitchen staff. Tables full of tipsy customers who ooh and ahhh as the food runners present spectacular dishes. Patrons at the bar laugh at the bartender's cynical jokes.

But today, as I offer my coat to a manager I don't recognize, it is very quiet. The new manager ushers us into a silent restaurant, empty except for one very long table. Remy sits at one end, glaring at Dare's father, who is sitting just to his right. There are a few open seats at the table, but the rest of them are filled with the usual cousins and cleaners that I am accustomed to seeing swirling around Remy. As soon as Remy spots us, he stops glaring at Dare's father and points to the seat immediately to his left. "Finally," Remy grouses. "I was wondering when either of my grandsons were going to get here."

We stroll up to the table and I take stock of the attendees. Remy is right; Burn and Daisy are nowhere to be seen.

Dare walks right up to the seat that Remy pointed out and

stares at the young woman sitting in the seat beside it. "Hillary. Be a dear and fuck off."

The young woman stands up and meekly moves aside, not even taking her wine glass as she moves to the end of the table. Dare makes a show of pulling out my chair and helping me sit down at the table. Then he finally takes his place. He arches a brow as he looks at Remy.

"Are we waiting on Burn, then?"

Remy checks his watch and scowls.

"No, we aren't waiting anymore." He twists around in his seat, looking for the waiter. To my surprise, the waiter is someone I recognize. He dressed me down once in the back hallway of this very restaurant. I catch his eye and he looks a bit puzzled as he steps forward, clearing his throat.

"Can I help, sir?"

"Tell them to bring in all the food. I'm hungry."

The waiter bows and turns, catching my eye again before vanishing toward the kitchen. I smooth my hand over the white linen tablecloth, taking the cloth napkin and pulling it into my lap. Dare catches my hand and laces his fingers through mine and puts our hands down on the table. Making a clear statement to anyone in the vicinity.

He swings his gaze over to Remy and picks up his glass of water. He takes a sip and then smiles.

"Is there a reason you called us here?" asks Remy.

Dare gives the ghost of a smile and shrugs a shoulder. "Let's eat first. If Burn still doesn't show up by the time we are finished, I can tell you our surprise."

I sip, feeling heat rise to my cheeks. Dare clenches my hand and silently reminds me not to show everyone my every thought.

Remy levels a glare at Dare, looking at him as if brushing invisible dirt away.

"It's your party, isn't it?"

Platters of spit-roasted game hens, raised beef, and grilled salmon steaks are soon brought to the table by several food runners. Bowls of linguine with bolognese and gnocchi with pine nut pesto soon follow. There are small plates of pan roasted mushrooms and blanched asparagus. And finally there are overflowing baskets of warm, crusty slices of focaccia bread slid onto any place that there is space. The wineglass that was left by cousin Helen is soon swept away, replaced by a fresh glass of dark purple wine.

I glance at Dare and he lets my hand go, but he does lean over and kiss me. The brief press of his lips is over before I even know it. But I feel the eyes of Dare's entire family on me as soon as he pulls away.

I busy myself taking a little salmon and pasta bolognese. I purposely keep my eyes on my plate, not looking up for long enough to catch anyone's gaze.

Dare and Remy talk a little, Dare's father leaning in and interjecting a few times. For the most part, everyone quickly seems to forget me, to my intense relief.

I don't hold much interest in this particular group of wealthy, self centered people. I can't do anything for them, and they lose focus on me very quickly.

But just when I start to relax, Burn and Daisy come in from the cold. Burn slides his arm around Daisy as they walk up to Remy, acting for all the world as though he is the only person here. Daisy sweeps her gaze over the table of twenty or so future relatives and smirks.

"Remy," Burn says very casually. "I see you started without us."

Remy scowls at Burn. "When I say one o'clock, I mean one o'clock."

Burn bows his head ever so slightly. Then he sweeps his gaze over the table. "Where should we sit?"

Remy looks at Dare's father and motions to him. "Trip, move down. Give Burn your seat."

"What?" Tripp howls. "He can sit at the end of the table!"

Remy gives Tripp a dour glance. He raises his hand, pointing it to the end of the table. "Don't make me repeat myself."

Tripp grimaces and then stands up, shoving his seat back so hard that it falls over. He stomps away, grabbing his wineglass and guzzling its contents, looking for all the world as if he were an oversized child. Burn taps the young man sitting in the next seat on the shoulder and the man jumps up, like a puppet that was yanked up by his marionette strings.

Burn sits down in the seat closest to Remy, letting Daisy seat herself. He leans in, looking around the table with a mischievous smirk. I drop my eyes to my plate just in time for him to focus on me.

"I didn't think you would be here, Talia. It's so nice to see you," he purrs.

My cheeks go red but I just lift my gaze and glare at Dare's twin. It's hard to believe that they are even related even though they share a face. I don't say anything, I just look at Burn, trying not to give too much away.

Dare moves his seat closer to mine and slides his arm around my shoulders, his gesture either protective or possessive depending on how you see it. He bares his teeth at his brother, silently warning him.

Burn snorts and grabs Daisy's hand, pulling it into his lap.

A flash of annoyance crosses Dare's features. He looks at Daisy. "Did my brother tell you that he was caught trying to undress my fiancé? Against her will, I might add. If he had his way, he would be a rapist."

Daisy's jaw drops. A dark and ominous cloud rolls over Burn, turning his glare into a spiteful look.

"That's a dirty lie," he hisses.

"It isn't. Ask anyone who was there that day. At the house that day. Burn tried to force himself on Talia. He can deny it if he wants to, but I think we all know the truth."

Dare's face says that he takes no pleasure in the accusation he levels. Burn growls, his gaze shifting to me. He starts to stand up, as if he is going to move to come around the table and get me. Dare stands up, unbuttoning his coat.

"Enough!" Remy bellows. "You two arguing about women is so fucking stupid. What a foolish thing for you to be at each other's throats about."

Dare and Burn keep glaring at each other and Remy raises both hands, pulling them down in a be seated gesture. "Sit down, you idiots."

As if pulled by forces beyond their own control, Dare and Burn both sink down into their seats. I can feel all eyes on me just now, staring at me, trying to figure out what my actual worth is. Basically, am I worthy of Burn's attention?

My lips thin and I grab Dare's hand, squeezing it tightly.

Remy sits back, his expression one of displeasure. "Get this food out of my face. Come on, come clear off the table."

Several food runners step forward, taking it all away. Then Remy puts his elbows on the table, leaning his head on his hands. He looks from one grandson to the other, his lips pursing.

"Dare, what did you call us here for today?"

I notice that he makes no reference to Burn's aggressive attempt to kiss me and undress me. Of course, I never expected Remy to give a shit about that. I am just a silly pawn in Burn's game as far as Remy is concerned.

Dare puts his arm around my shoulders, challenging Burn

to touch me with a glare. "I'm so glad you asked, Remy. Talia and I would like to announce that we are having a formal wedding in a week."

My eyebrows shoot up. I look at Dare, my eyes wide. If I am surprised, Daisy and Burn are aghast. Daisy audibly scoffs and Burn bleats out a laugh.

"You gotta be kidding me," he mutters.

"Nope, Dare says. "And now that our wedding is going to be so soon, I am actively trying to get Talia pregnant. We fuck like bunnies, practically day and night. Isn't that right, darling?"

My face goes red as a beet and I stare at my husband in horror.

What is he thinking?

Remy stands up, grabbing his cane. He leans over and claps Dare on the shoulder. "Atta boy. Congratulations on pulling ahead in the race to win my shares of the company. I thought that you were going to be single forever because your mother didn't raise you right. But it seems that this little competition for inheritance has fixed that."

I like to think that I have gotten to know Dare rather well. And I notice his smile slip away for just a fraction of a second before he leans forward, offering Remy his hands. He offers Remy a malicious smile.

"Thank you, sir. It's been an arduous journey, but I think we all know that it's practically a done deal by now."

Remy raises a brow and takes Dare's offered handshake, pumping it vigorously. He looks at Burn, who looks like he might explode at any moment.

"It seems like you might be right," Remy says.

Burn glares at Remy and Dare smiles at both of them.

Apparently, I'm going to be having my wedding ceremony in just a week's time. Dare gave me no warning… and the fact that I am the last person considered in any situation is starting to get really old.

I bite my lip and sink back in my chair, watching the men display dominance over one another.

Chapter Sixteen

TALIA

"Hey." I lean against the doorway to Dare's office, pulling on thick wool socks to match my dark jeans and heavy gray wool sweater.

Dare turns his chair around, his expression aggravated. His tone is snippy. "What?"

Stretching my back, I arch a brow. "I was just checking in on you. You've been locked in here all morning."

"I'm fine. The state of Maine, however, is not going to be fine after I am done raking them over the coals. When my lawyers are done with them, they will be so poor that they'll beg me for my fucking business."

I give a surprised laugh. "What did the state of Maine ever do to you?"

Dare gives me a long look, balling up a piece of paper in his fist.

"They are very against giving Morgan Drilling a license for offshore drilling. I hired a lobbying firm to persuade the state. But apparently the office of mineral rights is rigidly opposed to the plan." He hurls the piece of paper toward the wastebasket, but misses. It drifts to the ground and he groans loudly.

"That must be frustrating." I smooth my hand down the wool that covers my belly.

"It really fucking is." Dare stands up, shaking out his hands. "I'm tense all over."

I tilt my head, scanning him from head to feet. He seems really out of sorts. I would feel bad for him if I didn't secretly think that offshore drilling is a terrible, dangerous idea that threatens the entire planet. Pursing my lips, I make a decision.

"Do you have more work to do?"

He snorts. "Always. It never stops."

"Can it wait a while?"

Dare narrows his eyes. "Maybe."

I push off the doorsill, gently taking his arm. "You should come with me."

He slides his arm around my waist, mischief dancing in his eyes.

"Even though I already fucked you this morning, I could definitely go for another round. That's a good way to work off some of this tension."

I roll my eyes. "Easy, cowboy. I want you to come to the horse stables with me. I'm taking the kids from Hope House there."

Surprise ripples across his face.

"What for?"

"I've worked out a deal with the owner to allow them to groom the horses and eventually, to learn to ride. And before you say anything, you should know that I had something similar worked out with them when I was a kid. I really, really loved it."

He narrows his gaze. "I take it that some of my money is paying for this experience?"

I smile at him. "Not this time. But I was thinking that the children at Hope House could benefit from taking regular lessons at the stables. We would need your name and your money for that."

"You always think of others. You're never greedy. Charity is not what I ever expected my wife would care about."

I arch a brow, pulling out of his arms. But he holds me tighter, not letting me go.

"I guess I could see where my money is going." Dare drops a kiss to my lips and I try to repress a grin.

"You'll be charmed. I promise."

WHEN THE CHAUFFEUR pulls up outside the stables, a frisson runs through me. I can feel the goofy smile on my face. This place just radiates good vibes. It's impossible for me to be in a bad mood when I'm here.

I slide out of the car, walking over to the empty riding ring. Running my hands along the fence, I suck in deep lungfuls of rich leather and sweet horse feed. This place just feels like home.

Glancing over at Dare, I grin. "Isn't this place great?"

He casts a skeptical eye around the empty riding ring, the corrugated steel stable buildings, and the cliffs that drop into the vast, dark sea. I can tell that he's struggling not to make a face.

"Uh huh," he lies. "It's… nice."

Rolling my eyes, I grab him by the arm and pull him toward the stables. I made him change into a pair of jeans and a chunky-knit blue sweater under his usual dark wool coat. He looks like a fish out of water, but I find a dressed down Dare unusual and appealing.

I take his hand and interlace our fingers.

The short school bus that Hope House maintains is already here, unloaded and desolate. As I step into the warmth of the stable building, I can hear Gina's voice.

"My name is Gina. And this gorgeous lady is River."

I hurry my steps, coming into a large semi-circle of hay bales. About ten of the Hope House kids are seated there, with two of the grown-up volunteers standing nearby. Gina wears her usual uniform of a white silk button up shirt and black jodhpurs with knee-high black riding boots. Her brown hair is pulled back in a low ponytail and she holds the yellow bridle of a white-and-brown dappled horse.

She sees me coming and bursts into a smile. But then she sees Dare just behind me and her smile turns puzzled.

"Hi there," she calls.

Before she can continue, an adult volunteer named Linda turns around and spots us. She's wearing a faded pink dress and purple leggings under what looks like a men's trench coat. She beams from ear to ear.

"Hey, look! It's Miss Talia," she calls.

All the kids whip around and a few of them jump up, running to me. I grin, greeting the ones I know by name.

"Hi, hi. Denise, Craig, Sam. Hey there, Solana…" Most of the kids hug my legs. I spread my arms wide and try to make sure everyone gets their own hug.

To my surprise, Solana ducks out of my arms and heads straight for Dare. He lets out a whoof of breath when she collides with him, wrapping her arms around his legs and pressing her face against his denim-clad thigh.

"Dare!" Solana shouts. Her voice sounds like she's choking back tears. "You came back for me."

He pats her head, his expression saying that he's clearly out of his depth.

"Uhhh… yeah."

"Hey, everyone. Let's head back to our seats. Miss Gina is going to let you all pet an actual horse."

"Yes!" one of the kids that I don't recognize shouts. Linda shushes him, but he just kicks his legs excitedly. His brown curly hair and bright green t-shirt make his hyperactive squirming and loud outbursts seem normal.

All the kids find their seats again, including a very reluctant Solana.

"All right. As I was saying, this is River. Who can guess what kind of horse he is?"

Several hands shoot up and a couple of the kids start shouting out answers.

"Big!"

"German shepherd!"

"Okay. Remember what I said earlier. Horses don't like loud noises, so we are going to use our inside voices when we are here. Okay?"

"Yes, Miss Gina," the kid says in a stage whisper. "Sorry, River."

Gina laughs and starts talking about the horse. She gives some basic information like how old he is, what breed he is, and what he likes to eat.

"Yes?" she asks the girl with her hand raised.

"Can we pet him now?"

Gina smiles. "Let me tell you about how we are going to pet the horse. He likes to be touched here…" She pets his muzzle and all along his nose. "Here…" She pets his head and mane. "And here." She pets his shoulder and chest. "You will want to pet him with all five fingers together, like this. I like to call this my canoe. And like a canoe in a river, it only goes down. Never go against the current, in this direction. Horses don't really like that."

She flashes everyone her upright palm with no spaces between her fingers. Then she pets River again using the same technique.

"Now, if you're ready, I will have Miss Talia come up here and stand beside you while you pet River. Does that sound good? Does everyone have their canoes?"

She makes that same gesture, reminding everyone to pet with an upright and rigid palm.

A chorus of yeses is the gleeful reply. All the kids stand up. I turn to Dare, giving him a soft hug. His lips twitch. To his credit, he doesn't seem to be sulking over this morning's news anymore. He smiles at me and says nothing, but there is some unnamed emotion flickering in his eyes.

Leaving him, I head up to the front of the circle. For the next hour, I stand beside River, watching the kids respectfully pet him with stiff hands. River seems mellow about the experience, but the kids absolutely light up inside. It's so fun to watch them look up at River with wide eyes and a grin.

I gently correct a few of them when they forget to keep their hands like a canoe or when they pet against the grain of River's fur. But for the most part, the children behave themselves.

Gina cups her hands around her mouth. "I'm going to put our friend River away in his stall. Then how about you all help me feed the horses? Would you like that?"

"Yeah!" the curly-haired little boy shouts, still excited beyond measure. "Let's go!"

As I walk back to Dare, Solana comes barreling over to me. The kid throws her entire body weight at my legs and almost bowls me over. Only quick thinking on Dare's part to grab my arm and hold me up saves the day.

"Whoa, Solana!" I say, laughing. "What's going on?"

Solana shakes her long raven hair, tears threatening to pour from her velvety brown eyes. "My shoe is broke."

She sticks out her foot to show us both a dingy white sneaker with several Velcro straps. The Velcro is all bunched up on a couple and sticking to itself. I kneel down so I'm eye level with her. Then I spend a minute adjusting the straps, evening them out, and smoothing my touch over the top of her foot.

"All fixed." I smile at the girl. "I have a surprise for you. Are you ready?"

She glances at Dare, looking for his approval. He puts his hand on my shoulder, smiling at the girl. Apparently that's enough, because Solana whips her hand out and looks at me expectantly.

I reach in my coat pocket and produce a carrot. "Do you want to help me give this to River?"

Solana's eyes widen and she snatches the carrot from my open palm. She looks at me with a deep doubt. The kind of look that tells me that this kid has probably known a lot of hardship and disappointment in her short life.

"You hold onto it. We'll feed it to the horse together."

I hold out my hand, palm facing up. Solana stares at me for a second, trying to decide if I'm trustworthy. Then she takes my hand.

I wiggle my eyebrows. "Let's go look in the stalls and see which one River is in."

Solana nods and we walk over to feed River for a few minutes. At length, I leave Solana watching Gail and another little girl feed Black Beauty a carrot. When I head back to the circle, I find Dare leaning against the last stall with a watchful smile on his face.

"You look happy," he says.

I beam at him. "This is really filling me with joy. I'm so

happy to be here. Being able to come to the stables and help the kids feed the horses just fills my cup to the point of over-flowing."

Dare nods. "You're good at it. The kids love you, too." He pauses, hesitating. "I think you're going to be a really good mom."

I blink at him. "Me?"

"Yeah. You seem to genuinely enjoy helping them do things. You kneel down, get on their level. You really look at them and listen to what they are saying." He shoves his hands in his pockets, glancing away. "I didn't get that as a kid. I wonder what kind of person I would have turned out to be if I had."

I lean against the wall beside him, giving him a soft smile.

"Not as different as all that, I think."

He nods again. "At least I know that you're going to raise our child right."

I catch his eye, feeling a surge of emotion.

"Thanks. You'll be there too, though. You'll be taking part as much as me after I give birth."

Dare gives a haughty laugh. "What? No. I'm not good at that stuff like you are."

"You will be."

He cocks his head. "You're serious."

"I am." I fold my arms across my chest.

"You're crazy. You're the only person who thinks that I should ever spend more than a minute with a kid."

Taking his hand, I bring it to my belly. I lock eyes with him.

"You'll love her. The second she comes out and you see her face, you'll love her. I promise."

Dare narrows his eyes. "We'll see. And since when is the baby a 'her'?"

Shrugging, I let go of his hand.

"Just a feeling. Maybe I'm wrong." I hesitate. "Would that be a bad thing?"

He screws up his face, thoughtful. Then he shakes his head.

"Nah." His face shifts and he looks perplexed. "You know, when I met you, I didn't think you were much to look at."

"Way to ruin a great moment," I say, starting to pull away.

He tightens his hold, refusing to let me go. "Look at me. Look into my eyes."

I gulp and meet Dare's burning blue gaze. He cups my jaw and tucks a strand of hair behind my ear.

"I was wrong. You're perfect."

My pulse skyrockets. "What?"

"You're beautiful. You're sweet to me when I don't deserve it. You are the perfect little fake wife for me, darling girl. If I had to be married under false pretenses… I guess I'm saying that I could be stuck with someone… well, someone like Daisy."

My lips part. My heart pounds. I don't know what to make of his confession. Some parts are very nice to hear. For instance, it's nice to be put on a level above his cheating ex-girlfriend. I was low-key kind of worried that he still had feelings for her.

But other parts of his little confession make me want to push Dare down a flight of stairs.

The confusion shows on my face. "Thanks, I guess? I can't say I'm crazy about you calling me your fake wife."

He rolls his eyes. "You know what I mean."

I squint. "I guess so…"

Dare pulls me closer and kisses me. I don't kiss him back

but I don't pull away either. "Don't be a buzzkill during our wedding week."

"Don't remind me."

"What does that mean?"

"It means that I've spent the last few days dreading the wedding ceremony. But--"

Dare's eyebrows arch. "You're dreading the ceremony? Why?"

My cheeks heat. I flick my hand, gesturing that it doesn't really matter.

"It's not the biggest deal. I just don't feel like performing in front of a bunch of strangers. Your family already looks at me like I'm an exotic animal in a zoo. And not a spider monkey… like I'm one of those really terrifying-looking caterpillars with spikes. You know, the ones that scare away predators by looking like a nightmare? Being looked at like that is exhausting."

Just thinking about it leeches away a little of my joy. I screw up my face.

Dare shoves a hand through his short, dark hair.

"What if I made it up to you?"

I give him a side eye.

"What does that mean?"

"You suck it up for a few more days. Take part in this ceremony, pose in a bunch of photos, shake a million hands. And then I will make it up to you on our honeymoon."

I scrunch up my face. "You know that I'm going to smile during the ceremony. That's part of our deal. You don't have to do anything extra."

"I know. But maybe it will make grinning and bearing it a little bit better."

I purse my lips. "Maybe."

He pins me up against the stall and kisses me deeply. It's

on the verge of being inappropriate because we are in the open and the children could see if they came looking for us.

But damn if I'm going to stop Dare. He's got me right where he wants me, his body pressed against mine, his hot tongue working its magic. He growls just a little as he kisses me and I absolutely melt.

Chapter Seventeen

DARE

Using a hand to shade my eyes, I look out over the cliffs at my beach estate. The Cliffs estate seemed like the ideal place to have my assistant Jonathan organize the wedding festivities. But as I wait for Talia to present herself and walk down the aisle that's laid out behind me, I feel the flutter of my pulse. My body seems to think that I am sprinting, though I'm doing nothing of the sort.

There is no point in denying it. I'm nervous.

I run a hand down the vest of my elegant three-piece tuxedo, glancing at the crowd of seated guests. The ceremony attendees are a who's-who of wealth and glamor. There are several titans of industry seated in the audience, each a nebula with their wives and their assistants all around them. Filling in the rest of the audience are a mishmash of stars and starlets, business contacts, fashion designers, and countless other so-called important people.

All called here at the last minute to witness my lavish, extravagant wedding.

I see Remy seated in the first row. Next to him are my father, my uncle Felix, and two empty seats. Apparently they saved the spots for my brother Burn and my ex Daisy. I didn't invite them, but I am not foolish enough to think that they won't show up.

Remy will make sure that they do. He likes to see people squirm. And he has undoubtedly sensed that there is bad blood between Burn and I.

I am standing all the way at the very edge of the cliffs. The guests are seated in white folding chairs, the guest list so large that half the lawn from here to the house has been claimed for my audience. I run a finger underneath my bow tie, wishing that I had decided to wear a regular tie.

Tristen stands next to me, wearing an almost identical suit. He casts an eye over the large arbor trellis that has been set up for the wedding. It is a work of art in its own right, beautiful ash wood woven with thousands of pure white cherry blossom branches.

Tristen doesn't say anything, but I can tell by the look on his face that he is wondering whether the trellis will blow away if it gets any windier today. His gaze slides between the black-suited reverend and back to the trellis.

I look over at the reverend. "You think I should ask him to hold the trellis in place?" I joke. "It's not a religious ceremony, so he doesn't have any sacred texts to hold."

"You know, you get punchy when you're nervous," Tristen replies. "It's not your most attractive quality."

He runs his hand over his slicked back blonde hair and acts as if he hadn't contemplated the very same thing.

"I just need everything to go smoothly today." It's not a lie, exactly. "I have a lot riding on this ceremony."

He claps me on the shoulder. "I'm sure it will be okay." He glances up at the sky and purses his lips. "I'm not sure how you managed to pull all of this together in a week, though. I've been engaged three times and every single woman I was with set a date more than a year out. It takes a lot of energy to plan weddings, I guess."

"You sure that wasn't just a stalling tactic on their part? After all, you haven't actually gotten married."

"Fuck off."

He fiddles with his cuffs and looks out towards the back of the house, where the reception area is still having the final touches put on it. Wedding planners and caterers and florists practically sprint back and forth, trying to complete the vision that my personal assistant Jonathan told them to follow.

I shrug my shoulders. My assistant Jonathan planned the entire thing. And he has had more than a few months to plan it. I just moved the date up a little bit.

I start to say something further, but the front door to the house swings open. I turn my expectant gaze to the door, holding my breath for a second. I am all keyed up and expecting Talia to appear out that doorway any second now. But it's only one of the wedding coordinators.

"I have a flask in my pocket. You want to take a pull from it?" Tristen whispers.

I shoot him a look and run my hand down my vest for the hundredth time. "No, I'm good. Talia can't be much longer."

I look out of the crowd, who have started to turn around in their seats and fanning themselves, the bubble of their conversation washes over me like the sound of the ocean just behind me. I make a face and turn to look out over the ocean. Tristen turns too and slides me a concerned look.

"Should I go check on her?"

My lips thin. "Don't do anything. Everyone is watching us. I'll just text my assistant." But before I can do that, the squeaky front door opens again. The audience falls silent. I whip around to see Talia step out of the door. She's absolutely radiant in a dress that is as white as fresh-fallen snow.

The sleeveless bodice is wrapped in white satin. It has delicate lace cutouts around the sides and intricate pearl beading that trails down from Talia's waist while the skirt flares out dramatically at the knee. It has a train that flows out for a dozen feet behind her. Her head is swathed in a delicate white lace veil. As she steps out, two assistants rush to keep pace with her, keeping her train from touching the ground.

Her friend Olivia and her Aunt Minnie follow her, their pale peach silk gowns and professional hair and makeup making them look incredible. Olivia and Aunt Minnie hurry to step in front of Talia, each of them making their way down the aisle towards me.

My gaze is riveted on Talia's form as she slowly makes her way down the aisle. The guests have risen to their feet and watch in awe as Talia walks the last few steps towards me.

She's beautiful. Absolutely radiant.

Her facial features are clearer as she gets closer to me. By the time she sweeps up the steps and reaches the Arbor trellis, I am not anxious anymore.

No, I am excited, as ridiculous as it sounds. She steps close to me and my eyes scan her face. It's beautifully made up, but her features are totally blank. Is she shielding her emotions? Or does she feel as numb and uncaring as she looks?

I take her hand, leaning in close to whisper in her ear. "You look beautiful, darling girl."

Talia's blue eyes flash, her gaze skewering me. She doesn't look even a little bit happy to be here in front of all these people.

I'll admit, I'm a little taken aback. This is her wedding day. Shouldn't my bride be a tiny bit happy? When I start to pull away, she squeezes my hand hard and stares at me. She clearly means something with the gesture, though I'm at a loss as to what exactly.

Talia leans close to my ear and whispers, "Stay with me."

I grip her hand with both of mine, dropping a burning kiss onto the back. Then I hastily help pull the veil over Talia's head, revealing her beautiful face. She has never looked so lovely as she does today… but it is hard for me to think that there was ever a moment when I wasn't blown away by her elegance and grace.

She really is as close to perfect as a wife can be.

The reverend clears his throat and begins to speak. "Dearly beloved, we are gathered here today…"

I glance over to see Aunt Minnie standing beside Talia. She is glaring at me, her wild gray curls springing from her head like sea spray. A quick peek at Olivia's sulky expression makes me feel like I am missing something. Talia must have told them something to make them so mad.

I can't think of anything else I did to deserve their ire.

Tristen elbows me. I snap my eyes forward, looking at the reverend for help.

"Do you have the rings?" he asks.

My neck heats. "Tristen has them."

I hold out my hand impatiently. Tristen drops the rings in my palm. I feel like a robot as I take them, saying the words the reverend gives me as I slide the ring on her finger.

"Do you, Remington Darren Morgan, take Talia Rachel Chance to be your lawfully wedded wife?"

I look down into Talia's face. She is blushing, looking as though she wishes that an earthquake would come and sweep her into the sea. I take her hand and realize for the first time that she might not want to be here.

Turning her delicate wrist over in my hand, I place a kiss

on the pulse point of her wrist. Talia's expression softens and she reaches up to cup my jaw.

"I do," I swear. The words are a part of the ceremony that everyone is here to see. But I lock eyes with my wife, drawing her hand over my heart. Everyone might hear me speak, but my words are only meant for Talia.

The reverend intones, "And do you, Talia, take Dare to be your lawfully wedded husband?"

A tiny furrow appears between her eyebrows. "I do."

The reverend looks between Talia and I. He gives us a somber smile.

"By the power vested in me by God and the state of Maine, I am pleased to declare you husband and wife. You may kiss the bride."

I drag Talia in, kissing her like her lips are air and I'm a man who is suffocating. Her taste is sweet and minty, her tongue snaking against mine. She puts a hand on my chest, pushing me away gently. The reverend clears his throat and I reluctantly let her go.

"May I present to you, Mr. and Mrs. Morgan!" the reverend calls out.

Talia takes my hand and we turn to the crowd. There's a genuine smile creasing my mouth as we rush down the aisle. I slide my arm around my bride, the woman that I'm now given to protect.

Chapter Eighteen

I press my fingers against my tulle lace wedding dress and try to keep a straight face. I'm getting the worst stitches in my ribs just from standing here in the backyard of the beach estate at the Cliffs. I try to look the part of the cheerful bride as I stand next to Dare. It's just that my wedding dress doesn't allow me that much latitude of movement. And yet there are at least ten layers of clothing between my fingertips and my bare skin.

I sigh loudly.

Dare looks over at me, raising an eyebrow. He nods his head toward the man talking to us, indicating that perhaps I am being rude. He slips his hand around my waist and hugs me, putting his head close to my ear.

"Are you okay? I know Ms. Darcy is telling a very long-winded story, but I'm afraid I have to listen to it if I want any chance of doing business with them in the future."

I feel the eyes of Ms. Darcy on me. She's a dour looking woman in an undoubtedly very expensive yet still frumpy dress. I smile and take his hand, kissing his knuckles. "I'm going to the ladies room. And I should check on my Aunt

Minnie and my friend Olivia. Can I catch up with you in a little while?"

Dare's lips twitch and he makes a show of placing a single kiss on my bare neck.

"Be careful. I saw my brother Burn stroll in about twenty minutes ago so I know he's lurking around here somewhere. I hate to impose on your wedding day, but Frick and Frack have been given explicit instructions not to let you out of their sight."

I shiver at the feel of his lips on my skin and give him a lopsided grin, squeezing his hand one last time.

"Okay, I hear you. I'll be back soon."

Heading toward the house, I use the restroom fairly quickly and massage my ribs with great relief. I keep having painful pinpricks of sensation after I pull my dress down and exit the house again. I spot Frick standing just outside the door as I exit and nod to her. She straightens and gives me a nod in return.

I scan the crowd, looking for Olivia. And I quickly find her sitting at a table, a handsome young man on either side. Olivia picks at an imaginary piece of lint on her bridesmaid dress and nods at something one of the men says. As soon as she sees me, she perks up. Standing, she excuses herself and runs over to me.

"Hey, Mrs. Morgan," she teases. "It's weird that you go by a different name now."

"Not as strange as the fact that everyone seems to have assumed that I am Mrs. Morgan now. Dare and I haven't actually talked about whether I'll take his name or if our kids will have a hyphenated name."

She screws up her face. "I think we both know the answer to that."

Rolling my eyes, I nod. "I think you're right. Do you

think that we could find a quiet spot to sit down? My feet are killing me."

She beams and guides me toward the back of the party, to where there are festive white ribboned and blush pink netted tables spread out. "Aunt Minnie has already claimed a table at the very edge of the party. She waves off anyone that sits down with claims that she's saving the table for you."

"Ha! She's right, I'm afraid," I admit. "I'm exhausted."

We step around an elderly couple and I see my Aunt Minnie at a table by herself, an entire platter of hors d'oeuvres on the table in front of her. She pops one in her mouth just as I walk up. She looks up and sort of squeals with delight as she jumps up to hug me, her mouth still full.

I hug her gladly and then sink into the seat beside her. The white chair is the same type as the crowd of onlookers that is on the other side of the house. But it is the biggest relief to get off my aching feet and I lean back in the chair with the soft grunt of pleasure. Olive moves around me and pulls up another chair facing me. She pats the seat.

"You can put your feet up here."

I slide my gaze to the party guests milling around. If they knew I was pregnant, I think that putting my feet up on the chair would be something that they could overlook. But because my pregnancy is still under wraps, I feel like they will judge me.

I scrunch up my face and shake my head. "No thanks. It's better if I don't lose my composure while all the guests are still here."

Olive narrows her eyes at me but shrugs. She moves the chair a little so that she's sitting between me and Aunt Minnie and then slumps into it.

Aunt Minnie leans forward, holding out a cracker with a

blob of gray goo on it and a jaunty herb topping. "Would you like some pate?" she asks.

I turn a little green, shaking my head and putting my hand up like a wall to keep me separated from the offending cracker. "No way. Everything is making me nauseated today."

Minnie pouts for a second and then looks at me slyly. "How do you feel about some chocolate babka?"

The image of a fresh loaf of the sweet bread fresh from the oven, still steaming pops into my head. In my mind, I pull a piece of the bread away and smell the rich, dark cocoa mix with cinnamon that is inside. My mouth starts watering.

God, I wish that I had a piece. I could definitely stomach that.

Aunt Minnie stands up, holding her hand out to me and smiling mischievously. "I have some in the kitchen. I showed up with a few loaves and the Butler had a conniption fit. He made me hand them over to him for safekeeping." She rolls her eyes. "Let's go get a piece."

Jumping up and hugging my Aunt, I grin. "I can't believe you brought babka to my Waspy wedding. You know that they have always been my favorite dessert."

"Since you were a kid," Aunt Minnie says with a smile.

Aunt Minnie beckons Olive to follow and hurries me toward the house. We go in a wide arc around the wedding guests and are soon huddled in the kitchen and slicing into the decadent dessert.

Taking a slice of dessert from my aunt, I pop a chocolatey morsel into my mouth. The pastry is full of butter and honey, the cinnamony, chocolatey goodness almost too much to take. I close my eyes and let out a moan.

"Oh my God. It's so good," I manage between bites.

Olivia winks at me, her mouth too full of pastry to respond. Aunt Minnie gives me a little grin and guides me over to the overstuffed chair in the corner of the room. She and Olivia pull up two heavy dining room chairs and I sit down, feeling a little guilty as I try not to get crumbs on my wedding dress.

Aunt Minnie pops up from her chair and grabs a cloth napkin from a stack on the kitchen countertop, returning to hand it to me.

"Thanks," I say. "It's hard to convince myself not to have a second slice of Babka."

Olivia finishes her piece and dusts her hands off.

"Don't hold back on our account. There is no one here but us chickens." She grabs the matching ottoman and pushes it closer to the chair, smiling when I put my feet up on it.

"I'm going to get completely spoiled by the two of you taking such good care of me."

Aunt Minnie is looking at my feet with a skeptical expression. "I don't think I've ever seen you wear heels. And yet today, you have some serious spike heels on your feet. No wonder your whole body aches."

I make a face and rearrange my wedding dress, flicking it away from my feet and rubbing the skirts around themselves so that they don't hang on the floor.

"It's part of my makeover. It's taken me a few weeks to get used to them. Heels are definitely torture devices more than anything else."

Olivia chuckles. "I hope you're not going to change too much for your new husband. I happen to like everything about you. It would be a shame to bow to societal expectations, don't you think?"

I flush and set my dessert on the cloth napkin. "I'm afraid I didn't have a choice. It was one of the stipulations of agreeing to marry Dare."

Aunt Minnie huffs. "I don't want to speak ill of your new

husband. But I can't say that I'm crazy about all these new changes."

"But we're still crazy about you, Talia." Olive is quick to cut in. "And will support you in whatever you decide. Isn't that right, Aunt Minnie?"

Aunt Minnie rolls her eyes and flaps a hand at Olivia. "You're right, of course. I'm just cranky because I have been alone at the bookstore for too long. I can't wait until you come back from your honeymoon. I need your help changing the window display again."

I scrunch my nose up. "I don't know when I'm going to be able to do that, Aunt Minnie. I think we're going to have to hire you some outside help. You deserve to have someone at the shop more regularly than I can commit to."

Aunt Minnie looks a little surprised. "You're not coming back to work at the bookstore?"

I shake my head very slowly. "I don't think so. I will help whenever I can, of course. But you deserve somebody that can be at the shop whenever you need them." I bite my lip for a second. "Now that I am married to Dare, I have more money for things like getting you a shopkeeper. Isn't that nice?"

Aunt Minnie flushes. She stands up and puts her hand up to her hair. Patting the back of her head, she feigns a need to leave.

"You'll have to excuse me, dear. I want to use the ladies room and maybe swing by the drink station and grab a glass of Pinot. I'll see you in a bit."

"Aunt Minnie, wait!" I cry.

She shakes her head, her expression tormented. Before I can protest further, she sweeps out of the room, the back door banging as she exits.

Frustrated, I growl at the closed door. Olivia presses her

lips together and picks at an invisible piece of lint on her knee. I swing my head around and stare at her.

"She's being unreasonable. She had to have known that someday I would get married and start a family."

"Just give her time. Your whole relationship with Dare and decision to get married really threw her for a loop."

I give her a funny look. "It's been months."

"It doesn't feel like it."

"Are you telling me how she feels or are you speaking more from personal experience?" I ask.

Olivia blushes and shrugs, but she doesn't look away. "Oh, you know. Maybe both."

"Accepting Dare's proposal of marriage was your idea." I cross my arms and give her a stubborn stare. "You can't be hurt when the whole thing was your idea."

Her nose twitches. "I know. It's just… Everything changed almost overnight. I went from always having you in my corner to wondering when I would see you next. I didn't expect that."

The look of guilt on her face is almost painful and makes my heart ache.

I soften and sit up in my chair, reaching out a hand towards her. "I'm sorry about that. It's just been so crazy. But I will make a marked effort to be better about communication. I promise."

She flashes me a sad smile and looks down at her hands folded in her lap. "I'm not complaining. Really I'm not. But it's like I said. It's an adjustment."

"I know. I wrinkle my nose. It's been hard on everyone, myself and Dare included."

She laughs. "What do you mean? I thought nothing affected cold hearted Dare."

My head bobs. "I thought so, too, at first. It made me a

little crazy. But now that I know him better, I'm starting to see that the whole coldhearted act is just a front. Don't tell anybody, but Dare is definitely beginning to thaw out where I am concerned." I look around the kitchen, checking to make sure that we are still alone. Then I press my hand to my baby bump and smile. "He doesn't say it out loud, but I think that he's actually really excited for the baby."

Olivia's look of surprise couldn't be more perfect. I sit back, my thoughts drifting to my husband.

How excited he was when I stepped out the front door just hours before and started to walk down the aisle to where he stood beneath the trellis. He tries to hide it, but I have studied his face for months now. I know when he is secretly pleased and enthusiastic.

"Is there anything you'll miss about your old life? And I'm not asking for or digging for complements here. There's no need to reassure me that we will always be friends. I am not letting you go that easily."

"Nor should you," I reply. "And if you were to ask me what I miss most about my old life, it would be the simplicity of it all. My old life was so simple. I rarely had any cause to be angry or scared or sad. Now I have those feelings all the time." I pause. "But I suppose I have other feelings, too."

Olivia narrows her eyes on my face. "Such as?"

I shrug a shoulder, feeling blood rush to my cheeks.

She gets a self-satisfied little smirk on her face. "You like Dare. You actually like being Mrs. Morgan."

Embarrassed, I look down. "I didn't think that."

"You don't have to. We've been friends for our whole lives. You're always so bashful about liking guys. But I've seen you blush and stammer before. You didn't when we were in middle school. You did once a year in high school. And you didn't do it once in college." She holds up fingers to represent every crush I've ever had. Then she raises a finger and wiggles her eyebrows at me. "Now your latest is Dare Morgan. A little unexpected. After all, you seem so dead set against everything he stands for. But at the same time, it's actually kind of perfect. You might as well fall in love with the man you're married to, right?"

I groan aloud. "Don't even say the word to me."

"What? Love?" She slides me a sly smile. "I'm not saying that you are all the way in yet. But I have watched you fall in love over and over again. I recognize the first bloom of love when I see it."

I roll my eyes. "Please. I'm begging you, stop while you're ahead."

She pushes out her cheek with her tongue. She looks a little shifty, like a henchman that is calling something diabolical. But she just stands up and jerks her head toward the hallway. "I have to go grab something. But I'll be right back. Don't move a muscle."

I sink back into my chair and sigh. "That's not a problem. Although I may fall asleep right here."

"You want to wait till I get back. I have something for you." She picks up the skirts of her bridesmaid dress and hurries down the hall. She's gone for just a minute before returning with a small off white valise suitcase. She wiggled her eyebrows at me as she sits down, opening the suitcase so that I can't see what's inside. When she pulls out a long intricately carved T of wood with strings hanging down from each joint of the T. Hanging from the string are soft plush animal ornaments.

I narrow my eyes suspiciously.

Holding up the contraption and putting the valise aside, Olivia leans forward and shows me the ornaments. One is a rainbow, one a cat, one a dog. An elephant, a zebra, and a brown blob that I can't quite make out. I quirk my brow at her. Every single one of the ornaments is badly stitched and has been very messily colored, as if by a child.

"What is it?" I wonder. "Some kind of dream catcher?"

"It's a mobile to hang over a crib." She screws up her face. "Actually, I wouldn't hang it over a crib. I'm not sure if it's safe for a teething baby. But maybe by a baby's window? She touches one of the ornaments and smiles. Each toy was made by one of the kids at Hope House."

Tears spring to my eyes. "Oh my God," I say softly. I reach out and gently touched the brown blob which I now see has two lighter brown pieces coming out of the side of one end. "This is so adorable. You had them make it for me?"

Olivia's grin widens. "I did. And because I know you want to know, that toy you're holding is supposed to be a moose. That was actually made by Solana."

I look up at her and beckon her over to me for a hug. "Thank you so much. Really. I have to admit, I haven't actually bought a single thing for the baby yet."

She pulls back and looks at me with the prize. "Really? Why not? You have all this money now."

"Yeah. I don't know. I think… I think I wanted to make sure that things with Dare would stick. When I first agreed to the engagement, he was driving me up a wall on an hourly basis. I didn't know if I could really live like that. But he has really toned it down since then."

Olivia nudges her elbow into my ribs very gently and winks at me. "I got that when I saw you guys all over each other today. You two seem really happy. And I am thrilled for you."

I hug her again for good measure and then pull away. She sighs and takes the mobile out of my hand and puts it back in the little suitcase. She pats the side of it. "I'm going to go find the Butler and make sure that this gets put in your luggage. You just stay here and try to relax for a few more minutes."

Nodding, I give her a quiet smile. "I love you, Olivia."

She doesn't miss a beat. "You too, Talia. Always and forever."

She spends and heads off toward the hallway once more. I'm not in my chair for a whole two minutes before Dare opens the door and sticks his head in. He looks at me sitting down and grins at me. "There you are. If you care about me at all, you'll come save me from being bored to death."

"That bad?"

He rolls his eyes. "I got trapped talking to the company insurance agent. I was just trying to tell him that I wanted to make an appointment to change my life insurance policy. But he took the opportunity to give me a lot of very serious advice for how to treat a new wife."

"What, you didn't find that inspirational?"

He flashes me a smirk. "Can't say that I did. The worst part was that he wanted to meet with you, too. After twenty minutes, I ended up telling him that you're the only one that I give a damn about. So in ninety days, I'm going to put your name on my life insurance beneficiary form. Honestly, I almost chewed my own arm off because he had a grip and wouldn't let go until he was done dispensing his advice."

"So you give a damn about me?"

Dare frowns. "You know what I mean. It's just some official mumbo-jumbo."

"Oh. I get it. You can't even look me in the eye and tell me that you're glad that I am your wife."

"Talia," he intones. "Be reasonable."

I throw my hands up in the air, only partially serious. "I don't know what you expect me to do." He comes closer, picking up my hand. Squeezing my fingers, he looks down at me.

"I'm glad that you're my wife. Okay? Does that make you happy?"

I struggle out of my seat and then smooth down my dress. Then I wrap my arms around him and turn my face up, offering him my mouth. He kisses me then, long and slow and oh so passionately that my toes curl up inside my white high heels. Then he pulls back and takes my hand.

"Are you ready to go cut the cake, Mrs. Morgan?" Dare asks.

My heart thuds in my chest as I look at him. I don't know what to say so I just nod and kiss the back of his hand. We share another long look and then he guides me out of the house to the waiting crowd.

Chapter Nineteen

"Oh my god." I step out of the SUV, bringing my hand up to shade my eyes. The sun is warm against my skin, like I've just stepped into a warm coat. Below me, a number of bright white buildings with distinctive red roofs clustered on a gently sloping hill that eases right into the bluest sea I've ever seen. Palm trees dot the rocky terrain, leading suggestively to the beautiful tan stripe of sand that marks the start of the beach.

"It's a tropical paradise, straight out of a dream," I whisper.

"I told you I would surprise you." Dare comes around the SUV to grab my hand, a grin on his face. "Welcome to St. Barts."

"You really went all out." I kiss the back of his hand as he tugs me down the hill toward the bright blue front door to the sprawling villa. "Are there other people staying here?"

Dare opens the door, standing aside for me to enter and giving me a little bow. "The whole villa is all ours."

I walk into the villa's living room, my eyes widening at the beautifully clean light gray floors, cream colored walls, and blue slate overstuffed couches. This space looks like an art gallery and just shouts *money* to me. It has one wall made entirely of glass and looks out on a panoramic view of the beach.

"Wow." I feel a little out of breath just looking at the dark blue ocean swirling just below the window. "This was definitely worth the long plane ride."

Behind me, the chauffeur brings in the lightweight travel bags we brought on the plane. Dare throws his sunglasses on the teak coffee table and looks over at me.

"Want to check out the bedroom first?" he suggests. There is a playful kind of mischief in his gaze as he looks me up and down. "I've heard that the sex is better now that we are husband and wife. We can see for ourselves whether that's true."

I slide him a sly grin. "Can we eat first? I'm starving."

He nods. "It's important to fuel up for an extended sex session. I can call the private chef."

"I need something *now*." I scrunch my face up, feeling more than a little ridiculous. But my stomach is rumbling and I feel like if I don't eat right this second, I'm going to die.

"I'm sure there is something for you to nibble on in the kitchen." Dare jerks his head toward the back of the villa. "Let's go see."

I follow him into the kitchen, which is a masterpiece in its own right. This space is bright white. White countertops, white wood cabinets, white appliances, white pine on the floor. The only color in the room is the panoramic view that wraps around half of the room, looking out at the sandy walking path winding down beside the house and spreading out to the beach.

"What a view!" I say, a little awestruck. "Damn. This villa has got to be expensive. I know we don't really talk about money, but you have to tell me how much this costs per night."

Dare walks over to the refrigerator and pokes his head inside.

"I don't think it works like that. It belongs to a friend."

"You've got to be kidding." I spin, my white sundress fluttering. "What kind of a friend has this kind of beach house sitting around, unused?"

He shrugs, pulling out a bowl of tropical fruits and a container of yogurt. He sets them on the countertop and rustles through the pantry for a minute. Then he pulls out a plastic package of very expensive-looking granola and waves it at me.

"How does a parfait sound?"

I bite my lip and repress a smile. "I'm so hungry that I would be pretty much anything you put in front of me, given that it was edible."

His lips twitch and he starts to put a handful of blueberries in a bowl. I take a seat at the kitchen bar and watch him slice an Apple up and alternate it with layers of granola and thick dollops of Greek yogurt. My stomach rumbles and I run my hand over my growing baby bump, as if to soothe it somehow.

By the time Dare is done, I am absolutely ravenous. He sets the glass and a spoon on the counter in front of me and I wolf it down, barely tasting the bright, sweet notes of the fruit and the creaminess of the granola. Dare stands back and watches me with some amusement. I wolf down the whole parfait in less than three minutes. When I'm done, he takes the glass and spoon from me and sticks them near the sink.

"I take that as a compliment," he says.

I can't help but laugh. "Thank you for feeding me. I hate to even ask, but do you think that there are any salt and vinegar chips in this house? I'm having a crazy craving for them all of a sudden."

He smiles and shrugs his shoulders. "Whatever you want, they can get it for you. Salt and vinegar chips should be easy."

I bite my lip and lean forward, resting my arms on the counter. "Would it be too much to ask if they can get kettle chips?"

He whips out his cell phone and starts to text someone. "I'm sure they can figure something out."

He leans back against the cabinet and crosses his legs as he concentrates on his phone. I look Dare up and down, admiring his tall, trim physique. He is still wearing his usual black dress pants and his white button up, his suit jacket missing entirely. He's rolled up his sleeves at some point and I look at his strong forearms and his undoubtedly high end platinum watch. He's always handsome. But just at this moment, he is extremely attractive.

The fact that he is my husband doesn't hurt either.

I'm busy imagining my sexy husband shirtless and feeding me salt and vinegar potato chips when I catch movement out of the corner of my eye. I see two figures walking down the little path beside the house, a man leading the way and a woman holding his hand and lagging slightly behind. I can see the man's dark hair and looks are familiar to me. He clutches the hand of a woman whose blonde hair is tucked up in a red handkerchief. They are both dressed for a midday walk on the beach.

Why do I feel a sense of dread when I see them?

As I watch, the man stops and pulls the woman into his arms, kissing her dramatically and even dipping her backwards. I raise my hand to point them out to Dare, but then I see who the man and woman are.

It's Burn and Daisy. They are unmistakable from where I'm standing about forty feet away in the kitchen.

My jaw drops.

Dare turns his head to look, spotting Burn and Daisy in less than a second. He pushes off the cabinets and immediately his posture grows tense. His hands curl into fists and he spreads his legs, his gaze growing steely.

"What the fuck?" Dare hisses. "How do they even know where we are?"

I stand up and walk to stand beside him, pulling at one of his hands and lacing my fingers with his. I look up at Dare and take a deep breath. "They must've followed us. Or they knew that you had a plane booked to the island."

His eye twitches. Out the window, Burn pulls away from Daisy and looks in the window, making eye contact with us. Burn grins and heads down the path, toward the front of the house. I look at Dare, who looks like he is spoiling for a fight. Tugging at his hand, I try to talk him down.

"Dare? Look at me."

After a moment, he does. I gave him a soft smile and touch his cheek.

"You shouldn't fight with Burn. That's obviously what he wants."

Dare grits his teeth. He grimaces. "He touched you. He kissed you. He knew you were mine and he fucking did it anyway. No one lays a hand on you and walks away unscathed. I'll kill him for it."

I put my hands on his shoulders and try to calm him down.

"You're letting him win. You're letting Burn wind you up like a toy car. The only way that takes back the power right now is by not engaging."

He arches a brow. "The only way to win is not to play at all?"

I nod. "It seems that way."

Dare takes my hand, kissing the back of it. "You don't leave my side for a second. Got it?"

A sense of warmth slides through me. I nod and press up on my toes, seeking a kiss. He presents his lips against mine briefly and then sighs.

"Let's go see what they want, I guess."

He leads me through the house, seeming to know his way around. He steps out of the gorgeous living room into a luxurious pool area.

The whole area is open to the elements outside and Burn stands on one side, gazing out at the sea. There is a pensive look on his face which I've seen so many times before on his twin brother. Daisy is over by the pool, her sandals kicked to the side and her toes testing the water of the pool. She looks up as we come out of the villa, smirking a little.

"Well look who it is," she says.

Dare isn't interested in anything she has to say. He snaps his fingers at her, rushing past her and heading straight for his brother. This makes her eyes widen for a second and she hastily looks at Burn. I get the pleasure of watching her face as Dare stalks across the pool deck to where Burn is standing. I have no idea what's going on in her head exactly, but I get the feeling that she doesn't like Dare not pining after her.

Honestly, it's a little surprising even to me.

Burn turns and gives Dare a cocky little smile. Dare completely sidesteps my advice and punches his brother right in the mouth. Burn staggers back and looks at Dare with some horror, his hand over his lower jaw.

"Fuck?!" He cries. "What the fuck are you doing?"

Dare squares up, his fists in the air, his whole being ready to fight.

"Stand up. Put your fists up. Defend yourself."

Burn squints at him. "For what?"

Dare moves forward, pelting him with a one-two punch, a right hook then an uppercut.

He goes stumbling backwards and Dare puts his fists up, a sneer twisting his lips. "That's what you get for laying your hands on my wife. Now get up off the floor so I can hit you again. Come on, you fucking coward, I dare you."

My pulse races but I stay well clear of both men. The last thing anybody needs is for the pregnant lady to rush into the situation and get knocked down accidentally. Daisy on the other hand has no such reservations. She rushes in and tries to grab at Dare's arm.

"Leave him alone." Her voice sounds whiny. Dare shrugs her off and sidesteps her, not bothering to even look her way. A flash of rage washes over her features, there one second, gone the next. But I saw it.

She really doesn't like when Dare ignores her. Maybe it's a new phenomenon to her as well.

Burn wipes blood from his lip and looks at Dare, almost disbelieving. "What the fuck? I'm bleeding. You actually hit me."

Dare glares at him. "And I'll do it again. Get up. Or just come near my wife again, you fucking bastard. I'll do more than make you bleed. I'll wipe the floor with you and leave you in the forest where no one will ever find your body."

"Are you seriously going to act like that over her?" He gestures towards me. "You're a Morgan, for God's sake. You should be with someone worthy of your status. I'm just looking out for your best interest. Doing you a favor."

Something in Dare snaps. His face contorts and he heaves

himself at Burn hitting him and grappling with him. They roll across the floor, each one landing a few blows. It's not until they roll right off the edge of the deck onto the sand that Dare pulls himself off Burn. Daisy tries to help Dare up and Dare looks at her like she's insane. Like she's worth less than dirt.

"Get off me. Fucking creep," Dare spits. He points to his feet and backs away, wiping blood from his upper lip. Daisy looks hurt and angry, especially when Burn yells her name.

"Daisy!" He barks. "What the fuck are you doing?" He scrambles to his feet and yanks her toward him, off of her feet entirely. She seems shaken and Burn does little to soothe her. He just looks back and forth between her and Dare.

"What do you need? We have to hash this thing out."

Dare spits on the floor, glaring at his brother. "The fuck we do. Get off my property. The next time I see you down here, I'm gonna call the fucking cops. Or maybe I'll just call one of my security guards. They are armed and they aren't afraid."

Burn bleats out a laugh. "You're fucking crazy. You can't threaten me."

Before Burn says anything else, I step in, slicing my hand down through the air. "Get out of here. Get off our property. We are on our honeymoon, so just get lost."

Daisy sneers. Burn wipes his lower lip and growls at us. Dare makes a move toward him but I catch his arm and hold him back. Daisy tries to wrap her arm around Burn but he shrugs her off, whirling and storming down the beach.

Daisy looks at both of us, looking like a deer caught in the bright headlights of an oncoming semi truck. I arch a brow at her. Dare bears his teeth at her, walks over to me, and herds me inside. Once we close the sliding glass door, I pull Dare to a stop, grabbing his face. I look at his bloody lip and the raised, red contusion on his cheekbone.

"You're hurt," I whisper.

He slides his arms around me, grabbing my waist and pulling me close. "My brother deserves a lot worse than a punch to the face. He needs to know that if he messes with you, I will come after him with everything I've got."

I smooth my hands down his neck and across his shoulders. "I appreciate you protecting me, but I would rather just move on from the situation."

Dare's lips curve upward.

"I knew you would. I've been watching you try your hardest not to rock the boat since the first day I laid eyes on you. But this is between my brother and me."

I sigh and assess his injuries again. "Come on. Let's get you patched up. We can talk about your brother later."

Chapter Twenty

TALIA

The next morning, Dare sleeps in quite late. I wake early and spend the morning with a cup of steaming mint tea and a slice of locally made bread with a dab of sweetened butter. I don't know quite what to do with myself on this vacation. Usually when I am not busy with Dare, I have Hope House to occupy my time. And beyond that, I have Aunt Minnie and Olivia. They both entertain me and keep my hands busy with work.

But now I am at a loss for what to do with myself. I look out the window of the kitchen and try reading the copies of the latest issues of Vogue and Vanity Fair that are laid out near the window. I fidget and sit in a comfortable chair, then move to an expensive leather couch. At half past ten, I decide to check out the beach.

Dare is still asleep so I quickly change into a pale pink bikini and a pair of gray linen pants topped with a loose dark tank top and a chunky knit sweater. Then I put on a pair of tennis shoes and poke my head out into the room where the security guards are stationed. While I'm here, Frick and Frack are on vacation. But I smile at the armed guards, recognizing one of them.

"Can we help you?" The guard that I don't know asks.

I look at the guards that I recognize. "It's Bill, right?"

He straightens in his chair and nods. "Yes, ma'am. Can I help you with something?"

"I was wondering if you wouldn't mind accompanying me out onto the beach. Dare is still asleep, otherwise I would just ask him. I don't want to have any run-ins with his brother. I don't know if you know that Dare saw his brother and his brother's fiancé here yesterday... I'm not expecting any trouble, but better safe than sorry." I trail off.

Bill is already standing up. "Of course, ma'am. Let me grab my sunglasses."

He takes a second to find his glasses on the nearby table and also holsters his gun onto his belt. Then he jerks his chin towards the door.

"Lead the way," he says. "I'll follow at a distance. Just go about your regular day."

I give him a halfhearted smile then head outside, putting my own sunglasses on when I step into the sun. I walk by the swimming pool and head toward the beach, my eyes traveling down the shore. God, it's beautiful. I can see villas dotting the landscape here and there, but for the most part this is a very exclusive and secluded area of land.

As soon as I make it down onto the beach in earnest, I trudge through the sand and straight down to the water line. The water rolls in, lapping over the sand within inches of my feet. I glance out at the dark waters, noting that they are calm today. The ocean continues washing in and out like a woman's sighing. I stretch my arms up overhead and reach out, throwing my head back. The breeze whips all around me, ripping at my clothes.

This is the first time in what feels like forever that I have been alone. Well, alone except for the bodyguard trailing behind me. I suck in a breath and decide that I am going to walk down the beach for a while. I push up my sweater sleeves and start walking, the only gauge of distance is the gentle arc of land. I can see a far-off point where the land slips out from the island.

Strolling down the beach at a leisurely pace, I watch the seagulls as they land on the smooth beach before me.

Before I get very far in my walk, an all too familiar voice calls out to me. "Hey! Wait!"

Daisy's voice is as welcome to me as a bucket of ice water over my head. I grit my teeth and refuse to look around for her. Maybe if I just ignore her, she will simply disappear.

Before I have the chance to decide whether to actually speak to her or not, I hear her squawk. "Hey! Let go of me! Do you have any idea who I am?"

God, she is absolutely insufferable.

I turn around, finding Daisy struggling against Bill. Bill's looking at her with an intense glare and gripping her arm. "Ma'am, I need you to just step back."

I roll my eyes. "It's okay, Bill. You can let her by. She's not the one that I am worried about."

Daisy rips her arm from Bill's grip and glares at him. "I should have you fired," she threatens.

"Don't talk to him. He's doing his job." I run a hand through my hair and turn, shaking my head as I trudge on. Daisy hurries to catch up to me and then walks beside me. Although it's no more than eighty five degrees out, she's wearing a hot pink string bikini and a loose white knit cover-up that is ankle-length and completely unbolted. She wears nothing on her feet and has no sunglasses on. I don't know if that means that she just saw me on the beach and decided to come talk to me or what.

She walks beside me for a few steps, pursing her lips as she peers at me. I stare straight ahead and try my best to ignore her.

She sweeps back her hair and makes a face. "So that was something yesterday, huh?"

I stare off across the sea, intentionally not looking at her.

I realize now that my pulse is racing and it isn't because of my stroll down the beach.

Daisy bites her lips and looks me up and down. I can feel her gaze catch on my baby bump. She squints at it but doesn't say anything for a few seconds.

"I just came to say that I feel terrible. You probably hate me."

This draws my attention back to her. I arched an eyebrow. "Oh?"

She pushes the hair out of her face and gives me a wry smile. "Well, I'm the reason that Dare is probably still completely screwed up. You probably already know that he and I were together in college. We even talked about getting married. But… Then I met Burn. And we just had such undeniable chemistry that I couldn't lie to myself any longer. I broke up with Dare and Burn proposed to me the very same night." She pulls a face. "So yeah, Dare is probably still completely hung up on me."

I frown. "Dare said that you and Burn met before he actually met you. Is that not true?"

One glance at her suddenly red face tells me everything I want to know. She runs a hand down her stomach, poking out her cheek with her tongue.

"Well, sort of. I did know Burn when I met Dare. But I didn't know him well."

"And you got to know your boyfriend's brother well, after you had been dating him for three years? Is that it?"

I see a flush of disgust on her face but it's gone before I can comment on it. "You obviously don't understand the timeline that I'm talking about here." I shrug, "Maybe not. But I do know that you broke up with Dare after Burn proposed to you. Dare told me that you had that ring that's on your finger right now when you showed up to his house late at night and essentially dumped him. So that's two things that you have lied about in the space of a brief conversation." I turn my head, looking at her. "I'm not sure why you came out here to talk to me. But if it was just to fill my ear with these falsehoods that are easy to check the veracity of, you can just leave now." I pause, slowing my steps. "Or did Burn send you out to make peace with me? Is that what this is about?"

Daisy flushes scarlet red and her eyes tighten. "Are you calling me a liar?"

I roll my eyes. "If the name fits. Are we done here?"

"I just came out here to tell you that Dare still thinks about me all the time. There's no question about it. He has tried to get me back several times since I left him for Burn. Including right before you two met. I'm absolutely certain that he still dreams about me at night."

I whirled around, facing her. My pulse is high and I can feel my heart hammering against my chest.

"I don't know who you think you are fooling. I love that you think you're fooling everybody. I don't know if you are just trying to lie to me because I am the newest member of this fucked up family. But whatever spell you think you've cast over my husband has long since been broken. I know for a fact he didn't fall asleep thinking about you last night. Because we fucked until the early hours of the morning and he fell asleep satisfied after going all night with me. The fact that you seem to think that he has the brain space available to think of you is honestly pretty mind blowing."

Her mouth twists into a hard little ball. "I know one thing for sure. Dare hasn't told you he loved you. He said that to me so many times I lost count. But he told me he would never love any woman like he loves me. And I believe him."

My heart falls to my stomach. I lift my chin and open my mouth, speaking before I even think to stop myself.

"Of course he has said he loves me," I lie easily. "And I love him. We're married. And not only that, but I am pregnant. So whatever little schemes you have for the future, I would forget them. Focus on trying to love the fucked up man that you are engaged to. Because my husband and I are deeply in love and we're going to have a baby."

Her jaw drops. She looks down at my baby bump again and her eyes narrow viciously.

"Dare can't have children. I am living proof of it. We were together for three years and never used a condom once."

My heart is pounding so loudly in my ears that I am afraid that it will drown out the sound of my voice. "Maybe you should get yourself checked out then. Because Dare got me pregnant on purpose right away. Probably the first or second time that we tried to conceive."

The lies just roll off my tongue, each one surprising me more than the next.

Daisy looks furious and she steps to me, pushing me hard. I stumble back a step and my hands form fists. But two seconds later, Bill intervenes.

"Hey! Hey!" He runs up, pushing her away from me. He spins and spreads his hands out wide, caging Daisy and making her back up. "Get back. Get back!"

"This isn't over, bitch!" Daisy screams.

I turn away, my eyes welling up with unshed tears. I shove out a breath and dab at my eyes as Bill continues to back Daisy up.

"Ma'am? You need to start moving down the beach back toward the house. I radioed for help and Carl should be out here in a few seconds."

"Don't touch me!" Daisy snarls. "I swear to God, I will have your job for this. Don't you dare touch me."

Moving down the beach past Daisy, I start walking quickly toward the house and the safety of Dare's arms.

DARE

"Holy shit," Talia breathes as she looks up at the sleek white hull of the megayacht that I've brought her to. "This yacht is huge. It's gotta be six or seven decks and have multiple bedrooms too."

I walk her over to the ship's stairs, guiding her with a hand to her lower back. "We should've just stayed on the yacht instead of trying to have our honeymoon in St. Bart's. If I had put a minute's worth of thought into the plan, I would've realized that we were vulnerable to my brother and Daisy showing up."

Talia glances up at me and purses her hand over my arm. "There's no way you could've known."

"I should've prepared for an interruption. Instead, I just got wrapped up in the excitement of the wedding. I swear to you, it will not happen again."

Her lips thin and she glances away. I'm not sure how to interpret her expression so I straighten and hurry her forward. When I reach the steps, Captain. Weathers is waiting there for me. He greets us with a slight bow.

"Good morning, Mr. and Mrs. Morgan. Welcome to our ship, The Evangeline."

Talia smiles at the captain. "It's good to see you again. I must say, I didn't expect to find you waiting for us."

"Captain Weathers has been sailing with me for years. He works for the family full time. Any time that I have to sail somewhere and do not want to sail myself, Weathers is there for me."

I clap Weathers on the shoulder. He merely inclines his head again and gives me a cool little smile. "We have everything ready for you." He gestures to the stairs and I help Talia climb up, making sure that she doesn't somehow lose her footing.

"Weathers, we will show ourselves to the library. Let us know if you need our input at all."

"Yes, sir." Weathers inclines his head again and spots a uniformed steward walking across the deck. He hurries over to talk to the man, his movements brisk and efficient.

"Is this boat staffed, then?"

My lips twitch. "Yes. There are over twenty people working to make the trip as smooth as possible. I have a rule that staff should not interact with me unless it's an important issue. But feel free to talk to anyone that you see. They will be more than happy to help you with absolutely any request."

She wrinkles her nose. "To be totally honest with you, all I want right now is to sit down and relax."

"Well, you came to the right yacht. This yacht is all about relaxation."

The gentle, rolling waves rock the megayacht, luring me into a peaceful and soothing refuge. It's away from all the chaos that seemed to swirl around us.

The sparkling white exterior of the yacht glistens in the midday sun, its luxurious curves shimmering in the water.

The scent of the sea is a constant in the air. It was easy to forget at this moment that we aren't on a romantic holiday, but rather in the middle of a tumultuous and complicated situation involving my twin brother, Burn.

The thought turns my stomach sour and makes me want to physically punish someone.

I take a deep breath and savor the warmth and beauty of the yacht. Being here is like being in a second home. I have always loved sailing and yachting since I was a child, something about the open sea, with the horizon stretching out before me, that gives me an exhilaration like no other.

I stride around the deck with Talia's arm tucked in mine, determined to give her a tour. Cautiously I glance at her, my emotions swelling with a gruff protectiveness. "You don't have to worry," I say through tight lips. "Nobody will touch you while I'm here."

Even though I can admit to myself that Talia is indeed a capable and independent woman who can look after herself, something inside tells me I need to watch over her. A feeling at the pit of my stomach. I have no idea what it is, but whatever it is, it won't go away.

We arrive at the back of the yacht and I swing open the heavy door. A huge, opulent library awaits us. Everything is made from oak; a long table and matching chairs dominate the space, while its mahogany bookcases are filled with books and odd-looking trinkets. It's twice as big as the one I have back in Harwicke, and I'm forever in awe of its grandeur no matter how many times I see it.

"Oh my god!" Talia gasps with astonishment as we enter the room. The scent of books instantly fills our noses and I gesture for her to take a seat. She looks around in amazement, absorbing every detail of the vast selection of books on the shelves before her.

"This place is incredible," she breathes out in awe, eyes wide. I smirk and recline into the chair opposite her, studying her expression and silently laughing at how overwhelmed she seems.

"I'm glad you like it. This is one of my favorite spots onboard the yacht," I reply calmly, leaning forward again.

I walk up to one shelf and run my fingers across the spines of some of his favorite books, a wave of nostalgia washing over me. Talia quietly watches me, her expression soft and understanding as she realizes what this place means to me. "Do you want to talk about it?' she asks gently, her voice barely above a whisper.

I shake my head, not wanting to break the peaceful atmosphere we've created within this room by bringing up painful memories. Instead I gesture for us to have a seat at the large table in the center, away from all the reminders of my past life on board this yacht.

We settle into two chairs opposite each other and I take a moment to just breathe in all the happiness that is radiating from Talia's face. She looks so beautiful here in her natural surroundings; it's like watching someone come alive after years of suffocation by society's norms and expectations.

"I'm thinking about the future," Talia answers, her expression becoming thoughtful. "Just daydreaming, really. Nothing for you to worry about, Dare."

Talia smiles and leans into me, our hands touching as we sit in companionable silence for a few moments. It's nice to just be able to sit together without speaking—to simply enjoy each other's presence without having to say anything at all.

Suddenly she pulls away from me and looks up into my eyes with an impish grin on her face. "What are you thinking?" she asks teasingly.

I laugh softly and shake my head before answering honestly, "Just that it feels really nice being here with you."

Talia looks up at me, her face glowing with a radiant beauty that I'm finding hard to resist. Her eyes are like two deep pools of molten brown, her skin smooth and creamy like skimmed milk, and her hair is a glossy copper lion's mane that frames her delicate features perfectly. She's breathtaking, especially now that she is pregnant. I can't help but feel a swelling of pride in my chest at the thought of being the father of her baby.

I reach out and brush my thumb lightly over her cheek, the contact sending a forbidden jolt of electricity through me. The feelings pulse between us like an unspoken promise. One that is getting harder to ignore with each passing day.

We look into each other's eyes for what feels like an eternity before finally breaking away, as if remembering why it isn't wise to get too close. We're in a complicated marriage where emotion should take a back seat; I have to remind myself constantly that I'm in control.

Talia gives me a shy smile. I watch her silently from across the room, marveling at how such an angelic creature could be mine.

The atmosphere between us shifts suddenly as our gaze once more meets across the space. This time there is something different in the air. Something that neither one of us dare voice aloud.

Talia shifts uncomfortably in her seat, her gaze sliding away from mine as I sit across the room. I can tell she's nervous.

"What happened?" I ask softly, hoping to understand why she would make such an announcement without my permission or consent.

"It's just what Daisy said about you on the beach." Talia

takes another deep breath before explaining nervously, "She was saying all these horrible things about you. How you were too controlling, how you didn't care about my feelings. I just wanted to defend you. I wanted to tell her that what she was saying wasn't true." She pauses for a moment before adding softly, "Telling her that I was pregnant just popped out of my mouth."

I nod slowly in understanding as tears well up in Talia's eyes. I know she must be feeling scared and embarrassed by her lapse in judgment, but I'm also proud that she was willing to stand up for me. Even if it was done impulsively, I'm still blown away by her defense of me.

Reaching out my hand to hers, I give her fingers a gentle squeeze and utter the words earnestly.

"Thank you for being so brave. You don't need to apologize; you only did what any loyal wife would do."

She blushes and demurs. "I think any decent person would do the same thing."

"I don't think so, darling girl." I give her a long look. "Talia, I know I've been hard on you. I didn't expect to be married so suddenly and under these circumstances. But I want you to know that I'm trying. I'm trying to be an adequate husband." I can't help but look away, sliding my gaze to the horizon in the distance. It's uncomfortable being so exposed, even with a woman that I've spent nearly every waking hour near.

"I understand, Dare. I really do. You don't have to explain if you don't want to."

God, Talia is killing me right now. I catch her hand and kiss her palm. Then I nod, feeling my heart aching at her words. I can't believe I'm starting to depend on Talia so much, but I can't deny the feeling of connection that seems to grow every fucking day I spend with her.

I constantly question whether it's a good idea to be so deeply emotionally involved with this woman. And yet, I can't seem to help myself.

We sit in silence for a few moments, both lost in our own thoughts. Finally, I break the silence by asking hesitantly, "Talia... Why did you tell Daisy about the baby?"

She looks up at me with a guilty expression on her face, and I can almost see her thinking of all the reasons why she shouldn't have blurted out such sensitive information. Taking a deep breath, she answers slowly, "I guess it was just... the pressure of knowing that everyone would find out eventually. And what if... what if something were to happen to the baby?"

Her voice cracks as she says the last word. My heart swells with an overwhelming feeling of protectiveness. It's like something inside of me is pushing me to cocoon Talia from the world. I need to make sure no one takes advantage of her vulnerable state. With great effort, I suppress this instinct and instead reach out and lay my hand gently on hers.

"It's okay," I murmur softly. "Nothing is going to happen to him."

She blots at her eyes discreetly.

"What if it does, though? What... what will happen to our marriage then?"

I touch her knee and look deep into her eyes. "You're asking for answers that I don't have. I can't predict the future. But instead of worrying about all of the worst case scenarios, let's cross that bridge if we come to it. Can we agree on that?"

She blows out a breath and rolls her eyes at herself, shaking her head. "Of course. I just can't seem to help cata-strophizing everything."

"We're quite a pair. You're busy looking back at the past, worried about how everything will turn out in the future. And I'm only able to look at the future, never dwelling on the past. I'm forever on the lookout for the next gamble that I can make that will lead to vast fortunes."

"Hah!" Talia gives a small snort of laughter and shrugs a shoulder. "Well, so far as the baby goes, I'm afraid the cat is out of the bag now. I blurted the truth out when I was fighting with Daisy. So now I just have to prepare myself for everyone else to freak out about it."

Talia's admission hangs heavy in the air between us, as if it were a physical presence that neither of us want to acknowledge. The only sound is the ticking of a nearby clock and the distant rumble of traffic outside.

Finally, I speak up, "Well, there's no going back now. We just have to prepare ourselves for everyone else to freak out about it."

Talia nods her head in agreement and takes a deep breath. "Yeah... I know. We should probably let Remy and your father know first before anyone else finds out."

I nod in agreement, though I'm feeling apprehensive about how our families will react to the news. Talia must sense my unease because she gives me an encouraging smile.

"It's going to be okay," she assures me.

We spend the next few minutes discussing who we'll tell first and when would be the best time for that conversation. Soon enough we come up with a plan and I feel a bit more confident that we can make it through this announcement unscathed.

But once word gets out that Talia is pregnant, there's no telling how people will react or what kind of gossip will start circulating around town. People are notoriously nosy when it comes to other people's business and something like this is sure to set tongues wagging . The gossip could lead to serious consequences for our relationship and our unborn child if handled improperly.

Talia smiles gratefully, squeezing my hand in response before leaning into my shoulder and burying her face into it. I wrap an arm around her comfortingly and pull her closer, letting her draw strength from me as needed. We sit like this for a while longer until Talia finally pulls away and stands up abruptly.

"I'm dying of hunger all of a sudden," she announces.

I readily agree, my stomach grumbling at the thought of food. We make our way to the top deck, where a table is set with a gourmet meal prepared by the yacht's chef.

We sit down and as I tuck into my salmon and grilled vegetables, Talia watches me with amusement. She seems content just to enjoy the moment and not push me further on the topic of her pregnancy.

As conversation flows between us - ranging from topics such as books to music - I casually mention my mother, who loved the sea and often took me sailing when I was young.

"That sounds like it must have been really special," she says softly with a small smile.

I nod in agreement, feeling suddenly nostalgic for those trips that seemed so far away now.

"It was," I reply. "We'd take the boat out for days at a time and just enjoy being on the water together. It was the only place where I felt completely relaxed."

I can sense a newfound respect and understanding towards me from her as she listens intently while I regale her with tales of my childhood days spent sailing with my mother.

By the time dessert comes around, a rich cheesecake with

cream topping, I'm looking at Talia like she is going to be my nightcap. She looks beautiful in the soft light of the setting sun; her eyes sparkling and her lips curved into a gentle smile. Her smell is sweet and natural, her perfume light and airy. Her body smells of the sea, and fresh flowers. Her hair smells like vanilla, her skin is soft and warm.

As the night wears on, I request for a white-uniformed yacht steward to set up a classic movie in the yacht's home theater. The steward has almost every movie available, but I already know just what I want to watch.

"North By Northwest," I tell the young man. Turning to Talia, I arch a brow. "Have you seen it?"

She frowns, thinking. "Isn't it an old movie?"

"It was made by Alfred Hitchcock in the nineteen fifties. It stars Cary Grant as an ad exec who is mistaken for a spy and hunted by foreign operatives. You'll love it."

Her lips twitch. "I'm sure I will. I don't really watch many movies."

I smirk. "I'll introduce you to all the classics. You'll have plenty of downtime to catch up on movies before the baby comes."

She doesn't reply to that but her eyebrows arch ever so slightly, as if asking me silently, "will I?"

The young steward sets up the projector and dims the lights. I settle into my seat with a bowl of popcorn. Talia sits next to me, her gaze fixed on the screen as the opening credits roll. As the movie plays, Talia leans her head against my arm and I instinctively wrap mine around her. She softly relaxes against my chest, our hands entwined in one another. A moment of bliss washes over us, one I am desperate to hold onto for a little longer.

We watch in comfortable silence, only speaking up when we find something particularly amusing or captivating. It's so effortless to talk to her like this; no tension or hostilities between us.

Talia grins from ear to ear as the credits roll, her eyes dancing with delight. "That was amazing!" she exclaims, still snuggled up against my chest.

I chuckle at her enthusiasm. "I'm glad you liked it."

She looks up at me with a mischievous glint in her eyes. "Now I want to see more movies like this one! What other classics do you recommend?"

"I'll make you a list," I promise.

The movie leaves us both in a musing, dreamy state. As the credits roll, I absentmindedly stroke Talia's hair and say nothing. She is still snuggled up against my chest like a contented cat and I don't want to disturb her.

But then she begins to speak, her voice soft and reflective. "When I was little, my Aunt Minnie used to take me out on special days every month," she says with a hint of nostalgia in her voice. "We go out for lunch or dinner at some of the best spots around town—she always knows where the best food is."

I smile softly at Talia, glad that she is willing to share such personal memories with me.

"Aunt Minnie has an impeccable taste for culture and literature," Talia continues. "When I was younger, we would spend hours in bookstores or art galleries. We would talk about life and explore whatever new pieces of art piqued our interest. It was lovely."

My heart warmed at this image of Talia's childhood spent in such blissful pursuits. Her aunt clearly had done a good job in trying to make up for what Talia lacked from her parents' absence. It explained why she had an appreciation for helping the less fortunate, too.

I squeeze her hand gently as if to show my understanding

and support of what she is recounting to me. We sit together in peaceful silence until Talia finally pulls away from me with a yawn, ready for bed.

After the movie, we stumble into the yacht's bedroom, its plush silk sheets cool against our skin. As we make love, I can't help but feel that we're both doing a lot more than going through the motions.

But does Talia feel the same way? Or is it still fake to her?

When she rides my cock, it seems so fucking real. The way she leans back, arching her back, looking like a fucking goddess. Her hand touches her clit while I thrust up into her tight heat again and again, eventually making her come so hard that she screams my name.

I roar as I thrust my cock into her pussy a final time, filling every last fucking inch of the slit between her thighs with my hot, sticky cum. Marking her, making her mine.

All fucking mine.

I won't allow myself to feel anything more for Talia, even though she carries my child. It's all a sham, a game I'm playing to win approval from my family. I remind myself not to get attached to her, not to let my guard down.

Laying beside her, I watch her breathe in and out. The tug on my heartstrings can't be denied; a connection that could deepen over time. I know it's not what she hoped for, but maybe there is a hint of affection growing between us. I know that I don't love her the way she always dreamed of being loved, but...

Maybe.

Maybe something can live here, some small buds can begin to bloom.

But is it insane to think that I could cultivate a real intimacy with Talia?

I can feel the warmth radiating off of Talia as she drifts off to sleep in my arms. I know that if this arrangement were real, I could easily fall in love with her. But there is no point in getting my hopes up; this is a sham. This entire thing was forced upon us, and we both have our own agendas to fulfill.

But something inside me still wonders what it would be like if we did let ourselves feel something for each other. Before I can think about it any further, Talia's small voice speaks up from the darkness.

"Do you ever think we will fall in love?" she whispers softly, her voice heavy with exhaustion and emotion.

My heart flutters in my chest and I force myself to hide it from her, not wanting to give her any false hope.

"Let's keep our expectations low," I murmur into her hair, squeezing her gently against me. I'm bluffing, opening my mouth and letting a lie float out. "But that doesn't mean I'll ever let you go, darling girl. You're mine now."

"Hmm," she murmurs, too tired to open her eyes. She manages a barely there, "I guess so."

We settle into each other's embrace, tangled in a complex web of suspicion and attraction, our unknown fate looming heavily over us like a storm cloud on the horizon. I wonder if this strange connection between us will survive the night or fade away once morning light returns to our lives again.

Chapter Twenty-Two

TALIA

The sun is setting over Harwicke as we pull into town. I take a deep breath as the familiar sights of my hometown come into view. Even after what felt like a lifetime away, Harwicke feels just as homey and comforting as it ever did.

Dare's hand finds mine, his grip reassuringly strong. We both know our honeymoon is officially over and soon we will be entering a world of obligations and expectations that are so vastly different from what we experienced this past week.

I glance sidelong at Dare, who looks just as somber as me in the fading light. We haven't spoken about what this means for us—but that doesn't mean that I don't know what he's thinking; after all, we managed to build an unlikely connection over the past week that I don't think either of us expected.

We drive up the long driveway to Blythe Manor in silence, Dare's grip on my hand never loosening. As soon as the car stops, he turns towards me with an intent look on his face. His eyes search mine intently before he finally speaks up.

"Talia," He says softly, "I know it was never meant to be real between us, but..." he pauses and takes a deep breath before continuing "That doesn't mean there can't be something here."

I swallow thickly, my heart pounding in my chest and fear threatening to overwhelm me. What if I'm wishing for something that can never truly exist?

Taking a risk and hoping for the best, I reach out to touch his cheek hesitantly with my free hand. The warmth radiating from him also fills me with courage and hope and I force myself to keep looking into his eyes even though my cheeks are flushing red.

"Maybe," I whisper out loud before pulling away slightly to break the intensity of our gaze. I can't quite bring myself to say the words out loud, but Dare seems to understand me nonetheless. His hand gives mine a reassuring squeeze before he steps out of the car.

I follow his lead, stepping out of the car and hearing the chauffeur's low murmur of greeting. I can still feel Dare's hand around mine, but I don't have time to react as he leads me towards the front door of the manor. The house is gorgeous, like something out of a fairy tale. It has a sprawling front lawn that looks like it hasn't been cut in decades. The house itself is ivy-covered, the bricks a pale shade of red, the shutters and trim a faded white.

The estate is a sprawling, palatial mansion with a horseshoe staircase leading up to a multi-story glass atrium. The stairs and surrounding landings have wrought iron railings. The mansion is surrounded with a white picket fence and the front door is surrounded by a few stone statues of Greek Gods.

We enter the Morgan estate, and I can hardly keep my hands from trembling. I force myself to remember the bodyguards Frick and Frack are just behind us, that Dare is here with me, looking out for me. But it's hard to shake off the memories of the last time I was here—when Burn cornered me in a secret passageway and tried to kill me.

My heart is pounding as we make our way deeper into the manor. Here, everything is clean and fresh and new, from the hardwood floors to the bold modern sculptures. I hesitate as we approach the entrance. "What's wrong?" Dare asked. "I don't know if I can go inside that house," I reply, my voice barely audible. He smiles and it chills me to the bone. It reminds me of the glint of a dagger just before it slashes and stabs. "I dare someone to fuck with you tonight. I hope Burn pulls some shit so I can beat the fuck out of him in front of Remy and the rest of the clan." He catches my hand, kisses my palm, and then starts pulling me toward the house with an almost manic cheer. "Come on, darling girl, let's go."

Dare does not let go of me as we make our way up the stairs, and I'm not about to stop him. We enter the house and are immediately immersed in a large number of people, all dressed in immaculate suits and little black dresses. It is, after all, a cocktail party.

People are dancing slowly and swaying under twinkling lights. Black, white, and gray is standard, but an occasional color highlights a woman's dress or a man's tie. Men and women stand in small groups, laughing and chatting with each other. They drink from glasses of ice water and hold trays of appetizers, like sushi, proffered on white china plates.

I smell expensive perfume and cologne wafting from the crowd, the sweet floral notes of scents mingling together in a fog of alcohol and excess. Eau de cologne and perfume, leather and alcohol, and sweat.

It's impossible to escape the pounding rhythm of drum

and bass filling the air as people sway along to the music. The babble of hundreds of voices permeates the air.

"Here we go," Dare says softly, gesturing for me to walk ahead of him through the well-dressed crowd of people. I take a deep breath before beginning my descent into the unknown darkness below us.

We make our way through the crowd and enter a larger, more formal room. I gasp in awe as I take in the ornate décor that surrounds us. Velvet drapes hang from the walls and dyed silk pillows are scattered on plush couches. I notice a few of Remy Morgan's billionaire cronies are here, along with the entire extended Morgan family. I see Burn, Daisy, and Dare's father, Tripp. The only person missing is Dare's uncle Felix.

No doubt he's skulking in the shadows somewhere just out of sight.

The room suddenly falls silent as Remy makes his entrance. He is an elderly man, white-haired and wearing a tuxedo. He has the same piercing blue eyes as my husband and uses them to skewer people. People duck out of his way as he cuts a tunnel into the room, unperturbed by the sudden hush that has fallen upon the partygoers.

Remy soon walks right up to us. "The prodigal son returns. The last I heard, you were spending your honeymoon down at St. Barts."

"Happy Birthday, old man." Dare says, ignoring Remy's taunts. He pats Remy on the arm and then slides his hand around my waist.

Remy pins me with his icy gaze. He puckers his lips and I'm sure that he's about to say something about my pregnancy. But then he just flicks me a smile and turns away to greet someone else who has just arrived at the party.

"Remy! How are you this fine evening?" Burn shakes

Remy's hand with both of his, pasting on the fakest smile I've ever seen.

Burn is suave and charming as usual but I notice a hint of malice behind each word he speaks to Remy. It causes Dare's grip on my arm to tighten almost imperceptibly, like warning me not to trust this guy one bit.

Like I need Dare to remind me of that, I think.

As they exchange words it almost feels like they're on opposite ends of a battlefield - both trying desperately not to let their anger show while maintaining their composure and dignity in front of everyone else attending the party.

Dare whispers in my ear as we watch them cautiously size each other up: "I dare him to fuck with me tonight." His words send a shiver down my spine - I can sense the raw intensity beneath them. Smoothing down my black silk dress, I turn my face upward to him for a kiss. Dare gives me a peck on the lips, his eyes never leaving his brother.

Damn, that usually works as a good distraction.

That's when Remy starts moving. He floats through the room and a ripple of people move back to get out of his way. He's wearing a cruel smile.

He looks like a walking corpse, but he's surprisingly agile for someone in his eighties. His skin is wrinkled and looks like crumpled paper. His lips are dried and cracked, making it look like he hasn't had water in days.

His white hair is thinning from the top; his blue eyes are half-lidded, looking at me through a layer of cataracts.

I'm not fooled for a second by his appearance, though. I know there is a dangerous predator underneath the cardigans and the thick horn-rimmed glasses. He's one of the calculating men I've ever met, with a knack for sniffing out opportunities and exploiting them to his advantage.

I can see the calculating gleam in Remy's eye as he sees

Dare and Burn. They're pieces on a chessboard to him, and each of his moves is carefully thought out. Not to mention his venomous speech is as toxic as a superfund site.

One of Remy's cronies strolls into his path and shakes his hand. Remy's friend is plump and bald, dressed in a jacket with tails and a pair of matching slacks. He throws his arm around Remy and wheezes into his face. I can smell the booze on his breath from way over here.

I can feel the tension leak away from Dare's body as he sees his grandfather turn away. It makes me wonder if Dare even realizes how Remy affects him. It's not a positive relationship, that's for sure.

"Hey." I kiss Dare on the cheek, drawing his attention away from Remy. "I'm here with you. Okay?"

His lips turn upward at the corners and something sparkles in his eyes. He brings my hand up to his mouth and kisses my palm. "I know, darling girl."

But I only have his attention for a moment longer, because Tristen elbows his way through the crowd toward us. He looks as debonaire as always, his designer tux stylish, his rakish blonde locks swept carefully back. Tristen approaches with a swagger, his eyes taking in the scene.

Dare stands tall, pushing back his shoulders. "Tristen. What are you doing here?"

"Hey," Tristen greets Dare casually. "I thought I would come and see the newlyweds. It looks like your honeymoon was good." His eyes slide away to take in the room full of people, a smug smirk on his face.

"It was... eventful," Dare replies. "I don't want to get into it here."

Tristen shrugs, looking around the room again. "I'll just enjoy your grandfather's hospitality, then." His eyes finally land on me. "Talia," he intones. "You look well. I guess ten days of sex on the beach was good for you. I know Dare seemed excited by the prospect."

He turns to Dare and claps him on the shoulder before focusing on me again. His smirk is still in place as our gazes lock. I have to fight to keep my expression neutral as I remember how Tristen had helped Dare trick me into accepting his proposal of marriage only a few months ago.

My expression turns stony and I take a step back from Tristen. "You know, I was actually on my best behavior at our wedding," I remark coolly. "Considering what you did to me, I think it's amazing that I didn't make a scene."

Tristen's smirk fades away and his eyes widen as he takes in my serious expression. He takes a step back, looking almost guilty. "I'm sorry," he mutters. "I didn't mean..."

I cut him off. "You didn't mean to lie to me? You didn't mean to trick me into saying yes? You didn't mean to scare my Aunt Minnie half to death and cause thousands of dollars of damage to her bookstore?"

Tristen blinks. "Err... I guess I did. But I didn't think you would hold a grudge."

I tense up, so mad I could spit poison at the buffoonish man. Dare touches my shoulder, trying to hold me back.

"You two can hash things out later," Dare hisses, taking another protective step closer to me. "Now isn't the time or the place."

I glare at Tristen. Tristen bobs his head curtly and takes the hint. He steps away, blushing slightly. For a moment, I feel almost sorry for him; it looks like no one has ever called him out for his behavior before. But then I remember how he tricked me into accepting Dare's marriage proposal and all sympathy disappears.

He turns and disappears into the crowd without another word. Dare watches him go with an unreadable expression.

Once Tristen is gone, Dare turns back to me with a cool smile on his face.

"Let's just get through this party," he suggests. I lift a shoulder at his suggestion, my mouth pulling into a tight line.

I bite my lip, watching as Dare's grandfather Remy hobbles around the party, growling at people and spewing his hateful opinions. Every time he spouts off about something, I feel a wave of nausea wash over me. Dare is obviously very well-respected in this world that his family lives in, and yet he still seems so oblivious to how toxic Remy is.

I turn to face him, my heart pounding with anger and frustration. "Why can't you see how corrosive your grandfather is?" I say softly. "Do you not realize what kind of person he is? He's poisoning everything around him."

Dare blinks at me, taken aback by my outburst. He takes a step back and then shakes his head slightly.

"Talia," he says softly, reaching out to touch my arm lightly. "I understand why you're upset—but there's nothing I can do about it right now." He pauses for a moment, looking at the crowd of rich businessmen before continuing quietly. "This party represents their world; when we are here, we will just have to deal with it."

My mouth drops open as I stare at him incredulously. Deal with it? As if it's our burden to bear? The thought fills me with rage and indignation, but I swallow it down and take a deep breath to calm myself down.

I remember all too clearly the extensive makeover and etiquette lessons I had to endure in order to fit in here and pretend to be a part of this elite class of people. It's disgusting that I had to change in order to look like I belong standing next to Dare, and yet I wouldn't want to undo any of it. That would be like holding up a sign that screams, 'Pay Attention To My Differences'.

No thanks.

Looking away from Dare, I focus on the crowd of rich people who are laughing and having the time of their lives while all around them normal people are struggling just to make ends meet. They act like they own everything and everyone they see—and worse, it seems like no one even bats an eye when they do it! It makes me want to scream in frustration..

"How am I supposed to 'deal with it'?" I finally manage to ask through gritted teeth. Dare sighs before pulling me into his arms for a hug. He holds me tightly for a moment before speaking again, this time more sternly than before. "I know it's not easy, Talia, but we have to play their game if we want to survive in this world. I can protect you from Remy, but I can't change his beliefs or the way he acts. And as for the rest of them," he gestures towards the partygoers around us, "I can't fight every paper tiger for you. I have to focus on the battles in front of me."

His arm around my waist tightens and he pulls me closer for a second. But I resist the embrace.

Just because Dare is brainwashed doesn't mean I have to fall into line with all this elite nonsense.

A silky voice comes from just behind me.

"You're looking well, Talia."

I jump and spin, clutching at my chest. Burn smirks at me, seeming to enjoy my panic. My heart hammers against my chest and I go into full fight or flight mode. Luckily, Dare is right beside me, pushing me behind his big body.

"Don't talk to her," he grits out.

"Dare," Burn finally speaks up, his voice strained. "You

can't keep me from talking to her. We both know I didn't do anything wrong, I just...misunderstood."

I snort in disbelief and Dare's arm tightens around my waist as if to remind me that he is still here.

"She's clearly not misunderstanding," Dare says tersely. "She knows exactly what's going on here, and she knows you're a part of it." His voice is cold and firm but it carries an unmistakable undercurrent of anger.

Burn stares at us for a few moments before finally letting out an exasperated sigh. "Fine," he mutters under his breath before turning away from us.

Dare pulls me closer and I feel his rage radiating off him like heat from a fire. He might be trying to contain himself, but his emotions are so palpable I can almost taste them on the air.

But he does not move against his twin brother in any way; he only stands there with me tucked securely against him, silently defending my honor without resorting to violence or even raised voices. It's a stark contrast from the way Remy had treated me earlier and it makes my heart swell with admiration for Dare in spite of all the anger I'm feeling towards him right now.

It takes several long moments of silence before Dare finally speaks up again, this time with a calmer tone: "Burn, why don't you piss off? Unless you want Talia to start telling everybody here that you tried to assault her?"

Burn turns red and shoots me a glare. "This isn't over," he says through clenched teeth.

"It's over when I say it's over," Dare spits back.

Burn grimaces and turns away, heading through the party. My husband's grip on me loosens slightly but doesn't disappear entirely; the comfort of his embrace remains even as he sends his twin away with a polite request instead of an order or threat.

We mill around for a while, talking to wealthy party guests whenever they come up to congratulate us on our recent nuptials. While this is a slightly different set of wealthy people from our wedding guests, word has certainly gotten around about the lavish affair. My feet begin to ache and I start to regret my choice of stiletto high heels. They look great, but they are murder on my legs and back.

"There's Felix," Dare whispers into my ear. "Come on. I want to talk to him."

I compress my lips into a thin line and follow Dare's lead. He sidles up to Felix, who is just coming from one of the party's bars with a fresh cocktail.

"There you are!" Felix crowds when he locks his gaze on Dare. ""It's good to see you. How have you been?"

"Good," Dare replies, still tense from the confrontation with his brother earlier.

"I've got some good news from the state," Felix continues, his gaze flicking briefly over to me before returning to Dare. "My lobbying and legal efforts paid off; your project of offshore drilling off the coast of Maine is finally going to move forward."

Dare grins widely and claps Felix on the shoulder. "That's great! We can start construction soon then."

Felix nods and offers an encouraging smile in response. "Let's get down to business then, shall we? We need to start making plans." He turns back to Dare and fixes him with an intense gaze.

At first I think he's just addressing Dare, but then he adds "Ditch the wife and let's get down to business." There it is again; that term 'wife' being thrown around like I'm nothing more than an accessory or burden.

But I don't get angry at Felix like I did Remy earlier; instead I feel a swell of pride as Dare stands up for me without hesitating for even a second: "No, she can hear anything you need to say now," he responds firmly. "We're married."

Felix's expression softens slightly and he gives me a small nod of acknowledgement before addressing us both again.

"Very well," he says. "Let's talk about our next steps then."

He launches into a detailed description of the plans for offshore drilling in Maine, leaving Dare and me both thoroughly informed on every aspect of the project by the end of our discussion.

The conversation between Dare and Felix quickly turns to the project's finances. Felix is telling us that they will need a huge cash infusion for the next steps of the plan, when he suddenly stops mid-sentence.

He looks from Dare to me before saying in a low voice: "There is another way, but it's not exactly legal."

My heart sinks as I realize what Felix is suggesting - he's implying that Dare should consider killing his billionaire grandfather Remy for the inheritance money. It's a suggestion so extreme and shocking that I can barely comprehend it.

But before I have time to respond, Dare quickly interjects with a firm "No. That's out of the question." His tone leaves no room for argument; it's clear that there will be no discussion on this topic.

I'm relieved by Dare's decisive response, but also alarmed; what is it with Morgan men and their willingness to kill someone just to get ahead? It fills me with disgust, and I realize that we need to leave this situation immediately.

Taking advantage of the tense atmosphere, I pretend to feel faint and put my hand on Dare's arm. He notices right away and quickly moves away from Felix, ushering me away from the conversation.

Once we're out of earshot, he takes my hand and squeezes it tightly, reminding me of his love without saying a word. We make our way through the crowd towards the exit, thankful to have escaped this uncomfortable situation unscathed.

This party is really draining my remaining will to live. "How long do we have to stay?"

Dare looks at me, his shrewd gaze appraising me. "Not too much longer. Remy is notorious for leaving parties early, so we only have to stay until--"

"Dare!" Daisy calls, raising her arm and waving like he's a long lost friend. "There you are. I was hoping I would see you here!"

Dare takes a step back and he clutches my hand. His jaw tenses.

"It's Remy's birthday. Where else would we be?" I scoff.

Daisy's eyes narrow on my face as she sidles up to us. "I don't know. I thought perhaps you would be sidelined by your delicate state, Talia. I'm referring to your pregn--"

"Daisy!" Dare growls. "That's enough."

Daisy makes a scornful sound and rolls her eyes, putting a hand on her hip. "Talia gave that information away. There's no use in trying to safeguard it now."

The tension between Dare and Daisy is palpable, and I can feel my skin prickle with nervous energy. Dare keeps his stance steady, standing feet apart and his arms crossed over his chest in a defensive posture. His gaze is intense as he stares at Daisy.

He fixes Daisy with a piercing look, his voice loaded with menace. "I can't believe I wanted to marry you. What a waste of my life that would have been."

Daisy shifts uncomfortably under his gaze, her cheeks blazing pink. She looks as though she wants to lash out but she knows that won't do any good; Dare isn't the type of person to be intimidated by anyone.

Finally, breaking the silence, she speaks up. "What exactly are you implying?"

Her voice is shrill and her face is full of indignation. But Dare doesn't back down.

"I can't believe that you had me fooled. And I'm wondering if our relationship was ever real to you," he replies calmly but firmly. "Or were you just manipulating me the whole time we were together? Was every moment scripted for your own gain?"

His words are like a slap in the face for Daisy and I can tell that she's getting more and more angry by the second. She opens her mouth to speak but then quickly shuts it again as Dare glares at her with no signs of relenting.

"You are just mad because I ended up with the good brother. And you ended up with--"

"I dare you to finish that sentence," he spits. "Let's see if Burn is the only one who can strangle women in this house."

Her eyes widen, either from the threat or because that's not the version of the story of my assault that Burn fed her. Finally, fed up with Dare's accusations, Daisy takes a deep breath and stomps her foot before turning on her heel and stalking away from us. We both watch silently as she disappears into the crowd of people, leaving us alone in an awkward silence.

"We really should just leave," I whisper in Dare's ear. "Before we have another run-in with your father or grandfather."

He grits his teeth. "No. We have to play along." I bob my

head, shifting from one foot to another. Thinking to myself that it can't be much longer now.

The room falls silent as Remy clinks a knife against a champagne flute, calling for attention. "Friends, family..." He raises his glass. "I want to make a toast."

Remy stands in the center of the room, champagne flute in hand and his voice full of emotion. "Many of you know that my son Dare has a bit of a reputation around here. He's known as a complete bastard and a bit of a skirt-chaser."

I can feel my heart start to beat faster in my chest. I look nervously between Remy and Dare, while the rest of us just stand there, unsure of what is going to happen next.

Remy clears his throat and continues: "It is a pleasurable surprise then, that I have come to find out that my grandson has impregnated his new wife. I challenged both grandsons to marry and have children... and Dare seems to have risen to that challenge. I always suspected that Dare was a limp-dick sack of shit like my son Tripp. But perhaps I have been proven wrong."

Dare's face turns red with humiliation and anger as Remy continues. "I toast the union of my grandson and his new bride, Talia." He raises his glass and everyone else follows suit, raising their glasses to us.

Dare mumbles something under his breath but I can't make it out. We all wait for him to speak, trying not to be too uncomfortable. Finally, Dare manages to speak through gritted teeth.

"Thank you," he says stiffly. "Your words mean a lot to me." We all take a sip of our drinks in unison and the tension in the room begins to dissipate.

But then, Remy clears his throat again and turns towards me. "I must admit that when I first heard that you two were married, I was skeptical." He gives me a pointed look before continuing. "But you have proven yourself worthy of my grandson's affections."

I blush red as a beet, but I hold my head high despite the scrutiny I am receiving from Dare's grandfather. I can sense the hurt in my husband's eyes from Remy's words and I want to do something to make him feel better. So I take Dare's hand in my own and look into his eyes with love and admiration before turning back towards Remy.

"I may not come from a prestigious family like yours, but I love Dare more than anything else in this world." I pause for effect before continuing. "I'm proud of everything we've accomplished together - marrying each other despite our different backgrounds; proving those who tried to keep us apart wrong; building an amazing life together."

Remy's mouth pinches slightly at my words before he finally nods begrudgingly. It's more dismissive of me than it is an acceptance of Dare and I getting married and having a baby. I know that, but it still feels like a kind of victory to me.

After Remy's toast, I finally manage to drag Dare away from the estate and into the waiting SUV that will take us home. He settles in the back seat with a grumble. But when I put my head on his shoulder and intertwine my fingers with his, he runs his fingers through my hair and makes the quietest sigh of satisfaction.

Not a word is said on the car ride home. But I feel like I've figured out something vital. If I can make Dare happy enough when we are alone, it makes up for his family being a mess. Maybe if I can try to charm and enchant him, we can someday be free of the Morgans forever.

Chapter Twenty-Three

TALIA

I'm hurrying through the grocery store, trying to hunt for the exact brand of ramen I've been craving all day. In my mind's eye, I can see it. A yellow and orange packet with some Japanese writing down the right side. Frick and Frack are behind me, purposely giving me room to breathe. I have been cranky all day, so I appreciate it.

"Are you pregnant?"

When I hear the question, a chill slides down my spine. I turn around and see a woman in her thirties pointing at my stomach, as if I needed her to highlight my baby bump.

I give her a wry smile. "I am."

"Congrats!" She beams at me, then her expression sobers as she looks at the cheap ramen packets I'm holding. "You shouldn't have salty foods. Too much salt in your diet will basically pickle your baby."

"Are you taking over as my obstetrician?" I ask.

The woman's face colors. "Uh... no."

"Oh! That's good. I thought that you were trying to tell me what I should eat because you were going to take my actual doctor's place. But since you're not, and since I'm a complete stranger that you've never seen before, I think it would be in your best interest to stop giving out advice."

The woman's jaw drops. "I... I'm sorry?"

She turns and scurries away. I scowl after her as I take one of the packets off the shelf and head to the cash register. Frick and Frack are both pointedly avoiding my glare.

That's good, because I'm not looking for any more unsolicited input on my pregnancy.

I am five and a half months pregnant. When I go out shopping, I can feel the stares from passersby as I walk down the street. At the cash register in fancy stores, older women come up to me and tell me about the latest craze in pregnancy advice. What to eat, how much to exercise, what rituals will supposedly determine the sex or intelligence of my baby.

I'm overwhelmed. It's exhausting hearing all this unsolicited advice and it makes me feel like a broodmare - like all people see when they look at me as just a vessel for their opinions and expectations.

But despite all that, there's something else, too - a deep satisfaction in knowing that Dare and I are making this incredible life together. That there is something growing inside of me that we both created with love.

That thought keeps me going when times get tough and helps sustain my patience with all the intrusive comments from strangers. Because at the end of it all, Dare and I are creating something beautiful together for ourselves - our own little family unit with so much potential for a bright future ahead of us.

So despite feeling exhausted from carrying around this growing bump and dealing with endless belly rubs from strangers, I take comfort in the knowledge that Dare will love this baby.

He might not yet, but the second he sees his child, he'll fall for it. Or that's what I like to fantasize about, anyway.

I get a call from a number that I don't recognize one morning while I am leaving a maternity clothing store, bags hanging from both of my arms. It's a struggle to answer the phone but I get it out of my purse and shove it between my face and my shoulder.

"Hello?"

I almost drop my bags and Frack appears, as if summoned. He collects the bags and then hurries me into the SUV idling at the curb.

"Is this Miss Chance?" a strange woman asks. Her voice is high pitched and terse.

I hesitate. Is that the name I go by now? I still haven't decided. Will it be strange to change my name?

"Chance is my maiden name," I say, trying to see if it feels like too much of a lie to claim it. "I go by Mrs. Morgan now."

I prickle runs over my skin as I say the words. They sound nice rolling off my tongue.

"Mrs. Morgan, I'm calling from Our Lady of Penitent Faith Hospital. Minnie Chance has you listed as an emergency contact. She took a spill this morning and has several broken bones."

My heart stops for a second."Oh my god. Oh my god, is she okay?"

"She'll need surgery. But for now, she can go home and rest. She wanted to know if you could pick her up."

Tears spring to my eyes and I squeeze them closed. "Yes! Yes, of course. I'll be right there. Thank you so much for calling."

The woman responds briskly. "We'll let her know."

God, I feel like the worst niece in the world. Aunt Minnie probably hurt herself working in the store while I was out shopping, of all things. If I hadn't totally ignored her requests for help the last time I saw her, she would probably be perfectly fine.

I am so self-absorbed!

It's all I can do to hold it together while I head to the hospital.

Things get frantic for the rest of the day. The next four hours have me picking up a completely loopy Aunt Minnie from the hospital, getting her prescriptions for pain medication, and bringing her into the loft to stay in the spare bedroom.

"I can't stay here," she protests. "I have too much to do at the store!"

"You broke your leg in three places," I counter, tucking her into the guest bed. "You're on so many drugs right now that it would be irresponsible of me to let you leave. You need rest, Aunt Minnie."

Aunt Minnie catches my hand and grips it tightly.

"You're a wonderful person. And..."

"And what?"

"And I have a shipment of books waiting at the front of the bookstore. If they aren't brought inside someone will steal them."

I kiss her knuckles. "Don't worry about that. I'll have someone go to the shop right now."

Aunt Minnie purses her lips. "I don't want just anybody to have keys to my store."

"You don't have a choice. Your leg is broken. I am almost six months pregnant. I promise, I will get the books in the door somehow. And then the rest of the work can be figured out tomorrow."

Aunt Minnie wrinkles her nose. But I can tell that she is tired from her heavy-lidded eyes.

"Okay," she acquiesces. Her eyes slip shut. "I love you, Talia."

I grab her hand in both of mine and kiss it, then I sneak out of the spare bedroom. Calling a temp service, I get a young woman to come pick up the key to the bookshop from the loft and then go wrangle the packages.

Then I arrange to have a nurse come and stay with Aunt Minnie, to be at her beck and call.

Dare arrives home late that evening, and finds me stressing out in the living room. He takes one look at me and just knows that something is wrong.

"What's going on?" he asks. I hope he doesn't notice the worry lines that I'm afraid are etched on my face.

I explain what happened with Aunt Minnie and how I had arranged for a nurse to stay with her while she recovers. Dare listens silently, wrapping me in his strong embrace when I finish the story.

"I'm sure your aunt appreciates what you've done," he murmurs. He wraps me in a hug. "You look exhausted, though. Maybe you should lie down for a bit."

"I'm fine."

"Maybe you are, but what about the baby?" He slides his hand over my belly and looks down, a groove of worry appearing between his eyebrows. "I think I'm going to pull the 'Expectant Parent Card' and insist that you close your eyes for twenty minutes."

I try to shrug it off, but there's no denying the truth in his words. "I am a little tired."

He scoops me up in his arms and carries me to bed without another word. He lies down beside me and I curl up against his chest.

This feels so good. Being with him like this feels like a kind of completion that I've rarely felt in my life.

It's peaceful, where outside this room is so chaotic.

We lay there, quiet in the darkness. Dare's steady heartbeat lulls me into a trance-like state, and I feel all the stress of the day slowly melting away.

"Why do you feel the need to bend over backward for your aunt?" he asks.

I look at him and his brow is furrowed in confusion.

"What? What do you mean? She is the only family I've got."

Dare arches a brow. "No offense, but that doesn't really mean anything to me. You've met my family. They are all bastards. I wouldn't do nearly as much for them."

A startled laugh escapes me.

"Why do I feel like I owe Minnie so much?" I ask myself quietly, an intense feeling of guilt and admiration tugging at my heartstrings.

He looks at me intently, waiting for me to continue. Taking a deep breath, I tell him about the day my mother dropped me off at Hope House when I was six years old.

"I can't ever quite understand why she did it," I say sadly. "But looking back now, I think she must have been scared and desperate to give me a better life."

"That's when Minnie stepped in," I continue. "She took me in with an open embrace and offered me more stability than anyone else ever could have before or since. She wasn't a perfect parent. She is still terrible with money and impulsive about signing business deals with sketchy people. But she was there for me when I needed her. She put a roof over my head and food in my mouth. I can never, ever repay that kindness and generosity."

"I don't really see Aunt Minnie demanding that you repay

her. She loves you."

I take a deep breath, feeling tears pressing at the corners of my eyes.

"That doesn't make us even. My mom dropped me off at Hope House when I was six years old. She didn't even call the sister she had in town when she abandoned me. I... I must have been a burden to her."

Tears leak down my face. Dare pulls me against his big body, dropping a kiss against my temple.

"No one could mistake you for a burden, Talia."

"Y-you don't know that. You can't know what my mother felt the day she dropped me off."

He tips my face upward with a finger, his blue gaze piercing me straight through and holding me fast.

"I know. Okay? You're extremely lovable. It's impossible to know you and not to love you."

My eyes widen. Is Dare saying... that he loves me?

Dare seems to realize that he's misspoken. He clears his throat and breaks eye contact.

"What I'm trying to say is that you don't owe your aunt a thing... except maybe your own happiness. If my mom were still alive, that's what I think she would say about me."

He tightens his arms around me as if he knows this is what I need right now - just someone to hold onto while all the emotions wash over me like a wave.

I bury my face against his chest, my heart still pounding. His words are still ringing in my ears.

It's impossible to know you and not to love you.

What could that mean?

Somehow, despite my thrumming heart, I can't seem to keep my eyes open. The tiredness coupled with the emotional outburst absolutely does me in. I fall asleep in Dare's arms with his face buried in my hair.

My eyes flutter open, and for a brief moment I'm confused. This bed is too comfortable to be the cot at Hope House. Then I remember - I'm in Dare's bedroom. In Dare's arms.

But now he's gone. His side of the bed is cold and empty. Even the blanket has been thrown off on the floor. He must have left while I was sleeping.

I sit up slowly, feeling my heart sink in disappointment. Was he mad at me? Did he leave because he didn't want to be around me anymore? Or maybe he realized that we had shared an intimate moment and it scared him away.

Gathering up the blanket off the floor, I wrap it around myself and head out of his room in search of Dare or Aunt Minnie. When I step into the living room, I find both of them sitting together on the couch with steaming cups in their hands and a plate of cookies between them.

Aunt Minnie glances over her shoulder when she hears me come in, her face lighting up with a smile when she sees it's me. "Ah, Talia! Come join us. Dare was just telling me about his work."

My stomach does a little flip when I see Dare sitting next to Aunt Minnie on the couch. He looks up at me and gives me a small nod of acknowledgement, but his body language is tense and he doesn't quite meet my gaze.

Seeing him like this, it's hard not to feel a twinge of hurt. Did he regret what happened between us? Did it mean nothing to him?

Clearing his throat, Dare turns back to Aunt Minnie to continue his story about his latest business venture. As he explains the details of the deal and how much money it could possibly make, I can tell that Aunt Minnie is genuinely interested in what he has to say.

But even as Dare talks excitedly about the project, something feels off between us. There's an invisible barrier between us now that wasn't there before - a reminder of our differences in status and wealth that can't be ignored.

I try to listen attentively as Dare talks about the project, but my heart isn't in it. I know that this deal won't change who we both are deep down -I'm still just a girl from Hope House while he's still one of the wealthiest people in town- but it serves as a stark reminder that our worlds are miles apart, and it makes me sad.

After a few more minutes of talking, Dare stands up and declares that he needs to get back to work before the day ends. He says goodbye politely enough, but there's an icy distance in his voice that wasn't there before.

He leaves without any further words or gestures towards me, making my heart sink further into my chest. Obviously whatever happened between us this afternoon was just an emotion-filled moment with no real substance behind it. We're from different worlds and nothing we do will ever change that fact.

Pushing aside the feelings of rejection, I head to the guest bedroom. Aunt Minnie looks up and pats the spot beside her. I walk over to the bed and slump down onto the coverlet, feeling as mopey as a teen girl. Aunt Minnie's gentle voice draws me out of my thoughts and I look up to see her. She scoots over beside me and places her hand on mine in comfort.

"What's wrong Talia?", she says softly.

"Everything!" I say, feeling melodramatic. "My whole life is a wreck right now."

"Is this about Dare?" My heart stops as I hear her words and my eyes widen in shock. I try to look away, but I know it's futile. There is no escape now, so I exhale a deep breath and slowly let out the truth that has been burning inside me.

"I... I care for him," I murmur, my voice trembling with emotion. Tears stream from my eyes like a waterfall as I admit how much I have come to care for Dare - an emotion that defies logic yet infuses every part of me.

"But it's impossible," I wail, conscious of the insurmountable obstacles we face.

Aunt Minnie pulls me into a warm embrace before pushing away slightly and looking directly into my eyes. "Talia, don't be ridiculous! Dare is obviously head-over-heels for you!"

The scoff of ridicule that leaves my lips is unintentional. "He doesn't feel anything for me."

"That's crazy. You know what we chatted about? We talked about your childhood for almost twenty minutes before you came in. He asked me to tell him about when your mother left you with me. No man just casually asks for that kind of information about a woman he doesn't have feelings for. Dare is obsessed with you."

For the first time in weeks, I begin to consider the thought that maybe Aunt Minnie actually has a point after all. Dare does seem preoccupied with me every moment we're together.

I shake my head. "I don't know."

"Well, you should. The fact that you're in love with each other is painfully obvious to everyone but the two of you, I guess."

"How much pain medicine did that nurse give you? You're talking crazy."

I stubbornly hold my ground and tell her once again that I only feel friendship towards him. She just shakes her head before changing the subject back to her latest shipment of books.

Chapter Twenty-Four

DARE

As Aunt Minnie recuperates back home, I take Talia out to the coast. The ocean is a vast expanse of blue, stretching on for miles out towards the horizon. The wind blows waves upon waves of crashing white foam, which leaves the surf smelling fresh and salty. The sun shines brightly over us as we spend hours walking along the shoreline. The light glistens off the horizon and illuminates everything around me. The wind blows in our hair and causes it to fly about in the breeze. The sun burns into the back of my neck and warms my skin, my eyes squint from the light and I stare up into the sky.

The sweat on my skin brings a salty taste to my tongue. The sand is coarse and sharp when it rubs against my bare feet, a stinging feeling that feels like walking on shards of slate.

We spend the rest of the day walking along the shore, taking in the sights and sounds of nature. We talk about our childhoods and things that make us laugh. The sun eventually starts to dip low in the sky, bringing with it a deep orange hue that casts its warmth over us.

Talia takes my hand in hers and smiles up at me. "Thank you for bringing me out here," she says. "I feel so much better when I am away from the noise and the bustle of the city."

I groan, rolling my eyes and shaking my head. "It's for the health of the baby," I grumble in protest.

She giggles and squeezes my hand harder, her thumb caressing my knuckles in a comforting motion.

"I know," she says softly. "It's still nice."

The two of us walk until we find a secluded spot where we can watch the sunset over the horizon. We sit down together, watching as evening slowly creeps in on us and engulfs everything around us in long shadows. Talia leans closer to me and rests her head against my shoulder as we both gaze up at the first few stars and planets over our heads.

It's such a pure moment. All my worries seem to melt away. I'm content with just being here with Talia, enjoying each other's company without any distractions or expectations from either of us.

As we sit there together, I realize that no matter what happens between us in the future, this moment will stay with me forever. This moment of quiet calm is so stark when I consider that the only other people I ever brought to this beach were my brother and Daisy.

Like two little black holes, Burn and Daisy were each consumed by need and complaint, sucking everything around them in, crushing it without thought. But Talia?

Talia just enjoys the sunset without comment. Talia's skin is a warm, creamy ivory, like a pearl kissed by firelight. Her hair is a rich, fiery copper, more red than orange, like the sky itself is on fire.

Talia is as beautiful as the sunset we are watching. She wears a pair of black shorts and a simple white t-shirt that outlines her curves perfectly. She cradles her baby bump with one hand. Her expression is at once both thoughtful and unreadable.

The light of sunset and the clear blue of the sky is perfect, the sun a ball of pure light against the pure blue of the sky. She keeps her hand in mine, seeming to prefer some kind of skin contact with me. But her eyes are turned toward the horizon and her thoughts seem far away.

The sun is setting, painting the sky in a spectrum of fiery red and orange. It's the perfect backdrop for our adventure.

We wander around, hand-in-hand, exploring all that this hidden gem has to offer. At one end of the beach stands an old abandoned lighthouse - we climb up to the top and watch as the sun continues its descent into night.

As twilight fades away, Talia turns to me and smiles softly before saying, "This was worth it just for this moment alone."

We stand there for a few moments more before continuing our exploration around the island under starry skies above us.

The night sky is alive with stars. Sparkling diamonds against a velvety black canvas, they are like a million tiny beacons of hope and possibility.

We sit together at the beach, watching as the stars twinkle above us in the night sky. Talia marvels at the beauty of it all and I can't help but feel a sense of peace.

I take out my sextant and show Talia how to use it to sight stars and calculate our position on the sea. We laugh as we try to identify constellations and guess where we are.

Afterwards, I lay out a blanket for us to share and spread out some finger food that I had brought with me - dates, olives, cheese, cured ham - as we talk about our lives, our dreams and hopes for our future together. The moonlight illuminates our faces as we gaze into each other's eyes under the starry sky above us.

"If we see a falling star, you have to make a wish." Talia gives me a lopsided grin. "I wonder what your wish would be?"

I make a face. "Nothing, probably. I don't really believe in making wishes. Or maybe it's just that nothing I've ever really wished for has come true."

She gives me a surprised look.

That night, we fuck very slowly, forgetting everything else in the world. I slide my hands up her back, exploring her curves as our bodies glide together. We kiss deeply, our tongues tangling as we forget everything else in the world. I can't believe how perfect it feels to be here with her like this.

My hands wander lower and I grip her hips tightly, guiding them against me in a slow rhythm. Talia gasps into my mouth and arches her back, pressing herself against me intimately.

The sensation is exquisite; I can feel every inch of her body making contact with mine. Our movements become more urgent, faster, and soon we're both trembling with need. As the tension builds, I drop my head and bury my face in the crook of her neck for a moment, breathing in her scent and savoring this perfect moment between us. Nothing but bare skin and heated sighs, the press of hot mouths and exultant shouts when we finally come like a cascading avalanche down a mountain.

The next day, we spend most of the day sailing around the island. The gentle rocking of the boat and the salty breeze in our hair lulls us into a peaceful trance-like state. After a few hours, we stop for a swim and then make our way to an isolated beach for lunch.

We spread out the blanket and enjoy a simple meal of

cheese, bread, fresh fruit, and cold drinks. The warm sun beats down on us as we sit in comfortable silence.

After a few minutes, I tentatively break the silence by telling Talia stories from my childhood growing up near the sea. I talk about how my mother loved sailing and taught me all of her tricks for navigating these waters. I tell her about our old sailboat that she named after me, and how she'd take us out every weekend if she could get away with it.

Talia laughs at some of my embarrassing moments, but there are also sad parts, too.

"You know, I've never actually been here. My mother was interred here a year after she died."

She gives me a startled glance. "Really?"

"Yes. I've never been, but I've sailed by the island countless times. It makes me feel... closer to my mother, I guess."

"We should go visit the grave while we are here. Or we can walk to it and you can go alone. Either way."

I shoot her a scornful glare. "Why would I want to do something like that?"

Talia raises her hands. "It was just a suggestion, Dare. No one is going to make you do anything you don't want to do. I just thought it might be nice, since we are on the island."

Heat rises to my face. "Just drop it, Talia."

She looks disappointed at my reaction but doesn't push me any further on it.

As I am helping Talia back on the boat, she passes by an open foot locker that is bolted to the deck. She almost walks right by it, then stops and backs up. I look over her shoulder to see what she's noticed.

She's looking at the two dozen unused children's life vests, still wrapped in sheets of plastic.

"Are you planning on fathering a lot more children than I

anticipated?" she jokes. "If so, we need to have a serious talk."

"No." I give her an amused glance. "The vests are for Outbound Outriggers."

Talia throws up her hands.

"You're saying words that I recognize as English. But I have no idea what they mean and the order that you're saying them in has me stumped."

"It's a project that has been on the back burner for a couple of years. I want to bring a bunch of kids out to the boat."

She looks skeptical. "Where are you going to get these kids from? And what are they going to do once you've got them here?"

"I haven't really figured out the details. But sailing at a young age helped me gain confidence. It wasn't just about learning technical skills. It was also about building character, learning to trust and believe in myself, and connecting with nature."

Her jaw drops. For a moment, Talia is genuinely speechless.

"Are you saying that you would bring at-risk kids onto the boat and teach them life skills?"

My neck heats. "Yeah, sort of."

"You've been thinking about helping others, for no reason other than that you have the resources to do it?"

I scrub a hand through my hair. Her awe makes it seem like she didn't know I ever thought about anything other than how I can make more money. That isn't exactly flattering and I find her astonishment embarrassing.

"Yes."

Talia's face lights up with delight. She tackles me,

hugging me so hard that the breath is knocked from my lungs. I pat her back awkwardly, my face heating.

"Chill out. It's just a vague thought," I say.

Her arms loosen and she straightens.

"You named the organization. You also have started getting the gear you'll need. I would say it's definitely more than a stray thought."

My gaze slides away from her excited face and finds the horizon over her shoulder. I shrug noncommittally.

"Maybe."

Talia presses herself against me and uses two fingers to turn my cheek so that I am looking into her eyes. She stands on her tiptoes and kisses me passionately. I respond to her as I always do, by putting my arms around her waist and kissing her back like she's the only woman in the whole fucking world.

She does this to me every damn time.

When she pulls away, she cups my cheek.

"Remember when I got upset and called you selfish? This is what I needed to hear from you. I wanted to know that you had thoughts about anything other than money."

"Jesus, Talia. I'm as human as you are."

She pushes her fingers through my hair. "I didn't know that. Not for sure."

I press my lips into a tight line. Her words rip at my soft underbelly. Maybe I made a mistake telling her all of this.

"Hey." Talia runs her nails against my scalp. The gentle touch is meant to soothe me. "I'm glad you told me. We're still getting to know each other. I guess I didn't realize that there is still stuff about you left to surprise me."

"I hate that you just assumed that I only care about money."

She cocks her head to the side but continues to speak

gently. "Prove me wrong. You claim to be multifaceted, so show me the other sides you have been hiding." She brushes her fingers over my cheek and traces my cheekbone. "I want to know you, Dare."

Sucking in a breath, I put my hand over hers and kiss her palm.

"I'll try, little wife."

Talia steps back and looks around the boat, her expression thoughtful. I feel like I'm a boat that has sailed through the eye of a hurricane, battered and wind damaged.

"We should invite some of the kids from Hope House out for a sailing trip. It would be a really good way to test out your ideas for Outbound Outriggers." She wiggles her eyebrows, her eyes alight with excitement. "They would be so excited."

The image of Talia helping children navigate the steps of the boat blows away the remnants of our earlier conversation and my mood lifts.

"You think Solana would like it?"

Talia's brow furrows. "It will take a month or so to plan out activities and schedule an actual field trip. I can only hope that Solana isn't still at Hope House by the time we organize this event."

"Oh." My mouth twists. "Yeah, of course."

"But we can visit her!" Talia suggests. "Before her case is settled by the court and she moves on to a more permanent situation."

I bob my head and change the subject. But something about Solana's case sticks in the back of my brain, following me around like a shadow. I can't shake the feeling that something is off about it. Maybe it's just my distrust of the process. Maybe it's something else entirely. Either way, I will make a mental note to check it out later.

Chapter Twenty-Five

DARE

I clear my throat as I enter Gerard's Steakhouse, Remy's favorite restaurant. The décor is dated to the early nineteen hundreds with thick mahogany walls, old world paintings with rich detail, gilded frames with ornate wood carvings and golden trim. The tables are a dark, polished wood with blue and white linens atop.

The place is dimly-lit, with a deep mahogany wood paneling and red leather seats. The tables are far apart enough to allow for intimate conversation but close enough together to be sociable. The floor is made of a polished marble you can see your reflection in. The wait staff is dressed in formal suits, well maintained, pressed, and starched.

The dark paneling made of oak and marble floors are pristine in their presentation. Candles and sparkling silverware adorn the tables dressed in starched white linen. The walls are adorned with old paintings of groups of nobles on horseback, galloping to pursue some smaller, weaker prey. It's a chilling thing for a restaurant to boast about.

Gerard's has been the fanciest restaurant in town for ages. If you want to dine here, you'd better be ready to shell out some serious money. I don't like this place, but I've invited my grandfather as a way to butter him up.

I take a seat at a mahogany table with a white table cloth and a crystal vase holding a single red rose. The booth is tucked away in the corner, and my grandfather soon joins me.

He looks as sharp as ever in his custom suit and tie, though his hair is white with age. "Dare," he says gruffly. "It's been too long."

"Yes, sir," I reply. "I've been pretty busy getting married and producing that heir you requested."

He smirks at me and unfolds his napkin.

The waiter approaches our table and takes our orders. My grandfather orders the full rack of prime rib, his signature dish, while I order a New York strip, though I'm not really hungry. The smell of the steak wafts through the air, and my mouth salivates at the rich aroma.

We spend time catching up on family news as we wait for our meal. Mostly my grandfather brings up a relative and then proceeds to go into a vitriolic rant about how they are embarrassing him and living their life wrong.

I keep my mouth shut and listen, nodding every so often. A few months ago, I would have listened to Remy's diatribe without a critical thought. It's funny that it took Talia pointing out how toxic Remy can be for me to finally open my eyes to the fact.

The food arrives shortly after, juicy pieces of steak perfectly seasoned with spices like garlic powder and paprika before being cooked to perfection. The potatoes are buttery and light, while the salad is fresh and crisp. A glass of red wine is brought with both our steaks; it's truly an experience fit for royalty.

I take a deep breath before finally plunging into the conversation that will dictate my future. "Sir, I wanted to ask you for a favor. I want to fund a project that I'm passionate about: deep sea drilling."

He pauses, then takes another bite of steak. He looks at me with piercing eyes. "Out with it," he demands.

I take a deep breath and explain why this project is so important to me. Deep sea drilling can open up an entirely new frontier of energy resources, and it could revolutionize how we think about energy production in the future. It's something that not only interests me personally, but could have major implications on the global economy as well.

Remy considers what I've said for a moment before responding. "It's an interesting idea," he says slowly. "But why should I fund your project? What makes it worth my investment?"

I take another deep breath and explain how my research has been ongoing for years now, and how I have consulted with top scientists and engineers in the field to develop better technologies that make this possible. Not only is it economically viable, but it could also be very beneficial to the environment if done correctly.

Remy goes still, his faintly twitching muscles and rheumy eyes blinking slowly the only evidence that he isn't dead. He puts his hand on his chin, his expression pensive. I look at the ground, hoping he's mulling the idea over.

"I can't believe you have the nerve to bring this up to me again." He scratches his chin. "I already told you that Morgan Drilling isn't going to fund your stupid little fantasy."

I take a deep breath, trying to keep my cool. I know I'm not going to win this argument, but that doesn't mean I'm not going to try.

"Remy, when you're gone, who do you think is going to be in charge of Morgan Drilling?" I ask him pointedly. "Me."

Remy's eyes narrow. "And why should I trust you with my legacy?" he asks.

"Because when I'm in charge," I say confidently. "I plan on investing more money into research and development so we can find the next source for America's energy needs. We need to get away from relying on oil and gas so much because not only is it bad for the environment—it's also becoming increasingly unreliable."

Remy looks at me skeptically before taking another bite of his steak. He chews slowly as he considers my words. Finally, after what feels like an eternity, he speaks again. "You're an idiot," he says gruffly. "America will never give up oil and gas as our primary sources of energy—not while they still make money from it."

I slam my fist against the table in frustration—not hard enough to break anything, but enough to get Remy's attention. "That's the problem with you!" I shout angrily. "You are so short-sighted and stubborn! We need people with vision. People who can look towards the future and see where this industry needs to go next!"

Remy slams his fist on the table, and I have to take a step back. He is seething with rage, and I can feel the tension between us rising.

"I built Morgan Drilling from the ground up, Dare!" he shouts. "It took years of hard work and dedication to get it to where it is today! You should respect that!"

I take a deep breath, trying to remain calm despite his anger. "I do respect what you've done," I say firmly. "But times are changing, and we need to change with them if we want to stay competitive."

Remy looks at me skeptically, his expression unreadable. I can tell he's still not convinced.

"What are you planning to do differently?" he asks.

I take another deep breath and explain my vision for the company. "If I inherit Morgan Drilling, I want to expand our operations into oil and gas extraction," I say. "We could use traditional methods like drilling or fracking, but we could also look into other avenues like thermal stimulation or steam-assisted gravity drainage."

Remy's brow furrows in confusion. "Tell me more about the new processes," he says, his tone of voice gruff.

"Thermal stimulation involves using heat to help extract oil and natural gas from the ground," I explain. "And steam-assisted gravity drainage uses steam injection to loosen up deposits before pumping them out. Plus deep sea drilling, which is self-explanatory."

Remy continues to look skeptical, but at least he seems slightly curious now. He takes another sip of his wine as he considers my words. After a few moments of silence, he speaks again.

"Do you really think this will work?" he asks doubtfully. "I mean, how much additional market share do you think these methods could possibly get us? We already hold eleven and a half percent."

I nod slowly.

"At least four times our current market share," I reply firmly. "These methods are proven and reliable—and they're much more cost effective than traditional drilling techniques."

He doesn't look at all convinced. I lean forward, lowering my voice.

"Look, we have to think strategically about our future. Gas and oil will still be important in fifty or a hundred years. But they will not be the only resource. Someone is going to put the money into researching a new energy source. And I want to be part of the company that is smart enough to pull the trigger on it. It will make the billions we have now seem like chump change by comparison."

Remy looks down his nose at me, a wry smile appearing on his lips.

"Are you saying that I should have been funding research on these new technologies for years?"

I hesitate. "Well... it's a new and untapped market. No one has had a breakthrough yet. It seems risky, even though it really isn't."

Remy takes a full minute to wipe his mouth with his cloth napkin and then hurls it against his mostly-untouched meal.

"I make decisions based on what I know to be true. And you can't prove a fucking thing that research has provided for me."

My fingers tighten on my knife.

"That's just not true. There are dozens of small tweaks that our company lab has suggested to the extraction process. I'd wager those tweaks have earned millions of dollars, but they only cost about one hundred thousand in research."

"Bah." Remy waves his hand at me. "That's hardly the point."

The waiter turns to me, obviously trying not to show his distress. "Is everything okay here, sir? How is your meal?"

I smile politely. "It's quite good, thank you." Remy scoffs and rolls his eyes.

"Throw my plate in the trash," he barks at the waiter. "I've had better food at a gas station." The waiter looks horrified as he hurries away with the untouched food.

Remy turns back to me, his face smug. I feel my anger rising and take a few deep breaths before addressing him again.

"Look Remy, I understand your hesitancy towards investing in research, but this could be a huge money maker for us down the line." I try to keep my voice as even as possible despite my growing annoyance.

Remy pierces me with his glare, his eyes like daggers. "Does your grand scheme for our company's future involve moving the headquarters away from Harwicke? To somewhere like New York?" His voice is tight and wary, as if he already has an answer in mind.

I frown. The last thing I want is to falsely raise his hopes. "It's a real possibility," I reply. "We have to go where the money is, and unfortunately, Harwicke has never been much of a business option."

Remy stares at me with an expression of disbelief. "You truly think this is the right move? Without consulting me?"

I can feel my temper starting to rise, but I suppress it and remain level-headed. "Yes," I reply firmly. "When I take up the reins as CEO, my job will be to make sure that our company is successful and moving forward."

Remy snorts and shakes his head. "And what makes you think you're qualified to do that? You haven't ever been in a CEO position before. And you've never even worked for any company that wasn't the family business. You've been coddled for years. You're soft."

A bitter grimace appears on my face. "You're not immortal, Remy. Right now, you have the power to choose your successor. But every minute you delay announcing a name, you are taking a huge risk. Much bigger than deep sea drilling."

Remy stands abruptly, his chair scraping against the floor. He throws a bundle of cash on the table and glares at me with fire in his eyes. "You think you can make decisions about this company without my permission? I'm the CEO, goddamnit. The company will always have its headquarters in Harwicke!"

I rise, throwing my napkin on the table. "In order to grow, sometimes you have to take risks."

Remy snorts in disbelief. "Are you telling me that deep sea drilling is going to be profitable for us? What about the environmental impact? What about the safety hazards? A single nasty lawsuit could easily wipe out our entire fortune."

I open my mouth to answer but Remy cuts me off. "No," he says firmly, pointing a finger at me for emphasis. "I don't think you have what it takes to run a successful business. Until you sign a contract that keeps the company in this town, you will never be my successor."

He turns away from me and walks towards the door. Then he pauses dramatically.

"And don't expect any money from me for your grand plans. Not today, not tomorrow, not a thousand years in the future."

I lose my meticulously crafted cool. "You don't need to worry about that. You are going to die sooner or later. Sooner if you keep up this rhetoric. Someone is going to poison your coffee to be free of you."

The atmosphere in the room shifts immediately. Remy's face darkens and his voice becomes low and menacing. "What did you just say?" he growls, leaning over the table towards me.

I can feel my temper rising but I keep it under control. "I said that your decision-making days are numbered," I reply calmly. "You need to think about what is best for this company before your personal feelings get in the way."

Remy shakes his head incredulously. "It's obvious what's happened to you," he says, in disgust. "You've married that tramp of a wife. Now you're getting laid on the regular and it's giving you ideas. It's softened you up, made you think with your dick instead of your brain." He pauses, taking a breath before continuing in a low, dangerous voice. "You were raised by me to be a killer—to do what needs to be done for the success of this business. But now you are nothing but a disappointment, no better than Felix and Tripp."

My rage boils over and I slam my fist down hard on the table, making Remy jump in surprise. "That's not true!" I shout angrily. "I'm still as lethal as ever; it has nothing to do with Talia or sex! You know damn well that I am capable of making tough decisions when it matters most!"

Remy spits a wad of white phlegm onto the restaurant floor. "This is what I get for letting you marry outside of your own class. I thought you would pick someone more pure-minded, but it's obvious that she has warped your mind. The bitch has to be dealt with once she coughs up your spawn."

I glare at Remy, my anger boiling over. "You can not refer to Talia like that!" I growl, feeling my muscles tense as I take a menacing step forward. "She is family now—she is a Morgan. You will show her the respect she deserves or suffer the consequences."

He points a bony finger at me. "You had better get your house in order and quit playing by your own rules. Otherwise, your twin brother will take over in my place."

I turn away from Remy, unable to contain my anger any longer. I storm out of the restaurant, pushing past Felix and Tripp as they try to follow me. Outside, the chauffeured SUV is waiting for us, and I yank open the door and climb in.

Talia looks up at me, her eyes full of concern. "Was talking to your grandfather productive?" she asks quietly.

I take a deep breath before answering, trying to calm myself down. "Not at all," I reply coldly. "My grandfather is a bastard."

Talia puts her hand on my arm, but I shake it off angrily. She looks away, a hurt expression crossing her face as she realizes that talking isn't going to make a difference this time. We sit in silence as we ride back to our apartment building, until I finally break the silence by slamming my fist against the window in frustration.

"Remy is a bastard."

She glances at me. "Did the meeting go that badly?"

"Yes. And then Remy started insulting you. It took everything I had not to punch his wrinkled mouth and yellowing teeth down his throat."

Talia scrunches her face up. "I'm sorry, Dare. That sounds horrible."

She scoots closer and ducks under my arm, putting her head on my chest. The embrace soothes the beast that rages inside me, quieting my inner agony to a murmur.

I realize with a start that Remy was wrong. Talia hasn't softened me; having Talia at my side has made me stronger than ever before.

Her voice is soft and I can feel the reverberations against my chest as she speaks. "Wouldn't you be happier if you weren't always trying to win this inheritance race? What if you just got a business loan and started your own venture?"

I scoff. "Are you saying I should walk away from billions of dollars?"

She slips her arm around my waist and hugs me tightly.

"I'm just suggesting alternatives. You seem so unhappy right now. I hate to see it."

I stare out the window, my mind racing. Talia's words reverberate in my head; what if I didn't need Remy's money to make something of myself? Maybe I could start my own business and become successful that way. It was an intriguing idea but it seemed so risky.

How could I possibly pull it off on my own? Would I be

able to secure a loan without Remy's help? Could I really make it without relying on his connections or wealth?

As we arrived back at our apartment building, Talia pulls away from me and looks up into my eyes.

"Dare," she said softly, her voice full of compassion. "You don't have to do this for your grandfather's approval. You can still find your own success without him."

I just kiss the top of her head absently, nodding.

"Let's go inside."

But the idea reverberates inside my head, echoing and bouncing around for the rest of the day.

Chapter Twenty-Six

My heart races as the doctor wheels over the ultrasound machine. This fourth checkup looms in front of me, but instead of feeling nervous, I'm buzzing with excitement. The doctor helps me into the padded leather chair and I recline nervously.

Dare stands right behind me, putting his hand on my shoulder. I am glad of his steady presence. Without him here, I think I would float away somehow. But his touch anchors me.

I reach up and thread my fingers through his. He gives me a quick smile.

"You're okay," he reminds me.

I can only nod.

The white-coated doctor sits on a low stool. I pull my shirt up to expose my distended abdomen and the doctor squirts KY jelly on my belly. It's icy. The doctor smiles as I wriggle in my seat.

"Sorry."

"No problem," I murmur.

She begins scanning with the wand. I squeeze Dare's

fingers and stare at the blank screen before me. The whirring of the machine and the beep of the heart monitor fill the small exam room.

The jelly is warm on my stomach, and cold on my skin. The sensations are at odds with each other and create an uncomfortable, nauseous stirring in my gut.

"Let's see..." the doctor says, squinting at the screen. "Come on, baby."

Dare and I share a glance - this is the moment we've been waiting for. Our baby appears on screen in all its glory, limbs stretching and curling, tiny head bobbing up and down.

"There we go." The doctor presses the wand into my stomach, massaging tiny circles into my flesh. "Can you see?"

She angles the screen towards us more. I nod, astounded. I can't stop staring at the little person I'm growing inside my body.

Seeing the baby on the screen, it just seems more real now somehow. The sight of its little heart beating sends a jolt of pleasure straight through my heart.

"Oh my god." I look up at Dare, whose eyes are fixed on the screen, his brows furrowed in concentration. "What do you think?"

His jaw is clenched tight and he swallows.

"I don't know," he says. But it's clear that he is having a visceral emotional reaction.

"It looks like your baby is in great shape," the doctor says, reassuring me after a few more scans. "We made it to the six-month mark!" I exclaim excitedly. "Our little one is developing exactly as they should be."

The doctor nods with approval. "Let's take a closer look," she says, gesturing towards the advanced 4D machine.

It takes a minute to set up the wand over my belly

again. But when it's in place, my mind is blown. My jaw drops at the clarity of the images. I can make out each crease in the baby's lips and count every single finger and toe.

"Dare!" I gasp in awe, reaching for his hand. I tug on his hand. "That's amazing!"

The room is silent except for the beating of my heart and the low hum of the machine. Tears sting my eyes as I stare at our baby, finally becoming real before my very eyes.

I grip Dare's hand tightly as a new wave of emotions wash over me. His grip tightens in return and he looks up at me with a mixture of joy and awe.

We stay like that for a few moments before the doctor interrupts our reverie. "Well, everything looks good," she says gently. "Your baby's growing right on track with my projections."

I reach out and gently stroke the screen. "Hi, baby."

The doctor smiles and looks between Dare and me. "Do you want to know the gender of your baby?"

My heartbeat quickens in anticipation. But before I can answer either way, Dare blurts out, "Of course we want to know. Information is power."

His voice is strangely urgent and it catches me off guard. He glances at me before quickly looking away, a flush creeping up his cheeks.

I smile in surprise. I had been expecting Dare to be more ambivalent about the whole thing, but it seems like he's just as invested into having this baby as I am. I kiss his palm and he drops his hand to cup the back of my head.

The doctor smiles gently at our dynamic before going over the sonogram again with us. Finally, she pauses at a particular spot on the screen and points out a vague blob that looks like a hamburger patty.

"It looks like you're having a baby girl," she announces calmly.

"Really?" My pulse skyrockets at the news. Every little scrap of information, every moment I look at my baby on the screen, she becomes more real.

My heart swells with joy and tears of happiness prick my eyes. Dare squeezes my hand tightly in support as we both look up at each other with wide-eyed gazes. Dare seems as out of sorts as I am and nearly as emotional to boot.

The doctor smiles and prints out several screen grabs before switching gears to nutrition.

"I'm going to recommend that you cut salt from your diet, Talia," she says. "Too much sodium can cause complications such as dehydration during labor or preterm delivery."

She goes on to explain cord blood banking services, in case we decide to do so for our baby. Then she wipes the jelly from my stomach and pulls my shirt back down.

"Thank you," Dare says. I'm a little surprised. He's been reserved with the doctor for months. Now he is suddenly showing gratitude, which in itself is unusual for him.

The doctor gives a curt smile. "Of course. I'm available at any time for questions you may have."

I dress quickly, feeling a little uncomfortable with Dare's silence. He's staring at the ultrasound photo of our daughter like he's in a trance. I reach out to touch his arm and his head snaps up, meeting my gaze with a questioning look.

"Are you okay?" I ask softly.

He takes a deep breath and looks away, averting his eyes from mine. "I was just thinking… it feels real now, you know? This is someone else's baby. I don't know what that makes me… Am I responsible for this child now? Is it wise to claim her as my own even though she isn't biologically mine? It won't ever feel like she really belongs to me, will it?"

His voice is soft and painful and my heart aches for him. I take both of his hands in mine and squeeze gently. "It doesn't matter whose baby she is biologically, Dare. She is ours now —yours and mine—and no matter what happens we will love her just as much as if she were our own flesh and blood."

"You think?"

I touch his hand. "I know it for a fact. There will be a lot of things in the future that we will need to shield our little girl from. But I feel that having you on my team will make that much easier."

He looks up at me sharply, his face full of surprise before softening into gratefulness. He squeezes my hand back before turning away to wipe some moisture from his eyes without me seeing. His chest expands in a deep inhale before he turns back towards me with a smile on his face, albeit slightly forced still.

Dare takes my hand in his and brings it to his lips, pressing a gentle kiss into the top of my knuckles. I watch his face closely as he does this, marveling at the transformation that has taken place over the past few days. It has been an incredible journey, with countless moments of learning about each other and ourselves that have led us here.

"Talia," he says softly. "I want you to know that your vulnerability unlocked something inside me—something I didn't know was there until now." He pauses for a moment and closes his eyes before continuing. "When you told me you needed me, something in me… stretched open. A part of myself I had kept hidden away for so long."

He looks down at our joined hands before meeting my gaze again and smiling sadly. "Having this photo makes everything so real now—it's like it reached deep into my chest and opened something up inside of me." His voice is low and filled with emotion.

We sit there, looking at each other in silence for a few moments as we try to process everything that had been said. Dare eventually moves closer to me and wraps his arms around my waist. I lay my head against his chest and he leans down to kiss the top of my head.

The kiss slowly deepens from tenderness to something more intimate. I feel myself melting into him. His lips brush softly against mine, coaxing my own open with gentle pressure. For a few minutes we get lost in each other, lost in the moment until Dare pulls away with an embarrassed laugh.

"I'm not sure that the doctor's office is the place for what I want to do with you right now," he murmurs, gently brushing a strand of hair out of my face while his eyes remain locked on mine.

Letting out a laugh, I roll my eyes. "We'll save it for later." I smile up at him before standing up and taking his hand in mine.

On the way to the car, a store's display window catches my eye. It's full of gorgeous baby furniture, cute baby clothes, and squeezable plush toys. I touch Dare's arm and point to the store.

"Can we go look around?"

He screws up his face and checks out the display.

"Yeah, I guess..." he says, but he doesn't sound the least bit convincing.

I take Dare's hand in mine, squeezing it gently as we make our way into the store. The store is decorated in shades of baby beige, ivory, and cream. There are plush toys, rocking chairs, carriages, and cribs, all lined up for the taking.

The store is full of items—blankets, clothes, toys, cribs and car seats. There are items that range from the simplest, the plainest, to the most extravagant and expensive. Dare fingers a price tag on one of the fancier strollers and then gives a low whistle.

"Damn." He turns the price tag so I can see it. It says fifteen hundred dollars. My eyes go wide with shock.

"What?" I exclaim. "Does it also vacuum and dust your house for you?"

Dare chuckles. We haven't been shopping for baby items yet, and it feels so surreal to be here. Time is moving too fast —it's like sifted sand slipping through my fingers. I'm worried I'm going to blink and miss something important.

The store is buzzing with activity, customers bustling around and sales associates helping them pick out just the right items. I take my time, running my hands over a few rocking chairs and picking up some of the soft baby blankets that are for sale. Dare trails behind me, seeming to enjoy looking at all the possible options but not yet committing to anything in particular.

I turn to him and arch an eyebrow. "What do you think? Anything you like?"

He takes a deep breath and rubs his hands together nervously. "I think…well, everything looks really nice. But there's something about all this pink decor for the nursery and baby clothes that make me feel—" He stops mid sentence, embarrassed by what he was about to say.

"It's okay," I tell him gently, trying not to laugh. "You can admit that you're excited."

He looks relieved as he nods and smiles sheepishly at me. "I know it's weak to care about pink baby clothes."

I wheel around, looking at Dare like he's grown another head.

"Are you kidding? I'm really glad that you're starting to feel excited about the baby. I was afraid that you would be all weird about her parentage."

Dare stares at me for a beat, his face unreadable. Then he takes a deep breath and takes my hand in his, pressing it against my stomach. "I wish like hell I'd met you first," he says softly. "And that this baby was mine."

My heart swells with emotion and I take his other hand in mine, squeezing it gently.

"It doesn't matter," I tell him. "If you care for her—and I know you will—that's all that matters."

Dare presses a kiss to my wrist. I suspect that he is masking some emotion, but I don't know for sure.

We spend the next hour looking at furniture, clothing, toys, and other accessories for the nursery. Dare gets increasingly excited about each new item we come across until finally we've picked out everything we need for the baby's arrival—including an adorable stuffed giraffe for decoration!

As we walk through the checkout line, Dare turns to me with a smile on his face.

"Thanks for giving me this moment," he says softly, taking my hand in his own hand and squeezing it gently.

"Of course," I say. I smile back at him, feeling content with my life as it is right now.

Chapter Twenty-Seven

DARE

"Dare?"

My eyes open instantly when I hear Talia whisper my name. It's dark and we are both sprawled out in bed. I blink up at the faraway cement ceiling for a few moments before turning my head toward Talia. The very first thing I notice is that she's staring at me with her wide blue eyes.

Then I notice that her face is flushed. She chews on her lip and lightly rubs her hand on my chest.

"What's going on?" I ask, stifling a yawn. "Is everything okay?"

She gives me a sheepish smile and strokes my chest again. "It is. I just... I need you."

I screw up my face and rub the sleep from my eyes.

"Need me for what?" I ask.

Talia curls up to my body and caresses my thigh through my boxer briefs. Her blush darkens and she nervously swipes her tongue out to wet her bottom lip.

"I had a sexy dream about you. And now I can't stop thinking about how hot you are."

I raise an eyebrow. "Oh?"

"Yeah." She bites her lip and gives me a nervous smile. "I was just thinking how fun it would be to... to ride you."

My cock hardens in an instant. I reach down and reposition it as I look at my beautiful wife.

"Tell me what you want from me, sweetheart. I need to hear it from those pretty lips."

I love the way she blushes. I love the way she gets shy when she's turned on. I love that she's honest with me and won't hide her desires from me.

"I want to be the one in control," Talia whispers, biting her bottom lip. "I want to suck your cock. I want to ride your cock real slow and feel you come inside me."

I feel my cock jump. Putting my arms behind my head, I smirk at her.

"I'm here for your pleasure, darling girl. Suck my cock, ride me hard, drain my balls dry. Whatever you feel like."

She blushes and bites her lip, gathering up her hair and securing it with an elastic. I strip my dark boxer briefs off and then spread my legs wide, giving my cock a single stroke.

All I can think about now is how good her pussy will feel when it clenches around my dick. Talia moves toward me, hiking her teddy around her hips. I reach forward, pulling the skimpy strap down one of her shoulders.

"Take this off. I worked so damn hard to make you mine. Let me see all of you, every last inch of you, bare before me."

Talia's breathing grows shallow. She slowly reaches for the hem of the teddy and peels it off her gorgeous body. She kneels before me, completely naked, her skin so bare and perfect. She bows her head and strokes the top of her swollen belly.

She's so different from the girl I thought I was marrying. I thought she was a coarse-tongued harpy who would never appreciate the same things as me.

But I was wrong. Very wrong.

She's soft, feminine, and so beautiful. And she is growing used to being my little wife.

I can't wait to get inside her again, make her scream my name, fulfill every last need and want so that she never desires another man.

Looking at her makes me feel like a starving man with a feast laid out before him. All I can do is watch her, my mouth watering with urgency. I can't think straight. I *need* to taste her again.

"Kneel before me," I order. "Open your mouth."

Talia quickly complies, her eyes sparkling with lust. She opens her mouth wide, inviting me in. Leaning back on my elbows, I stroke my cock, enjoying the feel of bare flesh against my fingers.

It's been too long since I've had my cock in her mouth. I've missed feeling her warm lips, the wet slide of her tongue, the way she moans when she sucks my cock. I'm dying to feel it again.

Talia pushes me flat onto my back and knocks my hand away, gripping my hips. She runs her nails down my hips and teases my balls before framing my cock with her hand.

She looks right in my eye and opens her mouth, unfurling her tongue. Then she ever so gently trails her tongue along the thick vein on the underside of my cock, making me groan. She licks up to the tip and then licks the slit before sucking me into her warm mouth.

She is so gentle, so soft and slow. I didn't know she had this side to her. But I'm already dying to feel her mouth closing on my cock.

I look down to watch her. My cock slides along her lips as

she bobs up and down. I can see her lips stretch as she takes me in, her tongue working, her cheeks hollowing as she sucks me. She looks up at me, her big eyes sparkling, her lips stretched around my cock.

I thread my fingers through her hair and grip the back of her head, guiding her. She knows what I want, and she's more than eager to give it to me.

"That's it," I growl. "Take me in deep."

She does as I ask, bobbing her head quickly. Her movements are so eager, so hungry. I can tell that she wants my cock as much as I need her. I guide her head up and down, fucking her mouth. I like the way her lips feel when they're wrapped around my cock. She bobs her head faster and faster, taking me in deeper.

Talia shifts her position to take me deeper, bobbing her head so far down my shaft that I can feel the head of my cock touch the back of her throat. She gags just a little, but then I feel her swallow, and I groan.

I love that feeling, the sensation of being so deep inside of her that she can't help but gulp me down. I want to feel that over and over again. I want to feel her throat close around me, her tongue working me, her lips suctioning my cock.

"Fuck, sweetheart," I mutter. "You suck my cock like a champion."

Talia doesn't slow down at all. She wraps her hand around the base of my cock and continues to work the head and shaft in long strokes.

She's going to have to ease up or I'm going to blow my load in her mouth like an inexperienced boy getting head for the first time.

"This feels fucking incredible, wife." I pull my cock out of her mouth. She gasps, her lips red and her cheeks flushed.

"But I need more. I need to feel your pussy clenching against my cock."

Talia is on her knees in front of me, and she looks up at me with big eyes. I take a handful of her hair in my hand and bring her face closer to mine. I kiss her mouth, roughly, passionately.

"I've been thinking about your pussy all day, darling girl." I kiss her again, my tongue sliding against hers. "I've been thinking about what it's going to feel like to fuck you, to make you come. I've been thinking about how good my name will sound when you're screaming it while you come."

She inhales a shaky breath. "I want you so bad, Dare."

"I need to fuck you now," I utter.

I grab her ass with my other hand and haul her on top of me, straddling my hips. She flushes but smirks as she strokes my cock, finding it hard as a fucking rock.

I reach down and run my fingers along the lips of her pussy. She's damp but not drenched.

"This won't do," I say. "I need your pussy hot and ready to take this big cock."

Talia's eyes widen. Popping my fingers in my mouth, I suck on them and then run them back down her slit, parting her pussy lips. Her palm runs down my chest and her breathing halts.

"W-what are you doing?" she asks.

"Shh." I use my free hand to push against her belly, encouraging her to lean backwards and tilt her pelvis toward me. She takes my direction as if it comes naturally to her.

I love it when Talia takes my silent commands.

I part her lips and run my fingertips around her clit in a delicate swirl. "I'm going to make you so wet that your pussy is dripping with your juices. I'm going to make you so hot that when you straddle me, you're going to come all over my cock."

Her jaw drops. I shush her and rub her clit for a minute. Talia closes her eyes and touches her breasts, tweaking her nipples. She thrusts her hips forward a few times, her expression growing intense.

"Fuck, baby," she whispers. "Just like that."

I don't reply. I merely growl and continue my rhythmic flicking and swirling. I change the pressure a few times and then adjust the quick circles that I rub into her clit.

Talia's eyes fly open. "Oh, Dare. Oh, god."

She looks down at me and flicks her tongue against her upper lip. I quirk a brow.

"I want you to fuck me," she whispers. "I want you to fuck me like an evil, dominating billionaire."

I groan. "That's what I am, darling girl."

"Then fuck me like the wicked man you are."

I grab her hips and slide the head of my cock against her pussy but don't push inside her. It takes every single molecule of my being not to move.

But I stay still as a statue and stare her down.

She looks at me. "What is it?"

"I want you to beg me to fuck you," I grit out.

Her mouth pops open in surprise. "But I thought you said you wanted to fuck me."

"I do. God, I really fucking do. But does that mean I don't get to hear you beg?"

She blinks, her expression turning angry. "Fuck you, Dare."

I chuckle. "Now, now. There's no need for you to get upset, my little wife. If you want me to fuck you, all you have to do is beg."

"Fucking bastard," she mutters.

"But I'm your fucking bastard, darling girl." I smooth back a stray strand of hair that has escaped her bun, my expression taunting. "Say the words, Talia."

She sucks in a sharp breath. "Dare..."

I stare at her. "Beg."

Her self-consciousness is evident in the deep pink stain that tinges her cheeks. Her blue eyes pin me in place and she takes a deep breath.

"Please fuck me, Dare."

"Like you mean it, sweetheart."

"Please fuck me, Dare," she shouts. "I want your cock inside me, I want your cum inside me. Fuck me, Dare. Please?"

I don't bother replying. I push my cock up into her pussy, my eyes closing from the heavenly feel of pushing into her scorching, dripping, tight little channel.

"Fuck!" she gasps. "Oh, Dare... you're so fucking big. Stretching my pussy out, filling me to the goddamn brim."

There is no time for gentle lovemaking. I need to feel Talia clenching around my cock right fucking *now*.

I hammer into her pussy with hard, punishing strokes. She's so incredibly wet, her pussy juices coating my shaft, allowing me to fuck her like a piston gone mad.

I grunt, pushing my cock in and out of her tight channel, the enjoyment evident in my face.

"Don't you dare come yet," I mutter, my voice hard.

She blinks at me, panting. "W-what?"

I roll my hips, pushing my cock into her pussy, squeezing her ass cheeks in my hands. I can already feel my orgasm building up. Not yet. Not until I say so.

"You don't come until I say you can. Stay... on... the fucking... edge. Understand?"

"Fuck you," she pants.

"Good girl," I mutter, rolling my hips, making sure she knows who is in charge.

I lean down and capture her nipples, sucking hard on her pretty pink tips. The sensation travels straight down to her pussy and she tightens on my cock, squeezing my hard shaft.

She cries out and I release her nipples, giving her a hard slap on the ass.

"Stay on the edge."

She nods, her eyes hooded.

She is trying so hard not to come. I am so fucking turned on by her. I can feel the orgasm coming closer, hovering on the edge of my consciousness, ready to strike like a snake.

"I... I can't, Dare," she breathes, her eyes widening. "I'm so, so close. If you don't stop, I'm going to fucking come."

I slap her ass, squeezing it hard and pushing into her pussy in one hard, deep thrust.

"Come for me. Come for me, darling girl."

She shudders, her pussy clenching around my cock. I press my thumb onto her clit, rubbing it in hard circles, my cock buried deep in her pussy.

"Good girl," I coach, my voice strained. "That's a good little girl. Take it all for me, sweetheart."

"Dare! Dare... I'm coming! Fuck!"

I feel her tiny, hard pulses around my cock. She is coming for me and I devour the sight. Her head thrown back, her tits bouncing, the little half-moon of her swollen belly making me feel things that I don't even have a name for.

Talia is perfect. The perfect match, a perfect wife.

I feel her body spasm around my cock, her muscles contracting. My balls tighten and I know I'm a hair's breadth from orgasm.

I thrust into her hard, once, twice, three times and then give myself over to the orgasm, groaning her name.

"Fuck, Talia. I'm going to--"

I grit my teeth and squeeze my eyes closed. My cock erupts, sending my come into her pussy. It twitches deep inside her body as I pump into her once more. I can feel her pussy clenching and unclenching around my shaft, milking me for every last drop of come.

I sit up and put my arms around her, my cock still buried deep in her pussy. I hold her against my body and struggle to regain my breathing.

"That was amazing," she murmurs.

I grunt, nuzzling her shoulder. A wave of contentment and ease washes over me.

I don't want to let Talia out of my arms. I don't want to leave this room. In fact, I might never leave this bed again.

I must have reasons for existing outside this protective, cozy little bubble. But for the life of me? I can't think of a single one right now.

Talia pushes against my arms and eases back, separating our bodies. But in the next moment, she lies down and pulls me down next to her. I put my arm around her and she spoons my chest, her pregnant belly resting against my stomach.

I rest my free hand against her belly and drop a kiss into her hair. She releases a deep sigh and presses her face into my chest.

We drift off together, peaceful and content.

Chapter Twenty-Eight

DARE

"I can't believe I let you talk me into this," I gripe.

Talia is busy herding the children from Hope House out of the bus onto the sidewalk in front of the children's science museum. She rolls her eyes at my complaint and gives a soft laugh.

"Poor Dare. Won't anybody think of the billionaires? They have to be constantly coddled and entertained."

"Very funny."

I give her a sour look, but I can't be angry. The weather outside is unusually sunny and the sky a brilliant shade of robin's egg blue. Leaning against the bus, I casually look over the excited children and the Hope House volunteers that are gathering near the entrance to the museum.

Talia helps Solana out of the bus. "Long time, no see! Where have you been hiding?"

She tickles Solana gently on her belly. The little girl beams and dissolves into giggles.

"We're going to see all the sciences!" Solana crows.

"We sure are," Talia replies. She gestures to me. "Do you remember Dare?"

Solana's laughter subsides and she looks at me, thrusting her hands behind her back and peeking at me coquettishly. "Yeah..."

"We're all going to have a blast today. Now go line up on the sidewalk with the rest of the kids so we can head inside!"

"Okay!" Solana shouts. She takes off with a level of energy reserved for children alone, exaggerating the effort it takes to reach the line of kids and then playacting tiredness.

"That kid is something else," I say, my lips lifting at the corners.

"She's really great." Talia takes my hand as one of the volunteers does a quick headcount and then we all file inside the big brass double doors.

As we enter the building, I can't help but be impressed by its elegance and grandeur. The walls are lined with stunning works of art and sculptures, while a sparkling chandelier hangs from the ceiling. Talia leads the group through the main hall before finally stopping in front of a large door.

"This is it!" she announces, pushing open the door to reveal an impressive view of the two-story science museum packed with interactive exhibits. Everywhere I look, there are clusters of kids climbing all over dinosaurs, building an arch out of huge foam blocks, playing with dams in a large maze made with flowing water, and sitting inside a tiny movie theater.

A few of the children in our group scream. I laugh but I get it; full of bright colors, wacky sound effects, and thrilling textures, this place is made for nonstop fun.

The children rush in excitedly, eager to explore their new environment. Only Solana hangs back, seeming to have difficulty choosing between all the activities. She grabs Talia's shirt, her huge brown eyes taking in the entire room. Talia kneels down and looks at the little girl.

"What should we explore first?" Talia asks.

Solana's brow knits. "I don't know. I don't want to miss out on anything."

"Maybe you should start in one corner and work your way around the exhibits," I suggest. I point at the water maze. "Maybe you should start over there? The water looks cool."

Solana turns her wide brown eyes to me.

"Will you come with me?"

Her question makes something in my chest tighten. "Yeah. Of course. Maybe we can persuade Talia to come, too."

Talia stands up, twining her arm with mine and leaning her head against me briefly. "Lead the way, Solana."

Solana takes the lead, her little hand grasping tightly onto mine. I can't help but feel a sense of protectiveness over her. It's a foreign feeling, but one that I can't seem to shake. As we approach the water maze, Solana's eyes light up with excitement. She runs ahead, eager to play in the cascading water. I follow closely behind, watching her intently. Talia joins us a moment later, her eyes filled with wonder as she takes in the exhibit.

The sound of the rushing water gets louder as we approach, but it only adds to the excitement of the moment. Solana jumps and splashes , laughing and squealing with delight. I can't help but feel a warmth spread through me at the sight of her joy. Talia stands off to the side, her arms wrapped around herself, watching us with a small smile on her lips.

"Come on, Talia," I say, reaching out my hand to her. "It's not every day we get to have fun like this."

Talia hesitates for a moment before taking my hand and stepping into the water. Her gasp of surprise is music to my ears as the cool water splashes up onto her toes. Solana jumps up and down, coaxing Talia to play with her.

I take a deep breath and smile. I've been a little apprehensive about being around so many children. But as I watch Solana and Talia lift and lower gates to start and stop the flow of water in the river, I can't help but feel my anxiety melting away.

This isn't so bad.

Scratch that. This is something that I could get used to.

When Solana tires of the water maze, I point to the next exhibit twenty yards away. "How about we go over there to check out the dinosaur exhibit? It looks pretty cool."

"Yeah!" Solana shouts. "Let's go! Let's go! Hurry!"

"We are right behind you. You go ahead," Talia calls. She looks at me with a smile and shakes her head. "She's going to be so tired after we leave here."

I slide my arm around her waist and amble over to the earth sciences exhibit. Talia smoothes her hand over her belly with a gentle smile. When we get to the exhibit, Solana and another boy are busy climbing on the back of a small brontosaur.

"Look at me and Nathan!" Solana calls. "We're going into prehistoric times. Right, Nathan?"

"Right!" the boy shrieks. "We have Dino-Power!"

I start to pull back from Talia, but she flings her arms around my waist.

"Just another minute," she whispers. "This is comfortable."

She's right. It is comfortable. Being with her seems to make everything else disappear. The only thing that matters is her and the way she makes me feel. It's like a whirlwind of emotions that I can't control, but I don't want to. Not now, not ever.

This newfound sense of recklessness and lack of emotional control feels dangerous, but I refuse to put the brakes on. It seems doomed, like it can't go on for very long... but I'm testing that theory today, it appears.

Talia kisses my cheek and pulls away. She walks over to a messy arts and crafts area with a huge banner encouraging visitors to get their hands dirty.

"Look Solana," I call to her, pointing to the bags of plaster, clay and tools. "We can make our very own fossils!"

Solana slides off the brontosaur and hits the ground with a thump. She bounces back up and runs to where I stand, assessing the situation. Her friend Nathan is hot on her heels.

"Whoa! Cool! I'm going to make one, too."

I scan the directions printed on the wall.

"That's a great idea. This seems pretty simple. Here, let me hand you each the stuff you will need."

"Woohoo!" Solana exclaims, eagerly grabbing the supplies in her arms. Nathan follows with his supplies and we move to an open space on the floor.

"Alright," I say, mixing together some plaster and clay for Solana and Nathan. "Let's press this into your molds."

I guide Solana's hands as she presses down. Beside me, Talia kneels down and does the same for Nathan.

"This is so neat," she tells him. "This will make a really cool souvenir."

"Yeah!" he says, his excitement evident.

As I watch Talia work with Nathan, I can't help but feel a sense of pride. She's so good with children, and it's clear that Nathan trusts her. I'm glad that Talia brought me along today, even though our relationship is so complicated.

After we finish making our fossils, we wander around the museum. Solana and Nathan run ahead, giggling and pointing at the exhibits. Talia and I walk slowly behind them, taking in the displays.

"You know," Talia says, breaking the silence between us. "You're going to be an amazing dad. You have done a really good job today with Solana and Nathan."

I look at her, my brows rising. I'm a little taken aback.

"You think so?"

She nods. "Yes, I do. You have a kind heart and you're great with kids. And I can tell that you care about them."

I feel my chest swell with pride at her words. I never thought of myself as father material, but hearing Talia say that makes me feel like maybe I could be.

"Thanks," I say. I shake my head and shrug. "I have a lot to learn, but I'll do my best."

Talia smiles at me, and her expression softens. It's moments like these that make me forget everything else - the lies, the secrets, the mistrust. It's just Talia and me, and the great unknown expanse of the future.

After hours in the museum, the group heads out back to spend the rest of the day in the park attached to the museum, lounging in the sunshine. Though it's still windy and cool outside, the kids don't seem to know it.

We eat bagged lunches of peanut butter and jelly and apples. The adults have found spots under the dappled shade of the tall pine trees.

Solana and Nathan are running around, giggling and playing tag. Talia and I are lying side by side, soaking up the meager warmth of the afternoon sun.

Suddenly, Solana stops in her tracks and turns around. She runs back towards us and falls to her knees in the grass next to Talia. Talia raises her hands, ready to ask what's going on. But Solana snuggles up to Talia's baby bump, talking to it like it's an old friend.

"Hi baby," she coos. "Guess what? Talia said we can go on a trip to the zoo soon! I can't wait."

Talia laughs softly and strokes Solana's hair. "That's true. I did say that."

Solana looks at Talia, wrinkling her nose.

"How long until the baby gets here? Will it be here when we go to the zoo?"

"Uhh..." Talia stammers.

I sit up. "No, not quite yet. The baby won't be here for a few more months."

Talia flashes me a grateful look. I grab her hand and squeeze it.

"That's not fair." Solana makes a pouting expression. "I want to meet the baby."

"Solana!" a girl bleats from two hundred yards away. "Come play hide and seek with us!"

Fast as lightning, Solana is on her feet and dashing away. I watch her go, shaking my head.

"That kid is crazy."

Talia makes a soft sound and presses her palm against her belly. Her expression is puzzled.

"Is something wrong?" I ask.

She shakes her head and moves her palm a few inches up. "I don't know. I think... I think I can feel her moving."

Talia grabs my hand and presses it against her stomach. Sure enough, I can feel a soft fluttering sensation beneath my palm. Talia's eyes widen and she looks up at me in wonder.

"It's the baby," she whispers.

I feel a lump form in my throat and my heart swells with emotion. This is my child growing inside her. Our child.

"It's amazing," I say, my voice choking with emotion. "Absolutely incredible."

Talia nods, her eyes glistening with unshed tears. "I know. It's hard to believe that there's a little life inside of me."

I brush my thumb gently over the back of her hand, lost in thought. Despite the circumstances that brought us together, I can't help but feel a sense of wonder and awe at the life growing inside Talia. It's a reminder that, even in the midst of all the chaos and uncertainty in our lives, there is still something pure and beautiful.

Damn. I do everything right, this could really be life-changing. I know that things between Talia and I are far from perfect, but maybe we can actually make a family for our baby.

Loving, caring, supportive. The kind of family that I never had.

I kiss the back of Talia's hand and she looks up at me, her expression softening. For a moment, everything feels suspended in time, as if we're the only two people in the world.

But then, the sound of a car horn blaring outside jolts us back into reality. Talia jumps, startled.

I sit up straight and pull my arm away from Talia. My heart races as Felix's gaze shifts between the two of us with a knowing smirk. I clasp my hands together, desperately trying to keep a composed exterior.

"Uncle Felix," I say, voice strained. "What brings you here?"

"I called your personal assistant. He told me you were here." Felix takes a step forward and crosses his arms over his chest. "I have some news about deep sea drilling." He turns to Talia and smiles. "It's always nice to see you, Talia."

Talia nods politely and brushes a few blades of grass from her pants. "Hello, Felix."

"You two look like you were just caught fucking in the

park or something." Felix shifts his gaze to me and chuckles. "She's really got you by the balls, huh?"

Talia flushes a particular shade of maroon and clears her throat. "I'm going to go check on the kids."

She gets up and beats a hasty retreat to the other side of the park.

I give Felix a glare. "What is so damn important that it couldn't wait for me to get home, Felix?"

Felix continues to look at me for a few moments before he seems satisfied with what he sees. He shifts his attention back to the business at hand.

"I received a call from one of our partners in the drilling project," Felix says, his tone serious. "They've hit a snag. We need to invest more money to keep things moving forward."

I let out a frustrated groan. "How much more?"

"About fifty million," Felix says with a wince.

"What??"

"I know, it's a lot," Felix says with a shake of his head. "But we need to keep the project moving forward. If we don't pay some very important people, the project is dead in the water."

I nod slowly, my mind spinning with possibilities. I take a deep breath and look at Felix. "I had lunch with Remy a few days ago," I say.

Felix's brow furrows in concern. "How did that go?" he asks cautiously.

I sigh heavily, a mixture of anger and frustration bubbling in the pit of my stomach. "We had a heated argument about whether I should be CEO or if Burn should be promoted instead." I pause before pushing forward, needing to get it all out in the open. "Remy threatened to name Burn CEO if I didn't agree to his demands."

Felix runs a hand through his hair as he takes this information in. "That doesn't sound good," he finally says, sighing heavily.

"No," I agree grimly. "It's not." I frown, trying to think of some way out of this mess without having to make an enemy of Remy.

Felix nods, understanding the situation. "We have to find another way," he says thoughtfully. He pauses for a moment, thinking before continuing.

"We need to start making contacts with some private banks that finance huge loans like we would need for the project. I know a few people who can put us in touch with the right people." He looks at me expectantly.

I hesitate, not sure if I'm ready to take on such a risk. "Are you sure about this? What if it all goes wrong?" I ask reluctantly.

Felix nods firmly. "I know it's a risk, but we have no other choice. We can't let Remy bully us into doing something we don't want to do. We need to take control of the situation." He pokes his bottom lip out. "But if we are going to get a loan, you'll have to be the front man for our interests. I can do all of the footwork, but you will have to sign all the documents for the loan. My cache is blown with the banks. They won't give me a cent."

My eyes narrow on Felix's face. "I don't suppose that's a story I want to hear, is it?"

He shrugs a shoulder and looks unrepentant.

"Some other time, maybe."

I grimace and shake my head. "Why did I even ask?"

Felix chuckles, but the sound is devoid of humor. We both know that he is not someone to fool around with.

He turns away like he's about to leave. Then he pauses and turns back to me.

"You and Talia are pretty lovey-dovey all of a sudden,

huh? It makes you look weak. I'm not surprised that Remy is choosing your brother over you. If I were in your shoes, I would cool it on the kissy-touchy shit until my dad is dead."

I square my shoulders and hold his gaze, refusing to be cowed. My tone is as warm as arctic ice.

"Any other thoughts, Uncle Felix? Or are you ready to scurry along and secure our venture and loan?"

He looks like he wants to say something else, but instead he just walks away.

I stand there, my mind spinning like an out of control top. Felix's sneer sticks with me and his words thunder through my skull.

"You two are pretty lovey-dovey."

As much as it pains me to admit, he may be right. I have grown used to being my grandfather's golden child. But now that Remy has sensed weakness in his potential heir, I have to consider that there could be real competition. The thought makes my gut twist uncomfortably, a reminder of what I am up against.

Is Felix right? Maybe I should pull back from Talia just a little while I still have Remy's eyes on my back.

Later that evening when I finally head to bed, I'm still thinking about it. Talia is still up, reading with her small bedside light on. I kick off my shoes and rip my shirt over my head, then wrestle off my pants.

Talia arches a brow when I lie down beside her. She folds down her page to mark her place in her book and then puts it aside.

"You're awfully quiet tonight. Is everything okay with your drilling project?"

I wince. "Yeah. It's just complicated. These things always are."

She nods and curls up against me, settling her face against

my chest and drawing circles with two fingers on my ribs. Her touch is warm and relaxing. I could easily turn this moment into a night of hot sex by capturing her hand and kissing her deeply.

But I don't. I'm too keyed up for that. The words lovey-dovey are still ricocheting around in my head. I stare at the ceiling, trying to think of the best words to tell my wife that we have to tone down our affection in public.

"Dare?"

I screw up my face. "Yeah?"

There is a moment's hesitation.

"Can I tell you something?"

"Uhh, sure." I run my tongue over my teeth.

Talia takes a deep breath. I'm not sure what she's going to say, but when they come, her words stop me dead in my tracks.

"I think I might be falling in love with you," she says, her voice so soft that it's just above a whisper.

Fuck.

Fuck, fuck.

Of course it would be tonight of all nights that Talia decides to throw caution to the wind and declare her love for me.

Fuuuuccccck.

It's been too long since she stopped talking. I know that she's waiting for a response. I just can't come up with words to say that will satisfy Talia but not sound too...

Lovey-dovey.

"Dare?"

"Yeah. I heard you."

Talia lifts her head, looking at me with a tiny frown.

"Did I speak out of turn?"

This is killing me. The look on her face and the neediness

in her eyes are killing me. I'm hearing her voice when she told me she needed me... and then the sound of Felix's voice trying to drown her out.

Weak.

I clear my throat. "I feel something for you, Talia. There's no use denying that. But I don't want to put labels on our relationship. Love is... it's too messy and complicated. Christ, I loved Daisy. Look at how that all turned out! I don't want that to happen again."

It's partially a lie, mixed up in a fragment of what feels awfully close to the truth.

She picks up my hand and kisses his palm. "I know how you feel, even if you won't say the word. I can be patient with you. I... I just need you to tell me that I'm not crazy. I need to hear that you feel it, too."

"Don't put words in my mouth," I warn. "You can't just go around making up assumptions about what's going on in my head."

Talia looks at me like I'm a venomous viper who's just attacked her. She scoots away, creating space on the bed.

"What?" she asks, as if perhaps she misheard somehow.

Words just leap from my tongue. I can't seem to stop myself from twisting the knife even though the victim is my soft-hearted wife.

"Men don't like when you tell them what they feel," I argue, feeling imperious. "And they don't like being smothered, either. Maybe because you grew up without a father figure in your life--"

Her eyes widen. I stop mid-sentence, but the damage is already done. She gets up, sweeping the river of copper hair out of her face.

"Talia--" I try.

She shakes her head, her face contorting. "I'm going to go sleep in the guest bedroom with Aunt Minnie."

And as my punishment, I get to watch her dash for the door, looking for all the world like a woman fleeing her execution.

"Fuck!" I shout. I flop back on the bed, arms splayed wide.

That is not how I wanted to end an otherwise perfect day with my wife.

Chapter Twenty-Nine

TALIA

Olive and I walk outside in the bright autumn sunshine, enjoying a stroll down Madison Avenue. I grin at her.

"Can you believe how beautiful it is right now?"

She gives an astonished laugh. "No. It's such a perfect spring day to be in New York City. Thank you for flying me down here."

I take a deep breath and fling my arms wide. "I'm so happy that we escaped Harwicke for the morning! I desperately needed a girls' trip."

"I can't believe that you chartered a freaking helicopter to fly us here!"

I slide her a grin. "Would you believe that it's a company helicopter? It is always available at a moment's notice."

Olive gives an exaggerated sigh and an eye roll.

"Must be nice to be so well taken care of."

I consider that. "Yes, it is."

"Everything smells better here than back home. New York City smells like *freedom*," Olive remarks with a wide grin.

I smile back at her, enjoying her childlike enthusiasm. "And money," I add with a laugh.

We stop at the first store we come to, a designer French luxury brand that sells clothes and luggage. A tall man with salt and pepper hair approaches us from inside the store. He smiles graciously as he greets us both in a deep voice.

"Good afternoon ladies," he says warmly as he opens the door for us to enter the shop. "Welcome. Is there anything I can help you find today?"

We both glance up at him uncertainly before Olive begins to stammer out an answer. "Um... Well, actually... We were just looking around."

The man nods understandingly before adding: "Perhaps I can show you some of our newest arrivals? Or if you're looking for something specific--"

"No, thank you," I quickly reply before Olive can get drawn into any sales pitches. "We want to look around for a few minutes first."

The man gives us a tiny bow. "Of course. Please make yourselves comfortable and browse at your leisure. I will be right here if you need me."

"Oh, wow!" Olive exclaims as we step inside the store. She practically runs to the first rack of dresses and begins rifling through it. "These are beautiful."

The salesperson comes along with us, obviously ready to provide his best service. While we look through the racks, he refolds a stack of sweaters and tidies a display table full of sunglasses and valises.

"We should get dresses for tonight."

Olive looks up at me from where she is draping a pair of cashmere slacks against her leg, comparing the length. "What's tonight again?"

"That silly party that Dare is throwing to announce my pregnancy."

I hold up a pink taffeta dress, considering it for a moment before putting it back on the rack.

"I thought that Remy just blathered the truth out to everybody at that party you told me about."

She decides against the pants and moves on.

"He did. But Dare still wants to 'control the narrative of my pregnancy', whatever that word soup is supposed to mean."

"Hah!" Olive gives me a sympathetic look.

"What can I help you lovely ladies with?" he asks.

"We're looking for cocktail dresses for a party tonight," I reply, looking over at Olive who is still going through the rack of clothes.

The salesperson quickly gets to work, finding exactly what we are looking for. He also brings complementary accessories that could pull our looks together and hangs them outside our dressing rooms.

Olive can't contain her excitement, already pointing out several items she liked. "This one! And this one too!"

As we are changing in the elegant changing rooms, Olive can't seem to keep her curiosity contained any longer.

"Where did you say Dare is again?" she asks me suddenly after trying on several dresses without success.

I know Olive; she's been thinking about her question for a while.

I try to brush off the question, but I can feel my face heating up with embarrassment. "He's... busy," I mutter, not wanting to go into any more detail.

But Olive doesn't let it go. "Busy with what, Talia?" she presses, a mischievous glint in her eye.

I sigh, knowing that there's no way I can avoid answering

her. "He was called away for work," I say finally, trying to keep my tone neutral.

Olive narrows her eyes at me, clearly sensing that I'm not being entirely truthful. "Working or not, he should be here with his pregnant wife," she says pointedly, and I can feel myself getting defensive.

"He has a lot of responsibilities, Olive," I say, suddenly feeling defensive. "He can't just drop everything because I want him to."

Olive sticks her head out of her booth and holds her hands up in a gesture of defeat.

"I'm not trying to start any shit," she claims. She offers me a smile. "I just worry about you, you know? You're going through a lot right now."

I feel a lump forming in my throat at her words. They're true, of course. I'm pregnant with another man's baby, and I'm married to Dare - a man who, despite my best efforts to make him trust me, still clearly thinks I'm a gold-digging con artist. And that's not even to mention the fact that his twin brother, Burn, was my first one-night stand... and now he's the father of the baby growing inside.

Thinking of Burn in that context is actually super gross. I straight up don't like the guy. So maybe I should think of him as my sperm donor.

I sigh. "Money is the only thing that Dare understands. So if I rack up a huge bill, maybe it will give him pause. Maybe make him think twice about calling me a bastard."

Olive looks at me, her eyes wide. "He called you that?"

I shrug. "He implied that I lacked basic manners because I grew up not knowing who my father is. So... yeah, basically."

"Wow. I know I pushed you to accept Dare's proposal, but

that's unacceptable. No one gets to talk to my best friend like that."

"Thanks." I give her a tiny smile. "Now help me find the perfect outfit for tonight."

I start picking out things that catch my eye - dresses, shoes, accessories - until my arms are full of bags. Olive follows behind me with wide eyes as I pay with my glossy black AmEx card. Soon we hurry out of the store, giggling and excitedly gushing about our new purchases.

It feels good to splurge like this. I can finally let loose now that Dare isn't around to judge me. It's also the first time that I'm not really questioning and thinking twice about every penny I spend. For once in my life, it's nice to be able to do something without worrying about what anyone else thinks.

"So what happened last night?" Olive asks as we walk down the street, our arms laden with shopping bags.

I ball my fists up, unable to look at her. "Dare and I had a really great day," I say softly. "He was playing with the kids and it was so... nice." My cheeks are hot as I force myself to go on. "Then, like a fool, I told him I loved him." Her eyes widen in shock. "But he couldn't say it back," I finish, my voice barely more than a whisper. "He actually got really angry and accused me of putting words in his mouth. It got ugly very quickly."

Olive's eyes are wide, she says nothing for a moment. Her eyebrows knit together in concern.

"That's a big deal, Talia," she says seriously. "It sounds like he has some pretty deep-seated trust issues that he needs to work through before he can move forward in your relationship."

"I agree with you, sadly," I sigh. "I thought that maybe if I said those three little words he'd finally start trusting me, but clearly I was wrong. Now what do I do? Do I keep pushing him? Or do I just let it go?"

"I honestly don't know," Olive says. "I didn't even know that Dare had such a nasty side."

I close my eyes and take a deep, steadying breath. The thoughts of Dare, and his near-constant inability to open himself up to me flood my mind.

"He never seems to stop talking about my past. Yet his cruel words have done enough damage already. If he doesn't stop it, we will be over before we even start."

My eyes well up with tears and my throat begins to close. Dare has hit me where it hurts the most: I am an orphan, alone in this world. He has no idea how much pain his words cause me. Even though he doesn't mean to, it still cuts me a thousand times like a thousand knives.

"Oh, Talia," Olive whispers softly, drawing me into her embrace. She holds me while I weep, letting my tears soak her shirt as I attempt to take back control of myself.

"He says I'm smothering him," I whimper against her shoulder. "I wanted to show him that I care and want to be there for him. But he can't see that."

Olive runs her fingers through my hair comfortingly as she rubs circles on my back. "It's okay," she murmurs, gentle yet resolute. "You didn't do anything wrong. You were trying to express your love for him in the only way you know how."

I'm still feeling jittery from our conversation earlier, but Olive's warmth helps to steady my nerves.

Olive and I meander down the busy New York streets, taking in all the sights and sounds of the city. We occasionally make small talk, but mostly we just soak in our surroundings.

Most of my sorrow faded until we stumbled across Tiffany's massive wedding ring section. I take one look at the wedding-themed bridal decor and lose all my composure.

My heart plummets and the tears start streaming down my cheeks in an instant. The sight of all those radiant diamond rings makes me sick to my stomach.

"My life is a stupid joke," I weep. "It's a photocopy of a love story. Dare will never love me, no matter how much I love him."

I hear Olive's soothing voice, but I can't make out her words through the deafening roar inside my head. I'm too busy drowning in my own misery to listen or respond.

Olive takes my arm and leads me away from the jewelry section; it takes all of her strength to tug me along, as if some invisible force is holding me back from leaving this place.

Olive and I have been shopping for hours, but it hasn't taken away the pain. I feel an emptiness in my chest that intensifies with each passing minute. Despite all the luxurious clothes and jewelry, nothing could fill the void.

"Come on, let's get out of here," Olive urges. "We can go to the park and talk."

I nod, my throat too tight to speak.

The sea breeze is a welcome relief after the stuffy air of the mall. We sit down on the bench and Olive wraps her arms around me. She holds me close as I sob into her shoulder.

"It's okay," she murmurs, although I know she doesn't believe it. "Let it all out."

And so I do—all the pain, anger and grief that has been bottled up inside me since Dare told me he didn't love me. I tell Olive about how scared I am that no one will ever love me again, no matter how much I try to be perfect or how hard I work at making everyone happy.

I tell her about my fears of living a life alone and unloved, and of never having a family of my own. As my tears dry up, an unexpected calm settles over me; in that moment, all my worries seem to drift away like smoke in the wind.

"You deserve better than this," Olive says firmly, taking my hands in hers and squeezing them gently.

"Maybe deep down, he can tell that I'm damaged goods," I blubber. "I'll never be good enough, classy enough, tough enough. Maybe it's the same thing my mom sensed when she left me at a shelter all those years ago."

"Talia! You know that's not true."

"But what if it is? What if the baby I'm carrying realizes it, too? She'll know that I'm not a good mom."

A sob escapes me despite attempting to hold it back and Olive looks at me sadly as she hugs me tightly.

"It's ok," she says soothingly into my hair. "You're going to be an amazing mom. You love this baby so much already. Something tells me any child would be lucky to have you as their parent."

Her words make my tears fall even faster, but they also bring comfort. For a moment, gratitude overrides fear in me and I hug Olive back tightly while struggling to control my emotions.

After a few more minutes of composing myself, Olive suggests we go out for lunch somewhere nice. I nod in agreement and quickly call for Frick, my bodyguard. She soon appears at my side and I ask her to find us the closest expensive restaurant.

The restaurant Olive and I choose is an exclusive Italian eatery in the middle of downtown. While the outside of the building looks modest, the inside is decorated with exquisite art pieces and ornamentation. The tables are covered with pristine white tablecloths, and a maître'd stands at the entrance to welcome us.

He leads us to a cozy corner booth where we can enjoy our meal without being seen by other guests. The waiter brings out a menu for us to peruse, but Olive requests that he surprise us with whatever he thinks is best.

We sit in silence for a few moments before I finally pluck up the courage to speak again.

"I'm sorry," I say softly, tears stinging my eyes once more. "It's all my fault."

Olive shakes her head. "It's not your fault, Talia," she says firmly. "Dare was just too scared to be honest with you about his feelings. You don't deserve to be treated like this."

She reaches across the table and places her hand over mine as she speaks, her words washing over me like a balm for my broken heart. I take comfort in her nurturing presence; it's been too long since anyone has cared about me in this way and I cling onto what she says like it is an anchor in turbulent waters.

Soon after, our food arrives. Freshly made gnocchi reclining on beds of tomato sauce and topped off with generous shavings of parmesan cheese. We enjoy our lunch slowly, chatting away lightly between bites as if Dare never existed or mattered at all. By the end of our meal, I feel lighter somehow; my burden lifted somewhat by Olive's kind words and understanding smile.

The food is delightful, although I'm not very hungry. I'm more interested in my own thoughts than gnocchi. My phone buzzes in my purse. I make a face at Olive.

"Who the hell is texting me? You're the only one that I talk to."

Olive has a full mouth of pasta so she shrugs comically.

I pick it up and read the text message. Then my heart starts to pound. An icy shiver slides down my spine. The message just shows up as *UNKNOWN*. The same thing happened when an unknown number sent me photos as evidence that Dare and his friend Tristen tricked me into agreeing to this marriage.

My mouth goes dry. I open the text and my eyes go wide with horror.

My heart begins to race as I stare at the photos on my phone in disbelief. The photos are of Dare and I, in some car I don't recognize. The pictures are taken from an odd angle, making them seem extra seedy and illicit. There are several of me, looking extremely disheveled.

In one photo, I'm sitting on Dare's lap and kissing him, sticking my tongue down his throat and burying my hands in his hair. My brain seizes. When did Dare and I make out in a car?

Then I scroll to the next photo and gasp. It's a picture of me riding Dare's cock, my head tossed back, a shout leaving my lips.

My brain is clearly shorting out. I can't remember ever having sex with Dare in a car that looked like that. Wouldn't I remember a moment like that?

I'm so shocked that I don't even know how to feel. All I can do is stare at the photos in stunned silence while Olive looks on with concern etched into her features.

"Talia, what is this?" she asks gently, her voice full of worry.

I shake my head, my mouth opening. But I can't answer her question, because I don't understand what's happening. Before I can answer, my phone buzzes again, this time with a message from the same unknown number that sent me the photos. The message reads:

"I know your secret. If you don't want the whole world to find out, you'll do as I say. Instructions will follow in forty eight hours."

I choke on my bite of food as I gape at the pictures in

disbelief. Then I look at the pictures more closely. My hair is longer and more unkempt than I keep it. My clothes are dowdy and wrinkled. My fingernails are not manicured.

My eyes widen. "Oh my god."

There is no doubt that this picture was taken by someone who had deliberately tried to make me look bad. But the photos don't show me and Dare...

These pictures were taken when I had sex with Dare's twin brother, Burn.

"Oh god!"

Olive puts her fork down and touches my hand.

"Tell me what is going on, Talia. Clearly you're having a visceral reaction to whatever is on your phone."

My fingers shake as I shove the phone towards her. Olive gasps and pulls the phone closer.

"Photos of you and Dare together?" She trails off, her eyes narrowing. "Why are they taken like they are from some hidden camera or something? And why would anybody even take them? You guys are married, for god's sake."

I shake my head. "That's not Dare."

"What?" she squeaks. She leans down, staring at the photos. "Oh! Oh shit! That's what you were wearing that night..." She stops, looking up at me. Then she lowers her voice to a whisper. "These are photos of you and Burn?"

I nod. "Look at the text that came along with the photos. It's some kind of blackmail."

"What? From who?" Olive demands.

"I don't know!" I cry, throwing my hands up. "I didn't do anything illegal. Maybe morally gray at best. But... the black-mailer must know that these photos could be shown to Remy. It seems clear to me that they know the fortune that is at risk here."

"What are you going to do?" Olive asks me.

"I wish I knew," I reply. I feel overwhelmed, not sure what to do or who is behind the text messages. Whoever it is has gone to great lengths to hurt me.

I want to get to the bottom of it.

And I want to find Dare. To warn him, yes. But also because I want him to comfort me.

I want him to swear to me that he's going to make this blackmailer pay.

"We have to get back to Harwicke," I tell Olive. "Dare will know what to do."

At least I hope so.

Chapter Thirty

DARE

My heart swells with relief as Talia finally makes her way into the ballroom. She looks beautiful in a turquoise dress that hugs her curves just right. She looks more radiant than the sun, her eyes glittering like emeralds, her full lips a light pink and pouting. Talia's hair is pinned up to reveal her long, slender neck and her face is made up with a natural, glowing look. I can't help but smile at the sight of her, and I know that I'm the luckiest man alive.

I take her hands in mine and kiss her palm before pulling away. "You look amazing," I say, my voice full of admiration.

Talia sighs and gives me a weary smile. "Thank you. You look pretty nice in that suit."

There's an awkward moment where I realize that tonight, we are just pretending that we haven't argued. While it isn't my favorite, I can deal with it for the evening.

I nod in understanding. Before I can say anything, Talia leans closer and whispers in my ear.

"We need to talk privately. It's important."

I swallow hard and take a step back. I can sense the

distrust in her eyes - did I put it there? I force myself to give her an encouraging smile. "Of course," I reply softly.

My attention is drawn away from Talia as someone enters the ballroom with a flourish. Even before I lay my eyes on Felix, the stench of brandy accompanied by a stifling amount of cologne greets me. I see Felix's tall frame; his gaunt build fills out his black tailored suit perfectly. His silvering hair is slicked back, and his blue eyes have that sparkle of someone who is expecting to get exactly what he wants. His gaze lands on me, and I feel a chill down my spine. He raises his hand in greeting.

Felix has arrived with an obviously wealthy, rather pudgy man in tow. The man's tastefully tailored pinstripe suit bulges around the waistline, looking for all the world like a dam about to burst. Chunky gold rings threaten to be swallowed up by the man's fat hands. He clutches a white handkerchief in one hand, which he uses to wipe the prodigious sweat pouring from his brow and neck.

Felix notices me and beckons me over. Despite the fact that I don't really want to talk to my uncle right now, I obey his instructions and make my way towards him.

"Let's talk after the event is over," I say, looking at Talia.

She looks disappointed, an expression that I am not used to seeing coming from her. It eats me up inside. She nods slowly and steps away from me, purposely creating space.

That's what I wanted, isn't it? It crushes a part of my heart, though.

"I'll catch up with you later," Talia says softly. A strange mix of emotion flickers across her face before she turns away to greet other guests arriving at the ballroom. I see her Aunt Minnie enter the ballroom wearing a flowing dress of deep amethyst. The two women make eye contact and Talia practically runs into her aunt's open arms.

I rub my neck. I have done some real damage to my relationship with Talia. Even I can tell that much.

"Ah Dare!" He beams as I reach him. "Glad you could make it! You'll never guess who I've got here with me." He gestured towards his guests.

"Very impressive," I say politely, although internally I'm rolling my eyes at his antics. He wanted to show off - what else is new? Even though he looks happy in front of his peers, he still has an edge which almost everyone around him notices but chooses not to comment on it openly.

I approach Felix and the bank president, not entirely sure of what to expect. I spend my time schmoozing with him, telling him how great a business reputation his banking institution has. Basically kissing some serious ass. It's a strange experience for me, and it's as unwelcome as Talia's disappointment with me. It seems to do the trick, though... The sweaty man is all smiles and nods by the end of our conversation.

As for Felix, he takes a hands-off approach to letting me do my wooing of the perspiring executive. I notice him scanning the room looking for somebody. A few times he lingers on someone for a while before looking away again. As I get closer, I realize he's been staring at Talia. Seeing that makes me anxious and reminds me of the warning that I just got from my father about Felix.

Does Tripp know something that I don't?

While I'm still talking myself up, I can't help but notice Burn and Daisy make their entrance. They were not on the invite list, but I'm not going to make a fuss in order to have them kicked out. Besides, I want to really rub Talia's pregnancy in their smug faces.

I glance over at Burn and Daisy, but their conversation is too hushed to make out. Burn is gesturing repeatedly to Talia, which only fuels my suspicions. I can't shake the feeling that something isn't right.

I make a split-second decision to pull one of my bodyguards aside.

"Stay close to Talia," I order him in a hushed voice. "Don't let her out of your sight. If Burn touches her or gets too close, you have my permission to tackle him."

He nods and moves off into the crowd, taking up a post next to Talia while she talks with her aunt. I don't know what Burn is up to this time, but I don't want him causing trouble for Talia or anyone else tonight.

I take a deep breath and try to relax as I scan the room for any other threats that may be lurking around. But all appears to be quiet as the party continues.

I start looking at my watch. It's almost eight o'clock by now. I've been tentatively waiting for my grandfather to turn up before I start making a speech. But it's getting pretty late for early risers to wait around much longer.

The music is getting louder, and it's starting to interfere with my thoughts about what I should say during the speech. As I search for the words, a familiar voice suddenly startles me out of my reverie.

"Dare!" Daisy exclaims as she appears from out of nowhere. She wraps her arms around me and gives me an enthusiastic hug. "It's been so long since we've seen each other."

I pull away politely but firmly, trying not to appear rude. "Yes, it's been a while. I definitely didn't extend you an invitation. So what brings you here?"

Daisy bats her eyelashes coyly and then leans in close, breathing champagne-scented breath in my face. She effects a babyish voice that I remember her putting on for the first few months I knew her back in college.

"I came here to see you of course! To make sure that you are okay and to check up on you."

She slides her hand up my arm. I'm caught off guard and take a half step back, glaring at her. She pouts, still flirting with me.

"What, are you still mad? You know, if you want to come with me, we can find a closet where I can show you how much I've missed you..." Her voice trails off expectantly as she looks up at me with the widest eyes imaginable. She leans forward, smoothing my dress shirt with her hand. "Don't you want me, Dare?"

I can feel my neck flush as I take a step back, putting some distance between us. I don't need her to get the wrong idea. Frankly, I don't want her getting any ideas about me at all. Daisy obviously notices the change in my demeanor because she gives me an exaggerated pout before continuing.

"Look, Dare, I know that our relationship ended badly but... I can still be what you need," she says softly, almost pleadingly. "I can marry you and have your babies. I can be your sweet little trophy wife, like you always dreamed." She reaches out and touches my arm gently before continuing in an even softer voice, "I still think you're sexy, even though you've put on a few pounds since I met you."

I raise both hands up defensively and take another step back away from her persistent advances.

"You're crazy," I accuse her. "I can't believe you think I would have anything to do with you. First off, I'm married. Second off, you dumped me for my fucking brother!"

My voice rises as I talk until I'm practically shouting.

Daisy folds her arms across her chest and the sexy, pouty baby act vanishes. "You're just as much of a stick in the mud as I remembered."

"That's okay, because I am off the table where you are concerned. Go slobber all over my brother."

I wave a hand and Daisy makes an angry squeak before she huffs away. I watch her receding figure as she leaves through the back exit, opening the doorway to show a quick flash of a stairwell. After a second, I shrug and turn away.

I take a deep breath as I walk back inside. I told Daisy off, but now it's time to find Talia. I notice her almost immediately, though she has her back turned to me. She's standing with Burn and he has his hand on her arm. Her head is bent in what looks like an effort to escape his grasp.

The bodyguard I assigned to stand guard over Talia is nowhere to be seen.

"Let go of her," I demand as I stride over to them. Talia whips around at the sound of my voice and relief floods across her face when she sees it's me. Burn looks like he's about ready to explode but he takes his hand away from Talia's arm slowly, grudgingly accepting my presence.

Talia steps closer to me and whispers quickly, "Dare, it's important that we talk in private. *Please*."

I nod curtly, putting my arm around her waist. I pull her away from the prying eyes of the party-goers and toward the exit that Daisy just took.

But Remy has other plans for me, it seems. He finally enters the party, wearing a soft khaki cardigan, navy chinos, and a pair of sandals. He's extremely underdressed, leaning on his walking stick and being flanked by two very young female assistants.

"Fuck," I mutter. I nod to Remy, drawing Talia's attention to his arrival. "Of all the times to show up."

"Dare!" my grandfather bellows. "Where is Dare?"

Talia groans.

"I'm sorry. Let me go talk to him for a few minutes. I

promise that we will talk. Right after I make the announcement that we're expecting, we will slip out the back and you can tell me anything." I kiss Talia on the side of the head, moving so quickly that I make it exceptionally awkward between us.

She exhales heavily and pokes her cheek out with her tongue. I catch her hand and kiss her knuckles. She shrugs and turns away.

I take a deep breath and steel myself as I approach Remy. He glares at me, looking like an angry thundercloud about to burst into a hurricane.

"So glad that you made it, Remy," I say. I police my tone and try to keep my face completely neutral.

Remy snorts derisively. "I'm not here for your charade, Dare," he says gruffly. "I heard the news already."

I take another deep breath and try to keep my temper in check. I don't want to get into an argument with my grandfather tonight.

"It's still nice of you to come, Remy," I reply calmly.

"I'm not even sure why you and that girl need a gala to announce her pregnancy. I told everyone about it already!"

"I thought you might feel that way," I say, as a way of not saying anything at all. "If you don't mind, I'm going to announce it right now."

I turn around and make eye contact with the event planner. She is ready and quickly brings me a microphone. I take a deep breath and try to center myself. I can feel the energy in the room shift as Remy steps back and allows me to take center stage.

I clear my throat and look around the room. All eyes are on me. The crowd shifts anxiously, whispers rising in volume.

"I want to say a few words as to why we are all gathered

here tonight. Not just to give our money to Hope House, which is a worthy cause. But..."

My phone vibrates in my pocket, but I ignore it and keep going. There is a smattering of polite applause as I smile.

"I'm here to tell you that Talia..." I swing my gaze around the ballroom. "Where are you, darling?"

My heart sinks as I realize Talia isn't in the room. The crowd starts to whisper, and I feel my face flush with heat. I take a deep breath and scan the crowd for her familiar face.

"Just a moment..." I tell the crowd. My pulse starts racing. "Has anyone seen my wife?"

The crowd bursts into whispers. This is really not going as planned.

Talia is nowhere to be seen. Was she really so angry that I kept telling her that we could talk later?

Maybe she really had to use the restroom. Or maybe she texted me where she went? I fish my phone out of my pocket to check it for texts.

Time slows down. My heartbeat is ear-splittingly loud.

I see a single text from Talia. Opening it, I'm surprised to see just three digits.

911.

My mouth opens. What does *911* mean?

It means that Talia's in trouble.

My heart pounds in my chest as I yell out for all the security guards to search for Talia. They scurry off, but a few minutes later they return without her. I feel the air in the room grow heavy with disappointment and worry.

The guests start murmuring to themselves, shooting me sympathetic glances. I try not to think of what could have happened to her. What if she's hurt, or worse?

The only thing that matters right now is finding Talia and making sure she's safe. I take a deep breath and focus on the task at hand.

I turn to my security team and give them their orders. "You'll need to split up into groups of three and look everywhere you can think of. Alleyways, side streets, parks... Any place where someone might be hiding or in trouble."

The team nods and hurries away. My mind races as I worry about where Talia could be. Did she just need some time alone? Or was it something sinister?

I try calling her phone, but there's no answer. Then something occurs to me.

The text message that said *911*. Could it mean something more than just an emergency number? Tristen runs over to me, trying to see if he can help.

I scrub a hand through my hair, trying to think.

Think, goddamnit. Why won't my brain work?

"Mr. Morgan?" one of my security team calls. "I found something."

The security guard steps closer, motioning for me to come take a look. My heart skips a beat as I see what he is pointing at.

It's Talia's phone. Shattered and lying in pieces on the ground.

I reach down to pick up the phone and feel my heart sink. The screen of the phone is smashed, but the last text message still reads *911*.

My mind starts to race with fear and worry. She sent me that text, knowing that I would try to come find her.

But the fact that her phone is in my hand means that someone didn't want that to happen.

They didn't want me to get to Talia.

"What happened here? Where the fuck is my wife?" I shout.

"I don't know, sir. We should go downstairs and check if she fell somehow."

"You think she might have gone out this way?" I ask the guard, motioning to the emergency exit door next to the phone.

He nods and we head towards it, pushing it open cautiously before venturing down the stairwell. The stairs are dingy and damp. I can feel sweat dripping down my face from fear and anxiety as we make our way down further into the darkness of the stairwell.

It's six floors down the bottom of the stairs. Every time I come around the crook of the staircase, I am of two minds.

First, I pray that I'll see Talia's face.

And second, I hope against hope that she won't be harmed.

But when I turn the final time and step onto the downstairs landing, my breath coming in huffs, I haven't found her yet. The guard steps forward and yanks open the door. I cringe, expecting at any moment that I'm going to find Talia there, dead or dying.

But no.

I step through the doorway and look out into the back alley of the hotel. It's dark and drizzly, the night air chilly against my skin. I look both ways down the alley, but I see nothing but a few broken down cardboard boxes.

My heart seizes.

"She's not here," I breathe out. "Someone took her."

I stare into the darkness, panicking. My mind is dazed but two thoughts echo through my skull.

Where is Talia?

And who is responsible for her abduction?

Chapter Thirty-One

D are's and Talia's epic saga is not over. Raw, gripping, steamy, and emotional… Get ready for more of their story by grabbing VOW TO THE DEVIL on pre-order right now.

Vivian likes to write about troubled, deeply flawed alpha males and the fiery, kick-ass women who bring them to their knees.

Vivian's lasting motto in romance is a quote from a favorite song: "Soulmates never die."

Be sure to join her email list to keep up with all the awesome giveaways, author videos, ARC opportunities, and more!

VIVIAN'S WORKS

MARRIED AT MIDNIGHT SERIES
FORBIDDEN BILLIONAIRE ROMANCE
DEAL WITH THE DEVIL
WED TO THE DEVIL
VOW TO THE DEVIL

HIS AND HERS SERIES
HIS BEST FRIEND'S LITTLE SISTER
CLAIMING HER INNOCENCE
HIS TO KEEP
HIS VIRGIN

THE ADDICTION DUET
ADDICTION
OBSESSION

OTHER BOOKS
WILD HEARTS

For more information….
vivian-wood.com
info@vivian-wood.com